Faythe

Reclaimed

Hanaford Park #3

Lisa Sanchez

Tulipe Noire Press
CALIFORNIA 2012

For Sarah.

I couldn't have written this book without you.

Thank you for believing in me, and for being my best friend.

Faythe Reclaimed
Lisa Sanchez

Tulipe Noire Press

P.O. Box 815, Palo Alto, CA 94302

www.tulipenoirepress.com

First Print Edition, May 2012

First eBook Edition, May 2012

This work represents a work of fiction. References to real people, events, establishments, organizations or locales are intended only to provide a sense of authenticity, and are used fictitiously. All other characters, and all incidents and dialogue are drawn from the author's imagination and are not to be construed as real.

ISBN (print): 978-0-9839797-6-0
ISBN (electronic): 978-0-9839797-7-7

Chapter 1
·The Traveler·

Dark, viscous liquid pooled onto the rotting floorboards below her body, the blackened puddle oddly reminiscent of a Rorschach inkblot.

Suppressed memories and emotions I'd believed long dead amassed from deep within, slamming me with a powerful crescendo of...*Madre de Dios*...feeling. Something I hadn't experienced since the moment I'd lost my other half.

Nausea and desperation mimicked acid, burning a hole through my gut and my chest as I allowed my gaze to wander north. I knew what I'd find, and, *fuck it all to hell*, it scared me to death.

Taylor. The exotic beauty who'd breezed into my life just days before. The angel who'd awoken me from the state of numbness I'd resided in for three centuries. The woman who was an exact match in every way to my long deceased Faythe, hanged upside down and unconscious in front of me.

Thud...

Thud...

Thud...

My heartbeat... It echoed in my ears like a muted drumbeat. The rapid tympani so synonymous with anger and rage oddly diminished and muffled as though I were listening to it from deep within the bowels of the ocean.

How? How had I allowed my enemy to capture the beautiful

creature who'd breathed life into my pathetic existence?

I thrashed against the magical bonds holding me captive, every fiber of my being filled with panic, desperation—and rage. Supernatural throwdowns were a normal part of my everyday life. A warlock, an exiled member of one of Europe's most powerful covens, I'd been bred to do battle, to fight the dregs of the underworld—with magic.

Magic. It had been my saving grace, time and again. It was also the bane of my fucking existence. Much like time. I hated my magic, almost as much as I hated myself. Witchcraft, limitless power… Both proved worthless when they didn't allow you to save the one you loved. My magic hadn't kept Faythe's neck out of the hangman's noose.

My stomach seized as I took in the large gash at the back of Taylor's head. My magic hadn't kept her safe either.

Slow, heavy footfalls sounded in the far off distance, and it wasn't until a pair of black shoes slid into view opposite the crimson puddle staining the floor that I was able to tear my eyes from Taylor.

Lucian.

Heat burned beneath the surface of my skin as a ruddy, fury-induced haze clouded my vision. *Lucian.* His name alone sent an upsurge of hatred and disgust that fueled my rage. A long time enemy of my coven, and a complete shit in every sense of the word, he'd declared war against my coven-mate, my brother in magic, in a maniacal quest for power. Taylor, a mortal who'd only recently become aware of the existence of supernaturals, had been caught in the crossfire; another innocent harmed because of my fucked up legacy.

Dressed entirely in black, blue eyes darkened with malice, Lucian strutted around Taylor's limp body like a goddamned peacock on parade.

Every molecule of my being screamed to end him, to rip his head from his body, dance in his entrails, ensure he suffered massive amounts of pain before sending him to Hell. I closed my eyes, focused on my powers, fought to break free from the invisible bands he'd trapped me in.

I groaned in frustration. Nothing. Fucking nothing. The asshole had dampened my powers when he'd captured me. He was lucky. Lucky he'd managed to get the drop on me. Because if he hadn't, he'd be dead.

Fingertips pressed together, he arched a brow and sneered. "Gabriel, is it? I've heard of you and of the great loss you suffered." He cast a sidelong glance at Taylor, brow raised, then turned to face me once more. "She bears a remarkable likeness to your Faythe, does she not?"

Alarm flooded my system. My body shook. My jaw ached. My chest felt like it might explode.

Lucian's words echoed inside my head, gave voice to the troubled thoughts that consumed my every waking breath.

Was it possible?

Was Taylor, the woman I'd crossed paths with just days before, the same beauty I'd fallen in love with three hundred years ago?

The woman I'd sworn to protect?

The woman who'd died during the Salem Witch trials, a direct result of the wretched curse I carried?

Her physical similarities to Faythe were nothing short of astonishing. Aside from the modern clothing she wore, she was an exact duplicate in every way. Same long russet hair; same fine bone structure and flawless skin; same long, slender build. I'd never come across a doppelganger before and marveled, again, at the extraordinary woman before me.

Nausea tore at my gut as I took in Lucian's vile handiwork.

Slender arms dangling to the filthy floor below, skin pale, Taylor hanged limp before me, thick, dirty twine tearing the skin at her ankles as it suspended her unconscious body from a termite infested beam above.

Sharp, stabbing pain sliced at my chest, and though it tortured me, I couldn't look away.

I slammed my lids shut and groaned.

Fuck. Not the same, Gabriel. It's not the same as before. She's hanging by her ankles, not her neck.

And she's alive…barely. But for how long, I wasn't sure.

Ignorance, hatred and fear—fear of my magic, fear of the unknown—had taken Faythe from me so very long ago. Salem Village, a town filled with individuals seeking respite from religious persecution had become the epitome of that which they fled: intolerant and pious. Faythe had died along with nineteen other innocents, their necks snapped, in a chaotic hunt—for me.

Then, of course, there was my curse. The heinous affliction cast upon me by a vile, backstabbing bitch. The scourge that prevented me from finding everlasting happiness with Faythe.

"I curse you, Gabriel Castillo…"

The memory struck me like a pile driver. Venomous words spoken in anger and betrayal sliced across my psyche like a jagged knife, each intonation more painful than the last.

"In this life you shall know naught but pain and suffering. You will find love, Gabriel. You will find your soulmate and suffer a multitude of agony when she is ripped from your bosom. Your other half shall be torn from the life she knows, endure untold agony and persecution before fate finally steals her away. From that day forward, misery shall be your constant companion until the moment your heart beats no more."

I gnashed my teeth, bitterness and hatred waging a silent war within me. The curse I bore punished not just me, but an innocent soul as well. I was poisonous, unworthy.

Memories of my past crumbled to dust; every muscle in my body came alive as the familiar cadence of my enemy's voice yanked me back into the here and now.

"I wonder…" Lucian said, tapping his chin, "if she would suffer the same fate as your beloved Faythe? Shall we find out?"

"No!"

The flames that burned beneath the surface of my skin burst into a raging inferno, three centuries of pent up rage, despair and agony consuming me fully.

Power surged from deep within me, my control and my dominion over my magic—gone.

Clarity, born of fear and rage, pummeled me from all sides, the curse that clung to me like a second skin revealing the truth of the situation.

"Your other half shall be torn from the life she knows, endure untold agony and persecution before fate finally steals her away."

Realization, hope and terror intermingled as the reality of both my past and my present struck me.

I gaped, awestruck, at the woman who hanged bound and unconscious in front of me. Faythe, the beautiful outcast I'd fallen in love with in 1692, was not of that time. No. She was none other than the Taylor hanging a few scant feet in front of me. The curse, the festering plague thrust upon me, would send her backward in time via Lucian's evil hand.

Madre de Dios!

I'd been given a second chance.

A chance I didn't plan on wasting.

I would stop Lucian from sending Taylor back. I'd change her fate—and in doing so, mine as well.

Eyes dark with malice, Lucian pursed his lips and circled Taylor's body like a hungry vulture waiting to attack.

I thrashed against the invisible chains holding me captive. "If you touch her, I'll—"

"You'll what?" Lucian said, sounding bored. "I'm quite certain you won't give me a second thought." Eyes filled with mirth, he turned to face Taylor and flashed a wicked grin. "Let's test that theory." He flicked his wrist, and with a loud pop, Taylor was gone.

The room, Lucian, the circumstances leading up to my capture… everything faded away the moment Taylor disappeared.

Mortal man, when faced with the prospect of loss or great pain, has been known to perform great feats of strength, to risk everything to defeat that which threatens all he holds dear. Time and again, history has shown that when adrenaline combines with sheer will, the impossible becomes possible. Desperate fathers lift cars off children trapped beneath. Soldiers jump on grenades to save their comrades in arms. And lovers… Lovers place themselves in harm's way, run heart first into burning buildings, put themselves in the path of an oncoming bullet in order to save their better half.

Mortal man was capable of great things, indeed. But then, I was no mortal man. No. I was so much more.

I was a powerful warlock.

And I'd been given a second chance at happiness.

A chance I refused to let slip through my fingers.

I may have failed to stop Lucian from sending Taylor back to Salem circa 1692, but I refused to fail to save her from her upcoming date with death.

The windows scattered about the room exploded and glass blew inward, the force of my rage overpowering any hold Lucian had over me. Heat blistered my skin, threatening to melt muscle and bone as magical power coursed through me like supercharged bolts of lightning.

The present, the battle with Lucian, it all fell away, and with a roar, I followed Taylor into oblivion.

Chapter 2

· The Traveler ·

Chaos, both painful and familiar, grabbed me by the fucking balls and twisted. Trapped in a dark maelstrom and spinning out of control, my body disappeared, each cell exploding apart from its neighbor with the speed of magic. Teleportation, popping from one place to another, is one thing. That shit is quick, easy and relatively painless. Time travel, on the other hand, is a complete bitch. Your body? Shit, it stretches thin like a rubber band being tugged in a thousand different directions, then is catapulted through the fabric of time. It chafes like hell and leaves you with a wicked nasty after-taste.

Still, I knew I'd subject myself to the agony a thousand times over if it meant I'd be able to save Taylor. I'd do everything, anything, to never feel the loss of her again.

A rush of blinding light burned through my scattered anatomy, scorching heat threatening to reduce me to ash. Helpless to do anything but embrace the pain, I let go as multiple layers of time and space quickly peeled away and swallowed me whole.

Then, when I was sure all was lost, finally the world stilled. With a deep breath, I fought off the burning sensation blazing across my aching muscles and opened my eyes.

Moonlight filtered down through a thick spattering of hemlock and white pine trees. Their earthy scent jogged memories I'd locked away centuries ago—nightmares I'd fought to forget. "Home. Sweet, fucking home."

I'd vowed never to return, never to revisit this god-forsaken corner of earth. My memory of the ground, the trees... Hell, the very air, was tainted, haunted with the echo of what once was. Just standing on this miserable scrap of dirt made my stomach clench. No, I never intended on returning to Salem Village.

But that was before I crossed paths with Taylor. After suffering through three-hundred goddamn miserable years without her, she waltzed back into my life as though nothing had ever happened. And in Hanaford Park, California of all fucking places. Taylor—the reincarnation of Faythe—the only woman I'd ever loved.

And God, she was more beautiful than I remembered. Angelic with just the right amount of sin thrown in, Baby Girl sported a tall, thin frame with just enough curve in all the right places and a set of legs that went on forever. Legs I wanted wrapped around my waist while I drove myself deep into her. Taylor—with deep chocolate eyes and a mane of thick, mahogany hair my fingers itched to dive into while I laid siege to her soft, pouty lips.

Fear had placed me in a chokehold, blinded me to the truth of her identity until it was too late. Gentle, quirky and kind, she possessed an aura of overall goodness that comes along only once in a lifetime. Her soul's inner light was unmistakable. I should have known, should have recognized her as Faythe from the start.

Balling my hands into fists, I narrowed my eyes and shook my head. "I'll be damned if I lose her again."

The dark forest flew by me in a blur of movement as I raced through the brush toward the woman who owned my soul. I was a shadow in the night. A wraith bound by the laws of time, laws that had been set in stone a thousand millennia ago.

What is done cannot be undone. What will be cannot be changed.

I clenched my jaw and ran faster. "Fuck the laws of time." I'd failed her once before. I wouldn't make that mistake twice. "I—"

The forest disappeared, white light eating up the dark backdrop, blinding me and flooding the space with oppressive heat. Blown backward by a powerful blast of energy, my body seized up as an invisible force grasped me by the throat and lifted me off the ground.

"Sifting time is an abomination: therefore, forbidden."

Three voices echoed throughout the space, interwoven, layered, one on top of the other. Female in nature, the voices exuded power— primordial, unrestrained.

I struggled in vain against the unseen force gripping me in a chokehold, unsurprised when my attempts to escape by using my magic failed. I didn't have to see their ancient faces to know who'd muted my powers: the Fates.

My vision flickered in and out, lack of oxygen taking its toll. With the last bit of air in my lungs I managed to wheeze out a desperate plea. "I come…to save a…life."

"It is forbidden!"

The brilliant light that had bleached the forest alabaster receded, dim shadows of the surrounding woods a cool balm against my heat-singed eyes. No doubt satisfied they'd made their point, the Fates tossed me sideways like a rag doll, my body slamming against the base of a rotting tree with a loud crack.

Gritting through the pain, I pushed up onto my knees and craned my head toward the sky, a glutton for punishment. "I won't…let her die." I didn't care about the Fates, or their laws. My only thoughts were of Taylor and how to keep that precious neck of hers out of the hangman's noose.

The light returned, brighter than before, and with it fiery heat that threatened to melt the flesh from my bones. The ground shook beneath my hands and knees, and the sound of rolling thunder boomed overhead. The invisible force that held me captive just moments before returned, flattening me to the forest floor as the layered voices reverberated through my skull. Hot, searing wind whipped across my face and body.

"You think to spurn our word? Foolish, lowly creature. We are the Moirai. We are immemorial. Our word, irrefutable. Our law, absolute. What is done cannot be undone. What will be cannot be changed."

I clenched my jaw, struggling against their hold. *Fuck that.* I had a shit ton of power. The laws of time and space didn't apply to me. Teleportation, transmogrification... Those things were second nature to me, ingrained in the fabric of my being.

The Fates made no sense. Why saddle me with powerful magic, only to stifle me when I needed it? Why grant me the ability to bend time and space, then punish me for using that power to save the only woman I'd ever loved?

The blistering heat whipping across my face kicked up a notch, their sonorous voices clamoring throughout the space. "Mortal man was never meant to sift time. Such power demands a heavy price."

I grimaced, the heat blazing across my skin growing hotter, more intense. "A...price?" *Cristo!* What more did they want from me? I felt like I'd been paying the price for something or other my entire goddamn life.

The unseen force slammed me down onto the forest floor, choking the life from me once more. "Disregard the law, alter the past in any way, and you shall pay dearly— with your flesh."

The blinding light faded into nothing, taking with it the fire that blazed across my skin and the invisible vice cutting off my air supply. Power surged through my veins, whatever magic they'd used to suppress it vanishing with their eerie voices.

I slammed my hands onto the dirt floor at my sides before shooting up onto my feet. To hell with the Fates and their unyielding, fucked up laws. I'd be damned if I'd sit back and let that trio of bitches control Taylor's destiny—or mine. I didn't give a rat's ass about my flesh. I'd spent a year beneath the ancient grounds of Seville having the flesh torn from my body; my bones broken, then mended. If that were all the payment they demanded to alter the past, then so be it. They wouldn't be the first to sink their claws into me, and I was sure they wouldn't be the last.

Chapter 3

·Taylor·

"Ow, ow, ow! *Sheisa!*" I groaned, but it came out as more of a whimper than anything else. "Crap, that hurts." Pure, undiluted physical torment had ripped me from the blackness holding me under and shook me into consciousness. *Holy...Where am I?*

I sat bolt upright and immediately wished I hadn't. Searing pain tore through the base of my skull, each pulsating throb matching the steady drumbeat of my heart. It felt like my body had been sucked through a Swizzle straw, chewed on for a thousand years and spit out. An altogether unpleasant feeling.

Acting on instinct, I reached for the back of my head and winced when my fingers brushed across a large gash. The metallic stench of copper burned my nose as I pulled my hand away, and my stomach churned at the sight of my palm covered in dark, sticky goo. Blood. My blood. *Oh, God.* The world took on a vicious spin. If I was dizzy before, I felt positively loopy now.

A dark haze blocked my thoughts, sharp pain knifing through my head as I tried to recall how I got here. What happened to me? Where the hell was I, and why...why was I bleeding?

Darkness flooded my heavy-lidded eyes. I squinted at the towering shadows looming in front of me. Were those...trees? I whipped my head around, wishing like mad I had a pair of night vision goggles and cursing the stinging pain that came with each movement I made.

Note to self: turning head will result in copious amounts of pain.

Pain is bad, therefore, do not move if at all possible.

A small patch of light shone down between a handful of monstrous, black forms standing a few scant feet in front of me. The pungent smell of damp earth and deep woods flooded my senses as I dug my fingers into the ground, gritted my teeth and looked up into the night sky. Stars, brilliant white and blazing shone bright as fire through a spattering of clouds and cast a muted glow over the army of giant trees towering over me. A cutting breeze whipped through the enormous timbers, the icy air and eerie sound sending a scattering of goose bumps rippling across my flesh. *Okay. So, I'm in a forest.* I choked down the giant lump in my throat and wrapped my arms around myself in a tight hug. A fat tinge of panic wormed its way through my gut. *And I'm alone. Freezing to death.*

My thoughts were interrupted when a bomb exploded overhead.

Well, okay, maybe the noise I heard wasn't a bomb. But whatever it was, was loud. Loud enough to send me diving face first with a frightened shriek into a mixture of dirt and fallen pine needles. Tucking my head between my knees, I curled into the fetal position and slammed my eyes shut. Dammit, I was too young to die.

Unsure of how long I'd remained in the fetal position, I slowly lifted my head, expecting to see…well, I wasn't sure what I expected to see. The pearly gates? A sea of white? Where do you go after being eaten by a savage, woodland animal? The same eerie darkness that flooded my vision before overcame me the moment I opened my eyes. I was still in the woods—alive, presumably, and still completely clueless as to how I got there. *Fudgity! What a shitty way to go out. Stranded in the middle of Woop Woop with—*

Caaaaww!

I shot up off the forest floor with a breathy yelp, my eyes automatically traveling to the source of the unholy noise.

Moonlight bounced off a pair of yellow eyes staring at me from a barren tree branch above. The large bird squawked once more, leaned forward and took flight. The sound of its powerful wings beating against the air stole my breath away.

Okay, so a bomb hadn't gone off. And the unholy noise? Yeah, it was a damn bird. Pathetic. My stupid ass freaked out and lost its cool over a bird. *Fine feathered friend my ass.*

I closed my eyes and concentrated on breathing. "That's right, girl. Nice easy breaths will keep you calm. You just—"

My thoughts trailed off as the rhythmic sound of a woman crying out in the distance snared my attention. "What on earth?" I held my breath and focused, the musical chanting becoming louder and more frenzied with each passing second. I swallowed hard. What woman in her right mind would brave the woods alone at night?

A nagging thought wriggled throughout my consciousness. *You're alone in the woods at night.* I shook my head, wincing at the stabbing pain that shot through my skull as a result. "Yeah, no shit," I muttered to myself. Thing was, something told me I hadn't ended up in the middle of nowhere by choice. Maybe this woman, whoever she was, could lead me out of the backwoods and into town where I could get some help.

I stepped forward, ready to track down the distant voice when something sharp speared the ball of my foot. I pitched forward, clutching my injured extremity and swore like a sailor. Off kilter, I crash-landed into a gaggle of ferns and various shrubbery. "Mother freaking piss! Ouch!"

Yes, yes…I was more than aware that rocking back and forth while howling in pain did nothing to improve my situation. At that point, I didn't care. Whimpering felt natural, so I let go and had myself a good cry.

A large, jagged rock was deeply embedded in the ball of my foot and was protruding out at an odd angle. I slammed my lids shut and shook my head with a groan. There was no getting around it. That bad boy needed to come out or I wouldn't be walking anywhere.

Biting my lip to stifle my scream, I pulled the offending piece of rock from my tender flesh with a muffled yelp. A flash of color caught my eyes as I clutched my injured tootsie. I stared down at my polished toes with narrowed eyes. "Huh, whoever worked on my toes last did a fabu job. Love the polka…" I resisted the urge to smack myself on the forehead and shut my yap, disgusted with how easily I was distracted. *Concentrate, girlfriend.* Barefoot. Why in God's name was I barefoot?

Dizzy, freaked out and sporting a throbbing foot, I glanced down to reassure myself I was, indeed, wearing clothing. With the way things were going for me, a naked trip through the forest seemed entirely possible. I blew out a ragged breath, mentally thanking the good Lord above for small mercies. A faded pair of ripped jeans covered my legs, and I wore a yellow T-shirt, with the words "Spooning Leads to Forking" resting above a set of cartoon silverware.

My teeth chattered as I glanced around, soaking in my unfamiliar surroundings. Dense underbrush, ferns and the like, covered the forest floor. Dark shadows that could only be moss crawled up the sides of the multitude of huge timbers jutting upward into the night sky. I stared up at the ominous giants and shivered. *Jiminy freaking Christmas!* What in God's name had I been thinking when I got dressed this morning? Why wasn't I wearing a jacket or shoes?

I didn't ponder further. Sharp, shooting pain tore through my skull, bringing tears to my eyes. Frustrated, I tore at the bushes surrounding me and slammed my hands against the frigid forest floor. "Goddamn bloody bastard!" I was in the woods, alone, at night, with no shoes, no jacket and no idea how I got there.

I sucked in a deep breath, exhaled nice and slow, and shook my head, confused as all get out by the karmic spanking I'd been dealt. This shit was the stuff movies were made from. You know, finding yourself alone, stranded in some remote stretch of backwoods, with no clue how you got there and no weapon to defend yourself. I half expected a crazed maniac to come busting out of the brush with a body bag and a machete.

A blood-curdling scream wrenched through the air, and the chanting abruptly stopped. *Crappity.*

Billowing clouds of fog, thick like pea soup, rolled toward me at an alarming rate of speed, swallowing the forest whole. Dread wormed its way around my gut and an icy chill rippled across my flesh. *Not good. Time to move your ass, girl. Get gone.*

The throbbing ache at the back of my head made basic thought difficult, let alone hauling myself up off the ground. Seriously, it felt like someone had mistaken my noggin for a juicy steak and had taken a meat tenderizer to it.

The fear accelerating my pulse grew more intense the closer the strange vapor cloud grew. I had a minute, maybe, before it enveloped me, swallowed me whole. Something deep down told me I didn't want that to happen. *Up. I've got to get up.*

My already clammy hands grew stickier, and the cool sweat trickling down the back of my neck sent a wicked spasm barreling through my weakened frame. Woozy, I toppled sideways into the local flora, my vision fading in and out.

Okay, so I wasn't going to die at the fierce talons of a savage bird, but I was going to bleed out on the forest floor while disappearing into a strange, ominous mist. Yep, this shit was B movie material at its best, and lucky me, I got to play the lead role.

And dying? Yeah, it totally didn't feel like I'd expected. Weren't images of your life supposed to flash rapid fire before your eyes? My mind was oddly blank. I wasn't sure if it was a combination of the fear and confusion brought on from my current circumstances, or the massive head wound I sported that caused the odd wall of blackness in my mind. Whatever the reason, I couldn't remember shit, and it was more than a little frustrating.

A deafening roar splintered the air, sending a jolt of adrenaline barreling through my veins. I may have been bleeding out on the leafy floor of some backwoods wonderland, but I sure as hell didn't want to spend my last few minutes mimicking a chew toy for a hungry bear. Call me old-fashioned, but I was vehemently opposed to pain.

The vicious howling continued, the murky fog swelling through the trees, devouring me and the surrounding wildlife whole.

Jesus, Mary and Joseph. What is up with the creepy fog? How I managed, I wasn't sure, but I heaved myself up off the ground. The icy floor shook and swayed beneath my shaky feet, vertigo working its nasty mojo on me big time. Off balance, the sharp branch of a fallen tree sliced through the skin on my cheek and arm as I lurched sideways, crashing into the thick base of what I assumed was a pine tree. The familiar scent of Christmas burned my nose as the deadly beast I'd hoped to evade finally burst through the thick copse of trees, the fog doing little to mask its terrifying presence.

It dropped the limp woman in its arms onto the ground and was on me in an instant. Long, bony fingers topped off with razor-like claws gripped me easily about the neck and lifted me several feet off the ground. Staring into the face of the devil, a fleeting thought raced through my mind. Why…why couldn't it have been a bear?

Roughly eight feet tall, humanoid and skeletal, with an ashen gray pallor, the hell-beast tightened its grip around my throat, effectively stifling my breathy attempts at screaming. Glowing red eyes burned through me as I clawed at its monstrous hand, kicking and thrashing in vain as I tried to free myself.

The small reserve of energy sparking through me from my initial adrenaline rush waned quickly, and icy tears trailed down my cheeks. My time was up. The demon beast from hell was going to eat me.

Hot, rancid breath wafted over me as the beast leaned forward, pressed its bloody muzzle to my hair and inhaled.

The caustic stench of death and decomposition wafting off the creature's clammy hide sent the contents of my stomach rocketing upward. Choking on bile is never fun. Asphyxiating on your own puke while a deranged monster squeezes the life out of you, even less. Worse yet, on top of the heavy amount of "scared shitless" racing through my veins, I had an odd sense of déjà vu. I'd been in this type of situation before; I just had no clue where or when.

Fighting to suck in precious air, I watched in horror as the beast raised its other hand. Claws that looked more like Ginsu knives capable of filleting humans like sushi passed my line of sight and dug deep into the wound at the base of my skull.

The last bit of air in my lungs rushed out with a raspy scream as I cried out in agony. My vision warped in and out, threatening to pull me into a sea of blackness. I welcomed the dark, prayed for it even.

The beast smeared my crimson blood across its thin, rotting lips and snarled. A long, grotesque blue tongue swept out from between a set of gigantic needles that were its teeth, lapping up the sticky remains of my life force before throwing its head back and howling an unearthly, siren wail.

The inky blackness I'd been teetering over wrapped its stygian fingers around me and gave a hearty yank. I felt my eyes roll back and then… I was weightless, falling like a leaf floating on the breeze in the midst of chaos.

The fog continued rolling, thick and oppressive, and I was scarcely able to make out a dark form battling the hideous gray monster, several feet away from where I now laid, sheltered beneath a fallen tree. How I'd ended up there, I'd no clue.

A blur of movement off to the side caught my eye, a flash of gray skirt, dark skin, escaping into the forest. The demon's other victim. The woman who'd been chanting. She'd escaped. *Good for her.* At least one of us would live to see tomorrow.

The dark figure continued battling the demon, moving with supernatural speed. One minute he stood in front of the giant beast, blasting him with some sort of unseen energy pulse, the next he disappeared, only to reappear seconds later behind the demon, blasting away at it again. The beast faltered for a moment before swiping at my dark savior with its freakish claws once more.

Delirious. I had to be delirious, or on the brink of death. That was the only way I could explain the supernatural smackdown playing out before me. Hell beasts and evil, ominous fog didn't exist. And dark saviors who swooped in from out of nowhere just in the nick of time were the stuff of fairy tales. Not that I would have complained if my rescuer were, indeed, real. I was totally down with the whole "knight in shining armor" thing. With all that had happened, I wasn't sure I could trust my eyes.

"It's not real. It's not real. None of this is real." I repeated my new mantra over and over, hoping to squelch the odd sense of familiarity I was experiencing. For whatever reason, I couldn't let go of the idea that I'd been through something like this before. Talk about a disturbing revelation.

I narrowed my eyes and groaned. Clearly, I'd lost too much blood and my mind was in shock, acting out some odd fantasy moment before I kicked the bucket. *Bloody hell.* My mind couldn't come up with a better delusion than this? Weren't hero fantasies supposed to include heaving bosoms, hot kisses and a whole lot of lovin'? What kind of sick puppy was I?

"Enough!" The dark warrior extended his heavy arms upward, the air rippling and morphing as he blasted the creature with a massive energy pulse. The creature, in turn, let out an afflicted wail. It levitated off the ground and hung suspended in midair as though it were paralyzed, its hideous face marred with pain.

With my vision tunneling in and out, I barely registered the blur of movement coming toward me. The shadow savior crouched over me and with a tormented groan, barked out a slew of frantic words in a language I didn't understand.

An electric spark surged through me when the warrior cupped my cheek, my broken body easing and relaxing into the dirt. His touch… It was magical. Comfort, warmth and a fantastic sense of security flowed through me as his rough thumb gently brushed across the torn flesh from my earlier fight with the jagged tree branch. *Oh, God.* Could it be? Was I finally safe?

His scent was so familiar, spicy, woodsy—all masculine. I'd encountered it before. I was sure of it. *"Lo siento, mi dulce."* My angel's voice was smooth and deep, with a faint Latin accent so appealing, had I been even mildly coherent, I would have gone soft in the knees. He leaned down, his warm breath wafting across my face with each labored breath. "Baby, I'm here. I just…fuck!"

My shadow man let out a terrifying wail and pounded the earth beside my head with his heavy fists. Sizzling heat rolled off him in waves, an orange glow lighting his skin from the inside out, likening him to that of a human jack-o-lantern. He threw his head back and cried out, a horrific, tortured sound that made me fear for him and eviscerated my heart. What was happening to him?

He fell forward, his face mere centimeters from mine, his breaths coming in heavy, labored pants. "I...cannot stay, *mi dulce*. He... comes. They...ahhhh!" He fell back, writhing in pain, the brilliant orange light blaring from beneath his skin still seeping out from behind his dark eyes. With a labored groan suggesting he suffered immense pain, he lurched forward, hovering over me once more. Sadness and frustration shone behind the dark eyes that held my gaze. "I can't...they...they come." He glanced over his shoulder for a brief moment, then lowered his head and brushed his lips across my own in a desperate kiss.

An electrical shock that was both warm and tingly surged through me when his lips touched mine, heating my blood, speeding my heartbeat.

"Listen to me, *mi dulce*. I'm going to...fix this." His words came out rapid fire, clipped and almost incomprehensible. "Fix this. I will—Ahhh!" He threw his head back with an agonized groan and tore at his chest. Breaths coming fast, he quickly glanced over his shoulder before meeting my gaze once more. "Will change...fate. Promise you, baby. Trust no one but—"

There was a rustling in the brush, followed by the sounds of heavy footsteps barreling toward us. A brilliant orb of light broke through the dense fog shrouding the woods, blasting intense heat from its fiery core.

The shadow cursed beneath his breath and whispered a quick, "I won't rest until I know you're safe," before disappearing with a flash of light.

Weak, I struggled to reach for him, to beg him to stay, not to leave me alone in this wretched patch of woods with the devil himself.

But my arms were too heavy, and no sound came out when I tried to speak.

Running on empty, my head rolled to the side just as the new player burst through the dense copse of trees. Just like my shadow savior, his face was hidden from me by the night sky and oppressive fog. His giant, hulking frame circled the demon, which still hung in midair, shrouded by vapor, static and unmoving.

"Genitus hinc quod reverto haud magis!"

With a blinding flash of light, the creature was gone.

My lids finally gave out, and with a moan I closed my eyes. Tired. I was so tired. If this new stranger was going to kill me, at least I wouldn't be awake to suffer the pain.

Blackness overpowered me, and my body finally gave in.

Chapter 4

· The Traveler ·

"You were warned, Traveler." The Fates resonant voices blared throughout the small cave they'd sifted me to, echoing off the craggy stone walls. "Abide the law, or pay with your flesh."

My body flew backward, slamming against the rocky interior of the cave, a five-alarm fire igniting beneath my skin. With pain ruling my conscious thoughts, I forgot the Fates had muted my powers and threw up my hands to blast the unseen force burning me alive with an energy pulse.

Low chuckling vibrated throughout the small space, a heavy dose of salt to my burning wound.

"Your powers have no effect on us, Traveler. We are the Moirai— eternal, transcendent. You are nothing, a grain of sand that washes away with the waning tide."

Fire raged beneath my skin, and I screamed through gritted teeth, agonizing pain tearing away at what little control I clung to. Wisps of red and yellow burst from my fingertips, engulfing my arms, hungry for my flesh. My skin blackened to ash within seconds, the sooty remnants falling away with an invisible breeze I neither saw nor felt.

Fucking fire. Why? Why did my enemies always want to burn me?

I dropped to my knees, the stench of my burning tissue searing my nostrils. So this was it. The end. *Cristo!* I'd failed before I'd even fucking begun. Shock numbed me to the inferno gorging on my flesh and bone. My subconscious took over, hurtling me back to a time I'd fought hard to suppress. A time I'd no wish to remember.

I bit the inside of my cheek and squeezed my eyes tight, refusing to utter a sound as they hoisted my body high above the filthy stone floor. The unforgiving metal cuffs shackling my wrists and ankles bit into my raw flesh and my body sagged, reopening wounds that had only just healed.

My mind reeled, imagining all the grotesque possibilities that lay before me. I'd never been suspended from the ceiling before. Ivanov had planned something new for me.

The door to my chamber opened with a loud creak, soft footsteps creeping across the stone flooring. The faceless minions who'd hefted my failing body left quickly, slamming the iron door closed behind them.

I kept my eyes closed, refusing to seek out the face of my tormentor. What did he have planned for me this day? Would he cut out my tongue? Slice open my flesh and slowly bleed me dry? I prayed for death daily, but it never came. No. Death was too easy for the scourge holding me prisoner. He wanted me to pay, to suffer long and hard before allowing my body to succumb to endless sleep, to everlasting peace. For as much as I despised Ivanov for his deceit and betrayal, I knew his motivation. He hated me. Almost as much as I hated myself.

"Why do you keep your eyes closed, Gabriel?"

I stiffened, and my eyes shot open at the sound of Nadya's soft voice stealing away what little breath I had left. "Nadya," I groaned. "Release me. Kill me. Either way, this madness must end."

Ivanov's punishments were unbearable, yet somehow I always managed to endure. Nadya's were an entirely different matter. More agonizing than the physical torment she wrought upon me was the bitter pain of betrayal.

I'd loved this woman—cherished her, held her above all others. And she'd loved me. Or so I'd thought. A hollow ache vibrated inside my chest and my gut clenched, as memories both bittersweet and painful echoed inside my mind. How wrong I'd been to think she would forgive me my horrible transgression. I'd been just in my actions and could barely forgive myself.

A bitter laugh escaped her lips, ripping away any vestige of hope that she might comply. Nadya was every bit as cruel as her father, if not more so.

My body jerked, a wicked spasm tearing through my emaciated frame as she ran a fingertip down the raw, mangled flesh of my naked chest.

"Why would I set you free, Gabriel? We have yet to have any fun this morning." Venom coated her voice, her abhorrence for me evident in every poison filled word.

She danced beneath me, swirling in arcs and circles before stopping just in front of where my head hung low. Sharp fingernails bit into my skin as she grabbed my face, forcing me to look into her heated, obsidian eyes. "Father says you must be purified. Freed from the rot infesting your heart, your soul, and your flesh."

Animosity and outright loathing danced behind her ebony eyes, a wicked sneer crossing her mouth as she shoved my face away and crossed the room toward the far wall. She plucked one of the wooden torches illuminating the room from its metal bracket and cast me a satisfied smile as she sashayed back to where I hung. "And what better way to purify your wretched soul, than by fire?"

My head whipped back and I screamed a thick, guttural cry, unable to mask the excruciating pain that came when she thrust the torch at my bare chest.

Images of the past peeled away in an instant as my body was plucked from the cold, dirt floor of the cave and slammed against the rugged stone wall once more. Blinding light filled the cramped space, and I dropped my head to the side to avoid the heat of their presence.

"Heed our words, Traveler. To alter the past is to create chaos. What was done cannot be undone. What will be cannot be changed. Challenge our law again, make your presence known in any way, and the agony you just suffered shall be wrought upon you tenfold."

My back arched off the wall, acute physical suffering robbing the air from my lungs and shredding my vocal cords as I wailed in agony. New bone grew from the burned out stumps jutting from my upper body. Layer upon layer of muscle, fatty tissue and skin propagated before my eyes. Every inch of growth, every new cell compounded my agony, gave new meaning to the words "growing" and "pain."

The radiant glow the Fates cast diminished into a mere pinpoint before vanishing into nothing. With a final surge of energy, I was thrust out of the jagged opening of the hollowed out rock, falling several feet to the unforgiving forest floor below.

Lungs devoid of air, my mind and body still reeling from the horrors I'd endured inside the small cavern, I lay on the cold, earthen floor for what seemed an eternity, unsure if I was alive or dead.

Death, or what I'd imagined death to feel like, didn't involve pain, and my ass still felt like it was on fire. No, I was most definitely alive, no thanks to the vicious trio of bitches who sought to control me.

Twisted rage turned the corners of my mouth up.

Burn me.

Cut me.

Obliterate my body into a million pieces and sew me back together...

Nothing would change. I was a blank void, an empty shell, a ghost of a man, bitter and pathetic. Life without my other half, without Taylor, was unending, unrelenting torment, and I refused to suffer through that type of existence twice. The Moirai could slap a shock collar on me and take turns electrocuting me for the rest of eternity and I still wouldn't heel.

A tingling sensation rippled up and down the length of my arms, blood awakening the newly constructed veins and tissue. Magic...

my magic, anyway, was capable of vast, wondrous things. On top of transmutation, a kick ass electrical surge and the ability to sift, I could do things like knit broken bones, heal stab wounds and mend ravaged flesh with no more than a thought. Abilities I'd relied on, depended on, on numerous occasions.

Spontaneous regeneration, however, was a power I'd yet to possess, one I'd never heard of up until this moment. So, unless I'd imagined the entire fucking episode, which, given as painful as it was, I didn't think possible, I'd grown myself a new set of limbs.

I stared down at the bright pink flesh covering my hands and wriggled my fingers.

"Fates," I muttered under my breath. "Goddamn mythological bitches." Mere mortal or no, I knew their reasoning, understood why they'd destroy me to keep their law. The past was like a still pond, unmoving, unchanging. And I... I was a pebble, hurtling toward the glassy surface, hell bent on exacting change, altering the quiet fluidity of the water. From the moment of contact, no matter how small that contact may be, a ripple effect would take over, subtle changes altering the perfection of what once was. In other words, any change, no matter how small, could fuck up the future monumentally.

I shook my head and groaned. "*Madre de Dios.*" I didn't give a damn about altering the future, or any consequences that came with doing so. I knew what lay ahead of me: year after year of unending, unrelenting emptiness and pain. Pain that began the moment Taylor's neck snapped beneath the hangman's noose. Pain that wouldn't cease, that would repeat itself unless I became the pebble that cut through the glassy surface of the pond.

My jaw ached from clenching my teeth. If the Fates thought a little burning and regeneration would stop me from completing my mission, they were wrong. Dead wrong. Nothing short of death would keep me from doing all I could to change the course of Taylor's fate.

The faint memory of Nadya's voice cut across the breeze, slicing into my newly grown flesh like a sea of broken glass.

"I curse you, Gabriel Castillo. In this life you shall know naught but pain and suffering. You will find love, Gabriel. You will find your soulmate and suffer a multitude of agony when she is ripped from your bosom. Your other half shall be torn from the life she knows, endure untold agony and persecution before fate finally steals her away. From that day forward, misery shall be your constant companion until the moment your heart beats no more."

Centuries of pent up emptiness and hatred swelled inside my chest, the unforgiving ache a thousand times more painful than the Fates' cruel punishment. It would be so easy to crack, to falter under the weight of my fucked up destiny, to let the pressure, the loathing build until I imploded. Most days I prayed for oblivion. With death came peace and utter quiet. Two things I'd never known.

With a curse, I channeled the negative energy festering in my chest and gut, threw up my hands, and blasted the large boulder sitting atop the jagged cliff face. Dust, dirt and bits of debris rained down throughout the open space, my chest momentarily free of the ache that constantly hounded me, my resolve clear.

Misery and pain could stalk me all they wanted. I'd known them my entire life, had grown used to the bastards, and knew how to survive beneath their oppressive weight. But I'd be damned, damned to hell if that's what it took, before I'd let Taylor suffer a bitter curse meant to destroy me.

If I could free her from the twisted voodoo of Nadya's dying words, return her to the future, to the natural course of her life, then the hollow bubble I'd been surviving in, the half-life I'd been living, would finally have meaning, would finally have purpose. Even if it meant sacrificing myself to do so.

Thin, barren trees reminiscent of overgrown toothpicks jutted up from the ground all around me, soft light from the moon casting an eerie shadow through their naked branches.

I exploded off the ground, my jaw clenched, my hands balled into fists, determination igniting a new fire inside my veins. Unlike the

Fates' pyrotechnic torture session, this new flame fueled my anger and fed my resolve. Taylor would live, and God help the fool who tried to stop me.

Three centuries did little to dampen my memory of the wretched scrap of earth on which I stood. I knew exactly where the Fates had dumped me: The Witch caves outside of the Danforth Plantation, miles from where I'd found Taylor in Boxford Forest. *Mierda!*

Dawn was approaching. I felt it in my bones, saw it in the way the moon rode high and southerly in the heavens. I had just enough time to sift into town, just enough time to hide in the shadows where I could keep an eye on her—and the villagers.

A sharp, knifing pain flayed through my chest. *Cristo!* The echo of Taylor's frightened screams, the image of her broken body hanging limp in the demon's arms was more than I could bear. The red haze clouding my vision darkened, my hands balling into fists. "*Chinga!* Fuck!" Worse than the memory of her bleeding out on the forest floor was the fact I'd been torn from her side, pulled away and punished by the Fates before I could send the skeletal bastard that tormented her packing straight to hell. Heat engulfed me.

The large rock jutting out from the cliff face to my right exploded with a deafening bang, shards of rubble cutting into my skin, a cloud of fine dust stinging my eyes.

He'd saved her. *Damn, stupid bastard.*

The small tree that stood a few feet from me to my left burst into flames.

I shook my head and shoved my hands into my pockets. I didn't need Smoky the Goddamn Bear on my ass.

Life was hard, unforgiving, and its cruelty knew no bounds. I was no fool. I knew I couldn't reveal myself to Taylor again. Couldn't hold her close, couldn't breathe in her intoxicating citrus scent or run my hands over her silken flesh. *Madre de Dios*, that skin… So soft, so…

Sick over the reality of my situation, I shook my head and groaned.

I couldn't reveal myself to her. Not without risking everything. That much the Fates and I agreed on, though I'd never willingly admit it.

But what I could do, what I planned on doing every moment until I knew she was safe, was watch over her, protect her from anyone and anything that might do her harm. Including herself.

The familiar electrical surge that accompanied my magic hummed throughout my veins. Neurons pulsed and shot across synapses as I let it take over, teleporting to Ingersolls Ordinary in the heart of Salem Village.

The rising sun battled the scattered clouds peppering the sky. Warm, muted light shone down across the front of the house and nearby village. It wouldn't take long for the entire area to be bathed in sunlight, so I cloaked myself with invisibility and took up watch from high in the large tree that stood just to the left of the house.

I felt like a damn Peeping Tom, peering into the windows, hoping, praying for a glimpse, a brief look that would let me know Taylor was all right. Hiding in the shadows with my hands tied, unable to do anything but wait was a new form of torture, agonizing and infuriating at the same time. Every cell, every fiber of my being cried out for me to sift into her room, gather her into my arms and take her home, to her own time, her own life.

But I was bound, not only by the Fates and their unyielding laws, but by my own selfish desires. Stealing her away would rob my younger self of the chance to meet her, to know her and ultimately, to love her.

I shook my head. *Never fucking thought I'd be jealous of myself.* But jealous I was. And afraid. Because I knew what was coming, and it didn't bode well for Taylor or my younger self.

The early morning breeze, cool and crisp, caressed the side of my face, carrying with it the faint sound of whispering.

What the...

I turned my head just in time to see a flash of dark skin and gray skirting duck behind a tree across the road, disappearing out of sight.

"Tituba."

More disturbing than discovering the Reverend's slave skulking about during the wee hours of the morning was the thick sea of mist billowing toward the village. The same heavy fog that had engulfed the woods earlier crept forward like an ominous scourge, swallowing the sun's rays and blanketing the opposite side of town in misery as far as the eye could see.

Brows furrowed, I thought back to the grizzly scene in the woods earlier that morning. She'd been skulking around where she shouldn't have been then as well. I'd heard her chanting, saw her steal away during my fight with the demon. What the hell had she been up to? Had to be something shady. Women in the seventeenth century didn't wander through the woods in the dead of night alone. Hell, women in the twenty-first century didn't do that shit either. At least, none with half a brain.

I'd sensed magic, dark and angry, when I first entered the forest. Magic I knew Taylor didn't have. Magic I knew Parris's slave was capable of.

The blood-curdling scream that pierced the morning's calm confirmed my suspicions.

Tituba was up to no good.

Chapter 5

· The Traveler ·

My fist slammed into the crusty bark coating the tree in which I sat.

"Fuck!"

Stinging pain burned across my newly grown knuckles, warm blood seeping from the split skin and torn fissures.

I glanced at Taylor's window, then out at the sea of fog blanketing the opposite side of the road, electrical pulses sparking through my blood, the thick vapor taunting me, rousing my power. Magic was responsible. Dark magic…twisted, angry and full of revenge. I'd battled enough blood-thirsty demons, enough malignant, power hungry spirits to recognize the smell of evil when I came across it.

"Fucking Tituba." It didn't take a genius to put two and two together. She'd been sneaking around, chanting, deep in the woods in Boxford Forest when the ominous fog showed up. She and Taylor both had been attacked shortly thereafter. Little Girl had conjured up some bad ju-ju, put a hex on the village, summoned a demon. A monster she couldn't control.

"Fool!" The thick branch I'd been holding onto snapped from its base with a loud crack, falling from my fingers to the hard ground below with a loud thump.

So it was true then. Reverend Parris's West Indies slave had kick-started the mass hysteria that swept through Salem Village. Her blackened soul would be responsible for the deaths of twenty innocent people when all was said and done, including Taylor.

The indecision weighing heavily on my chest vanished in an instant as I dropped from my roost, the bones in my legs jarring, dry leaves crackling beneath my boots as they slammed onto the granite hard dirt below.

Keeping watch over Taylor, protecting her from harm, was all that mattered, my only goal. But the sound of Tituba's faint whispering, that goddamn fog and that hair-splitting scream… They tore at my psyche, grated at my conscience like gritty sandpaper against skin. If there was another demon, some dark force roaming about the village hell bent on destruction, I had no choice but to step in, no choice but to fight.

I glanced up at Taylor's window, chest aching. I hated leaving her side. Didn't matter she'd no idea I was here. Didn't matter I knew my younger self would be with her and she'd come to no harm this day. The idea of being separated from her for any reason now that I had her within my reach grated on my soul.

Fingers pressed to my lips, I blew a kiss toward her window, sending with it a bit of magic—a memory. The Fates said I couldn't reveal myself to her in person. But, they'd never said anything about a dream. If I couldn't be by her side in the flesh, at least she'd have me with her subconsciously.

Electricity sparked between the tips of my fingers, my body juiced and humming with unleashed power. *Time to kick some ass.* I closed my eyes, embraced the chaotic rush that came with sifting, and smiled before vanishing altogether.

Tituba and me? Yeah, we had some business to attend to. Right after I sent whatever demon she'd unleashed packing straight to hell.

****

Common sense combined with centuries of kicking demon ass told me I'd find what I was searching for if I just followed the screaming. I materialized moments later in front of the Cobley farm, the dense fog shrouding everything in sight, eclipsing the sun.

Energy, supercharged and dark, snapped through the coagulated mist, sending my already heightened senses into overdrive.

Frightened whimpering leaked out from the direction of the barn. I moved toward the structure when a low, baleful growl rent the air, another high-pitched scream nearly drowning out the monster's cry.

Mierda! I sifted to the entryway of the aging barn and nearly dropped to my knees. The caustic stench of death choked the air from my lungs, the scene before me shrouding my vision in a deep red haze.

The interior barn walls, once an aging gray, were now bathed in deep crimson. Old Man Cobley's oxen, his bay mare and newborn foal lay slaughtered on the hay-covered floor, viscera spattered over every square inch of space.

The beast, the same skeletal nightmare from the previous night, had cornered Cobley's teen daughter, backed her into one of the horse stalls preventing her escape. Blood from its killing spree dripped from its raised claws, seeped from inside its open muzzle. Evidently, Cobley's livestock wasn't enough to wet the bastard's whistle because it lunged forward with a deadly growl.

I didn't think. One minute I stood at the entrance to the barn, the next I was in front of the demon, blasting it with an energy pulse. The demon flew up and back, crashing through the flooring of the loft above. Chunks of wood crashed to the floor, bits of hay and dust littering the air. *To hell with the Fates and their ridiculous laws!* There was no way in hell I was going to just sit back and watch while an innocent girl suffered through a demon attack.

Only fools waited for their injured opponents to rise. Anger fueling my magic, I sifted to the loft above, eyes narrowing when I failed to see the massive creature I intended to kill.

I spun in a tight circle, brows furrowed, a loaded ball of energy sparking between my hands.

An unearthly wail split the air as the beast dropped on top of me from the rafters above. Taken by surprise, the power surge intended for the demon careened out of my hands, burning a large hole through the nearby barn wall as it sailed into oblivion.

Jagged claws tore through my chest, ripping and shredding skin and muscle before picking me up and hefting me from the loft toward the blood-soaked floor below.

Thank fuck for my magic. I managed to sift—mid fall—to the opposite side of the barn before hitting the ground, avoiding broken bones and a shit ton of pain.

I eyed the heavy iron pick ax hanging from the wall to my left and clenched my jaw. *Time to put an end to this bullshit.* Iron was the only thing that would put a Wendigo demon down. A fact I was damn sure my younger self was ignorant to, and something I needed to remedy ASAP.

Willing the iron weapon into my hand, I stalked toward the underworld shit-for-brains ready to put the damn thing in the ground. Cobley's daughter, who'd passed out early on into the fight, lay unmoving atop a pile of hay, the demon hovering over her, eager for a human snack.

One fucking second, that was all I needed. Cloaking myself with invisibility, I sifted behind the hulking sack of death and destruction, a fast, clean kill foremost on my mind. Hovering several feet off the floor, I lifted the weapon high and, with a battle cry, drove the deadly blade straight down, cleaving the monster in two from the top of its bony skull to the center of its cavernous chest.

The demon dropped to its knees, a sick gurgling noise bubbling from its partially severed body.

Placing my foot on the beast's chest, I wrenched the pick ax from the warm carcass, kicking its lifeless body backward into its own sticky pool of blood.

Chest heaving, panting for breath, I slung the ax off to the side, the sound of metal skidding through dirt echoing through the open space.

That's when I heard the soft gasp.

My eyes shot to the entrance of the barn in time to see Abigail Williams, Reverend Parris's niece, shaking in silent fear, hands smothering her mouth. With a whimper, she darted away into the now dissipating fog.

I looked down at my hands and cursed. "Fuck." Without realizing it, I'd released the cloaking spell that kept me invisible.

Abigail had seen me.

Chapter 6

· Taylor ·

"Do you think it's her? Is it possible?"

"I know not. Perhaps the Wampanoag took her captive? Look at her strange manner of dress. She wears breeches. And her feet... Look, they are bare, just like the savages."

"No, Goody Godbert. Not a captive, I think. She is not damaged aside from the scratches and rash."

I gnashed my teeth together. On and on the whispering went. Hushed voices spoke in clipped sentences that didn't make any sense. *Wampanoag captive? Strange manner of dress?* And what was that they said about a rash? Criminy! Why wouldn't they be quiet? I had it on good authority there was someone in the room sporting a nasty headache.

The wicked pounding in my skull made it impossible to feign sleep any longer. But worse than the headache was the unbearable, burning itch setting fire to my face and arms. *Ah, okay, the rash.*

With a labored moan, I shifted atop a soft, warm surface. Curious about my whereabouts, I trailed my fingers along the cushioned surface and fisted a handful of cotton bedding. I nearly cried with joy when I realized I no longer lay on the forest floor but in an actual bed.

My cheek felt like it was on fire, so I raised my hand to scratch at the nagging tickle. Where was I, and how did I get here? The last thing I remembered was—

"Cease thy scratching."

A cool hand gripped my wrist, effectively putting the kibosh on my scratching attempt. *Criminy!* I wriggled atop the bed, doing my best to create friction between my inflamed, itchy body and the warm sheets.

I opened my eyes, my lids fluttering against the bright morning light that shone in from a nearby window. It didn't take long for them to focus and zero in on the source of the austere voice ringing in my ear.

Cold, gray eyes, topped off with a wicked looking mono-brow, bore down on me with visible disgust. Pasty skin pulled tight over a plump face, and thin lips pulled down into a frown.

What was her damage? Why on earth was she so mad at me? And holy crap, had she never heard of tweezers? The poor woman looked like she had a matching set of fuzzy caterpillars attached to her face.

Her thin lips wriggled and pressed tightly together before parting with a quick intake of breath. The woman shook her head and made a "humph" sound low in her throat. "Scratching will serve only to make your condition worse." One side of the mono-brow shot up, and the already hard angles of her face pinched even further.

My heart went out to the poor woman. She wasn't just smacked upside the head with an ugly branch, she'd been beaten heavily with the whole damn tree. And damn… What was with her funky clothes? She looked like an extra out of an early colonial period piece, dressed in a long-sleeved, ankle length, brown dress that buttoned down the front. Uglier still were the beige apron and aging shawl she wore on top of the hideous Olde English garb. Her graying hair was pulled back into a severe bun and topped off with a fugly bonnet type cap, reminiscent of a nun's habit.

Sheesh! No wonder the woman wore a scowl. If I was forced to wear that ensemble, I'd be bitchy, too.

She shook her head and readjusted her frown. "Ye should know better than to roll around in poison ivy."

"Poison…ivy?" My voice cracked, and my mouth felt like it was full of cotton. I sucked in a quick breath and moaned. So that was why my skin felt like it was on fire. I'd unwittingly taken a wild romp through the poisonous brush and was now suffering for it. *Fudgity!* Seemed I couldn't catch a damn break.

The aging woman threw her hands up in annoyance and rolled her eyes. "Oh, for goodness sakes, child. Leaves of three, quickly flee. Leaves of five, stay and thrive." A large vein protruding out from beneath the white cap she wore throbbed and pulsated, and she stared at me like as though her little rhyme was common knowledge.

Unsure of what to say, I beamed her with an apologetic smile and shrugged.

"Oh, God." I winced and reached for the source of the pain at the back of my neck. "That smarts like a beeyotch." I wouldn't be shrugging again anytime soon.

"Of course it hurts," the woman said with a snarl as she yanked my hand away once more. "You have a giant, gaping wound at the back of your head. 'Tis no doubt affecting your mind, for ye make no sense." She cast me another reproving frown and grumbled low in her throat. "Your manner of speech is odd and ye possess a viper's tongue. Do ye not know the commandments? Taking our good Lord's name in vain. For shame!" Her round face pinched and contorted, and she scowled at me as though I were an uneducated heathen.

She leaned over me, her hot breath wafting across my irritated skin.

"I know not what a 'beeyotch' is, but I'll thank ye to not repeat the word. It sounds blasphemous, it does. You have an odd way about you. Your speech… You do not sound as though you come from England. There be an odd lilt to your words."

The patch of skin between her eyebrows creased as she quietly surveyed me.

I had zero clue what she was talking about. I thought I sounded just fine. In fact, if anyone sounded odd, it was her. Who in the hell threw around words like "ye" and "blasphemous" nowadays? And for crap's sake! Wasn't there anyone in this place with a tube of anti-itch cream? I was ready to tear my skin off with my bare fingers I itched so badly.

The woman grumbled at me. "I suppose your odd mannerisms matter not in the grand scheme of things. Now, lay still. Mistress Loveguard will be in shortly with some of my boneset tea, a bath and a poultice. I must take my leave. There are others that need tending."

I raised a brow. *Loveguard? What an odd name. And others?* Someone else had been attacked by that…thing?

Images, fragmented and confusing, flashed behind my eyes. A skeletal creature with sickly, gray skin, and long, razor-sharp claws. A woman with long, dark hair and chocolate skin, hanging limp in its arms. I shook my head and moaned. The woman from the woods, the one that got away. Had she been injured? Was that who Monobrow was referring to?

Still grumbling, the stout woman waddled over to the door, the thick layers of her woolen dress rustling with the movement. She stopped just beneath the doorway and pierced me with yet another savage glare. It was clear this woman, whoever she was, meant business and wasn't often trifled with. She glared at me through narrowed, suspicious eyes. "I suggest you sleep if you can, child. For when I return, it will be with the Reverend Parris and the magistrate, Goodman Hathorne."

If she meant to frighten me with her superior tone and "bow beneath me you groveling swine" demeanor, she was succeeding. I swallowed down the fat lump in my throat. *Magistrate?* I wasn't sure what or who that was, but regardless, it didn't sound good.

Monobrow eyed me warily, her cool gray eyes mimicking a set of lasers as they burned into my flesh. She jabbed a stout finger through the air in my direction. "And no scratching. Heed me this or suffer."

I bit the inside of my lip and gave her a nod, relieved when she trotted off. Truth was, the woman scared me a little, and I would have agreed to anything at that point to make her leave. The sooner I could get myself up, out of bed and out of this strange nightmare world, the better.

Absolute silence covered me like a blanket, and let me tell you, I was nothing but thankful for it. The constant whispering from before made my already pounding head ache further. I was sure there'd been more than one person in the room. *Huh*... Maybe I'd imagined it. After all, I did have a "giant gaping wound" at the back of my head.

With a groan, I hefted myself up into a sitting position and braced myself as the dark, wooden ceiling and walls tilted and swayed. Once the amusement park spinning wore off, I took a good, long look at my surroundings.

The room was sparsely furnished. And by that, I mean aside from the large wooden bed I lay on and a simple dresser sitting just to its side, the room was largely empty. A lone rocking chair with a faded brown quilt draped over the back sat in the far corner of the room. The wooden walls were barren. No pictures, no mirrors. I scanned the ceiling, then the floor. *No central heat or air and no carpeting.* It was obvious I was in a remote cabin out in the middle of Asscrackistan. *Great.* I may not have been able to remember diddly, but I knew instinctually I was most definitely an indoor girl. Roughing it in some remote cabin out in the wild was not my idea of fun. And indoor plumbing? Yeah, it was essential.

I clenched my thighs together and wriggled in place, a familiar, urgent sensation making itself known. *Crap.* Where the hell was the loo, anyway? I was about to float away.

Reluctant to leave the warm cocoon I'd made, I closed my eyes and sighed. Blocking out my body's desperate urge along with thoughts of running water (I really had to pee), I focused, trying to remember something, anything, beyond my jaunt through the forest last night that would clue me in to my whereabouts. All I got for my efforts was a brain-splitting ache that tore through my skull as though someone had taken a hack-saw to it. Nauseated and tired, I eased back onto the soft feather bedding and groaned.

"Will change…fate. Promise you, baby. Trust no one but—"

Whoa. The memory of my rescuer's Latin voice? I remembered that just fine. I also remembered the way his warm breath wafted across my skin, the sense of safety brought about by his touch. Who was he, and when would I see him again?

I snuggled further into the warm bedding and let the memory have its way with me. "Mmmm…tall, dark and Latin," I whispered to myself. "I don't know who you are, but I hope I see you again."

A gust of wind whipped through the nearby window, a hint of pine floating on the cool breeze. The small room, the bed, time itself—fell away in fragmented layers, the heady scent of pine and rich spices triggering a vivid fantasy.

Rough bark cut through the layers of wool and cotton, the unforgiving surface chafing at the tender skin on my back. I twined my fingers through the thick layers of hair at the back of his neck and held him to me, his glorious lips a perfect balm to the nagging irritation at my back.

The scent of rich spices, fresh air and pine swirled around him like some kind of erotic love drug, luring me in. It was intoxicating. He was intoxicating, and the only thing I cared about at that moment.

Goosebumps spattered across my skin, my heart fluttering like a hummingbird's wings inside my ribs as he pulled his lips from my mouth, trailing soft, whisper-light kisses down my jaw.

He groaned, a deep, masculine sound that sent my blood boiling and my nether regions screaming for attention. There wasn't an inch of skin covering my body that didn't ache for his touch, cry out for his kiss. He was a master in the art of sexual warfare, a damn guerilla fighter—lethal, proficient and fucking sexy as hell.

The buttons holding the top portion of my dress closed exploded from the annoying fabric keeping us apart, and it was all I could do to breathe, to keep my wits about me, when he laid siege to my chest with his mouth.

Strong, capable hands tugged at the layers of fabric covering my legs, the hideous skirt an unwanted barrier between my ready and willing girlie bits and the salvation that was him. Warm, rough fingers grasped both sides of my ass, lifting me off the ground. My legs snaked around his waist, and I cried out in exquisite relief as he ground his swollen cock against my aching core. Oh, God. I was so ready. I wanted him. No! I needed him...like air. Without him I'd asphyxiate, I'd cease to live... I'd die. I sucked in a ragged breath. "Please, Gabriel..."

"Ah, I see you're awake now."

Startled, my body jerked sideways atop the bed and I let out a breathy yelp. *Holy freaking crap. What the hell just happened? What was that? Scratch that. Who was that, and why...why did this chick have to interrupt? The dream was just getting good. Really good.*

Heart still hammering and flushed from the erotic vision that had swept me away, I sucked in a deep breath, wishing the young woman sauntering in was someone else altogether.

Twenty years old, if even that, she bustled toward me with a large tray in her hands, and a set of clothing draped across her arm. Taking care not to spill her load, she set the wooden caddy down on the nearby dresser. After gently laying the drab clothing at the foot of the bed, she turned to face me and offered up a gentle smile. "Good morrow to ye, Mistress..." She trailed off, her sky-blue eyes drinking me in with stout curiosity.

Just like Ol' Granny Sourpuss who'd tended me earlier, this new woman swathed herself in bizarre pilgrim garb. A pale green dress, also sporting long-sleeves, covered her slight frame and complimented the paleness of her skin. She, too, wore an apron and sported a bonnet that tied beneath her chin.

I frowned. *What is up with the weird pioneer clothing?* Felt like I'd landed in the middle of a *Little House on the Prairie* convention.

She raised her eyebrows and inclined her head toward me. It was clear she was waiting for me to give her my name, which, for the life of me, I couldn't remember. A thick wall of blackness and pain shrouded my aching head, and I couldn't make my way past it to find any answers. This, of course, was beyond frustrating, and I let out a ragged gasp as warm tears welled in my eyes. Why couldn't I remember? Not only did I not know where I was, I couldn't remember my damn name.

I couldn't meet her eyes, so I picked at a stray piece of fluff on the bedding like it was my sole purpose for living. Heat blasted across my cheeks and I gasped, unable to keep it together. "Jesus Christ! I can't remember my name. I can't remember anything." I finally looked up, frantic. "What's wrong with me?"

The young woman's pale blue eyes grew wide. "Merciful heavens. Goody Godbert warned me of your viper tongue, but I was hard pressed to believe her." She glanced over toward the door before leaning in close. A wisp of blond hair fell out from beneath her stark white cap and she quickly tucked it back under.

She raised a brow as though she were gearing up to tell me a juicy secret and gave a nod toward the now empty doorway. "No need to work yourself into a fit, Mistress. I overheard Goody Godbert gossiping with Goody Pope. It matters not that ye have damaged your head and cannot remember yourself. They are fairly certain they know who ye are and are right thankful to see you alive and whole. Here," she said and offered up a steaming cup of tea.

I eyed the steaming liquid with trepidation. Taking in any kind of liquid was a bad idea.

Curious, the woman drew back and narrowed her eyes. "What ails ye, Mistress? Ye are dancing in place like… Oh! Ye poor thing. I expect ye need to relieve yourself?"

The breath I'd been holding burst out in a relieved whoosh. Bladder burning, I barked out a desperate "Yes! God, yes. Please. Where's the loo? I think I'm going to float away."

Pity crossed the young woman's face as she hurriedly set down the teacup. She bent over, pulled a large, stone pot from beneath the bed and shoved it into my empty hands.

"Here you are, Mistress. I would send ye outdoors, but judging by the way ye are dancing atop the bed, I fear ye would not make it." The corner of her mouth lifted ever so slightly, making me wonder if she didn't find my predicament more than a little funny.

I peered into the dark earthenware pot and threw my head back a millisecond later, gasping for air. The damn thing stank to high heaven. "What am I supposed to do with this? It smells like someone..." Oh, good God. Girlfriend wanted me to piss in the pot. Seriously?

The woman gave me a single nod and eyed me like I was a loon.

I whimpered, briefly considering the amount of time it would take me to make it outside, before sighing in defeat. "Where do I...uh...go, for...you know, privacy?" Talk about your horrifying, humiliating experiences. I wanted to cry. First I wake up, barefoot and alone in a strange forest. Then I'm attacked by a ravenous flesh-eating demon, and now...now I'm being forced to empty my bladder into a stanky, funk-laden pot. Damn, freaking gross.

"Oh," she said and shuffled in place for a moment, looking almost as embarrassed as I was. "Forgive me, Mistress. I shall take my leave, and leave you to your..." She inclined her head toward the pot. "Will ye be needing a corn cob?"

My head shot back. "A corn cob? What would I..." I didn't bother to finish my sentence and instead shook my head. I waved her off. "On second thought, don't answer that. I really don't want to know."

With a nod she turned and left the room, closing the door behind her.

She returned after a long stretch of time, for which I was extremely thankful, and found me snuggled once again under the goose down bedding.

As to my experience with the pot... Well, let's just say it was an experience I'd rather not think or speak of...ever. I shuddered as

I remembered how my nursemaid had tossed its contents out the window like it was no big deal. Yeah, I'd rather not think about that either.

With pressing bodily functions out of the way, my young nurse renewed her ministrations and shoved a no-longer-steaming cup of tea beneath my nose. "Drink, Mistress."

A bit woozy, I propped myself up on one elbow and sipped some of the liquid she so desperately wanted me to drink. "Ugh," I said with a grimace and pushed the small porcelain cup away. "That tastes like…" A vision of the stoneware pot I'd become familiar with just minutes before raced through my head. Gross. I scrunched up my nose. "That tastes like piss. I'll pass, thanks."

With a raised brow, she shoved the cup under my nose once again and shook her head. "I know not what piss is. This here is Goody Godbert's boneset tea. Twill rid the pounding in your head."

My eyes shot open. *Oh, hell to the yes.* I didn't need to be told twice and downed the repellent liquid in one huge gulp. The tea was rank and nasty, but if it would rid me of the mind-splitting ache, I'd drink a gallon of the septic crap. Excedrin would have worked much better, but I was of the mindset that beggars shouldn't be choosers. If the piss-flavored potion worked, then I was a happy camper.

"Hold up." I jabbed a finger through the air, the words she'd spoken moments before just now sinking in. While I enjoyed this new woman's soft voice and happy demeanor, her rapid speech left me a tad dizzy. "Who were you yammering about a minute ago? Monobrow? And really, they know my name?" *Huzzah!* I was desperate for some answers.

She jerked her head back and narrowed her eyes in confusion. "Mono…what?"

I frowned. "Monobrow. You know…the large, round woman with caterpillars for eyebrows." How could she not know whom I was talking about? You couldn't miss those unlandscaped nightmares if you tried.

She stared at me for a second, after which a light bulb must have gone off somewhere inside her brain, because her eyes grew large, her lips turned up into a smile and she nodded at me furiously. "Yes. Goody Godbert. She does have a dreadful spattering of hair across her forehead, does she not?"

I bit back a laugh despite my miserable condition. "Yes. Dreadful, indeed." This girl, whoever she was, was beyond adorable, and I took an instant liking to her regardless of her strange appearance and odd lingo.

"As to your other question, I am afraid I cannot say. I did not hear a name spoken, only that they thought ye dead this past fortnight." She rustled with something on the tray she brought in, then came at me with an odd looking paste in her hands. "I am sorry for the smell, Mistress, but there is naught to be done about it. I must dress your wounds." She cast me a sympathetic eye and proceeded to slather the thick paste across the gash on my cheek.

The rancid smell made my eyes water and sent the contents of my stomach hurtling upward into my throat. "Oh…God, that's awful. Do you—"

She lobbed a thick smear of the goop on the wound at the base of my skull, using her fingers to spread the paste to just behind my ears. "Oh!" she said and drew her hand back with a gasp.

I raised a brow. "Something wrong?"

She eyed me, brows drawn together as she rubbed at her fingers as though she'd been shocked. "No, Mistress. There is…there is nothing amiss."

I wasn't sure I believed her but kept my mouth shut as she reached for another blob of the disgusting goop and started smearing it across the gash on my arm.

She made a show of clearing her throat before speaking again. "And to answer your question, yes. I must administer this paste if ye wish to heal."

Free of Goody Godbert's watchful eyes, and covered in stinky goop, I clawed at my arms and neck, wishing like hell I had some sandpaper, or a bottle-brush, or at the very least, another set of hands with which to scratch. Poison ivy was one vicious bitch and I felt like crawling out of my skin. *Wait…another set of hands.*

I eagle-eyed the young blonde and did my best to appear pathetic and desperate. Which, I suppose in my case, wasn't a far stretch; I was beyond pitiful. "Oh, my God. Please," I whimpered. "Help me scratch. The itching… It's unbearable."

The young woman's eyes widened with horror. "Have a care, Mistress, with how freely you misuse our Good Lord's name. You will find little tolerance for that type of speech in these parts." She shook her head and made a "tsk" sound. "These are dark days we live in," she whispered. "Blasphemous talk will only serve to draw accusations of witchcraft and bedevilment."

Was girlfriend serious? Witchcraft? Bedevilment? What the hell was bedevilment anyways? I frowned. Would these strange people really banish me for tossing out a random OMG? Seemed a bit puritanical to me, but I apologized anyway. No need to draw further negative attention to myself. My little jaunt through the woods and subsequent attack had likely stirred the gossip pot just fine.

"I'm sorry," I said, desperate for some relief. "The itching is so bad. I can't think straight."

Her expression softened. "I expect it is. Oh!" Her face fell for just a moment and she mumbled something under her breath. "Curse my scattered thoughts, I have gone and done it again. Here," she said and turned her back to me for a moment as she reached for a large bowl on the tray she brought in. "You shall continue to itch if we do not get the oil from the plant off your skin. After we wash you, we will have to reapply the poultice. I am truly sorry."

I was sorry, too. The idea of her plastering more of that rank paste on my skin made my stomach turn.

She plunged a cloth into the bowl full of water and wrung out the excess. "This here has goldenseal in it to help ease your discomfort. Goody Godbert's been schooling me about herbs and such. She is the village healer, and I am to follow in her footsteps."

I scrunched up my nose. Village healer? Where the hell were we, medieval England? I half expected her to bust out a bowl full of leeches any moment, or worse, try her hand at a bit of bloodletting. Eeck!

I scanned the small room once more, wondering where the heck I'd managed to land myself. The North Forty? Timbuktu? And really, hadn't she ever heard of Cortisone cream? That stuff was fab at getting rid of pesky itching. Why'd she have to bathe me in herbal crap?

My body sagged into the mattress after the first swipe of the cloth, and for the moment, I no longer cared where I was or what she said. *Sweet blessed relief!* The cool water combined with the friction from the cloth felt like heaven and it took everything I had not to whimper like a baby. As it was, I moaned a little, but I didn't see how that could be helped. In fact, I'd challenge a three-hundred pound warrior to keep his trap shut while suffering from an unbearable itch.

The young woman smiled, the left corner of her mouth pulling up into a crooked grin. "My name is Prudence Loveguard. Forgive me for not introducing myself sooner."

All I could think about was the relief the cool cloth was giving me. Her late introduction, her unusual Olde English name, the foul smelling paste... None of those things mattered to me in the least. As far as I was concerned, Prudence Loveguard was an angel sent from above. "It's okay," I said, waving her off. "It's nice to meet you, Prudence."

Her blue eyes held my attention as she plunged the cloth into the bowl once more. "Can you really remember nothing? How it is you came to be here? Your name?" She held the cloth forward, gesturing for me to wash my face.

I closed my eyes, swiped the damp cotton across my skin and focused all my energy on remembering.

I blew out a ragged breath. Nothing. Zip. Nada. Zilch.

Beyond the crap storm that was my night in the forest and the comforting voice of my Latin hero, I remembered nothing. Wait, scratch that. I knew what year it was... Two thousand... "Crap!" I slammed the moist towel onto my lap with an aggravated huff. I couldn't even remember the damn year. Everything, and I mean everything was, well, fuzzy. What the hell happened to me? Why couldn't I remember people? Did I have any family? Friends? And if I did, were they searching for me? Did they know I was missing?

The line of questions racing through my mind seemed endless, and the scary thing was, I saw no answers to any of them in my immediate future. I was alone—with no one to trust, no one to turn to, and that frightened me more than anything. Even more than the monster that attacked me the night before.

Frustrated and defeated, I reached over, dropped the cloth into the bowl and blew out a sigh. "Sorry. I don't remember anything before last night, and parts of that are fuzzy." I held up a hand and circled it through the air. "Who brought me here?" I glanced around the room before meeting her blue eyes once again. "And where *is* here, anyway?" Maybe she knew my Good Samaritan and could tell me how to get in contact with him. I had a fat thank you to dole out.

Surprise flickered across her face, and the corner of her mouth lifted into a soft smile. "Ye have taken shelter at Ingersolls Ordinary, silly."

Ingersolls Ordinary. I sat back and pondered her answer for a minute. Seriously, between the head wound, rash and widespread memory loss, I wasn't sure why it came as a surprise I didn't recognize the name. Seemed I had the world's shittiest luck.

After reapplying the rancid poultice to my wounds, she plucked a thin linen slip from the pile of clothing she brought in and motioned for me to remove my dirty shirt. "Quickly now. We must get you out of these filthy rags and into something more befitting a gentlewoman. What were you thinking, donning men's breeches?"

I frowned, wanting to point out that my shirt, though agreeably filthy, was not a rag. Why T-shirts had a bad rep for being sloppy I'd never know. They were comfy as sin and cute. Well, not so much the boxy styles but—

"And as to who brought you here, well, I'm quite surprised you have no memory of it. 'Tis a rare woman who can forget the likes of Gabriel Castillo. And with the events of the past week…"

My pulse kicked up a notch the moment the name passed her lips and I no longer heard a word she spoke. "Gabriel," I whispered. Flashes of my earlier vision raced behind my eyes, my own, breathy voice ringing in my ear. *Please. Gabriel…*

I gasped. *God, could it be?* Was the man from my vision the same man who rescued me last night? His name felt so familiar, intimate almost. Just uttering the masculine name sent a rush of heat pooling between my thighs and a hot zing of desire racing through my veins. My skin flushed and a dull, needy ache grew from my center, ripples of excitement sparking off every inch of my skin.

A flash of something—a pair of vivid green eyes—danced behind my lids for a split second, the scent of pine and deep, rich spices flooding my already overloaded senses. *Whoa. There it is again. That wonderful, masculine smell. God…who is this guy?*

More than a little confused by my body's blatant sexual response to the mention of my rescuer's name, I shrugged off the thought, concluding that if this Gabriel character had been the one to bring me to safety, that's where the familiarity and "appreciation" came from. I yanked my yellow tee over my head and…

"What?" I asked, curious about the odd expression slathered across Prudence's face. I looked down at myself and frowned. The twins were holstered nicely in a white, lacy bra. What was the problem? I looked up. "What's the matter?"

Prudence shook her head and fiddled with the linen slip in her hands. "Nothing is amiss. I have just never seen such a…fancy undergarment before. 'Tis so very small…*and* made of lace. Surely it must have cost you a fortune."

"My bra?" Was she kidding? I cocked my head to the side and eyed her with a whole lot of "you've got to be shitting me." "Are you telling me you've never seen a bra before?" Was this girl for real?

"Bra…" She mouthed the word slowly as though it was new and foreign to her. "No. I have never seen the likes of your bra before." She thrust the thin scrap of fabric at me and shook her hands. "Quick! We must cover you up before one of the Goodwives discover ye and accuse you of harlotry! Or worse, witchcraft!"

Witchcraft? People would accuse me of witchcraft and harlotry for wearing a bra? Girlfriend's too-tight bonnet must have been squeezing the sense right out of her. I snatched the slip from her hands and drew it over my head. "Relax, Prue." I pulled my arms through the slip and raised an eyebrow. "Is that cool? Me calling you Prue?"

She gave me a sober nod and I continued on. "Sheesh! You'd think you'd never seen someone's undergarments before." I slid off the bed, ignoring the dull ache in my injured foot. It took some maneuvering, but I managed to hike the slip around my waist and wriggle my jeans down the length of my legs, before kicking them off completely.

Cool, blue eyes burned into the top of my head, and I stood up, unsurprised at that point to see Prue shaking her head at me once more. "I have seen plenty enough undergarments, thank you very much. Just none that look like that," she said, pointing to the pair of matching white, lacy panties covering my girlie bits.

I rolled my eyes and shoved the slip's gauzy fabric down, letting the cotton drape down past my knees. "Well, if you don't wear a bra and panties, then what do you wear beneath your clothing? Don't tell me you walk around free styling it?"

She snatched a gray, woolen skirt from the bed and handed it to me. "I cannot say I know what this 'free styling' is. But as far as undergarments are concerned, the women here," she tugged at the hem of the linen slip I wore, "wear shifts."

Shifts? I opened my mouth to question her further when a ruckus from the first story down below caught my attention. Holy Lord. It sounded like a bomb had gone off.

Goody Godbert's robust voice blasted up through the wooden flooring, ringing in my ears and grating on my senses. "Stop right there, Good Sir. I have told ye, the mistress is still recovering. She is not receiving guests this day. Goodman Castillo!"

Goodman Castillo? Wait a minute. Castillo... My body stiffened with a jolt as realization hit me. Jesus, Mary and Joseph... Gabriel Castillo, the man who plucked me from the jaws of death, the man I'd had a lusty fantasy about just a short time before, was headed my way.

Anticipation, excitement and a staggering amount of "oh shit, what do I do?" whirled throughout my gut, leaving me breathless and more than a little dizzy.

The air in the room thinned, my heart slamming a staccato beat against my ribs as heavy footsteps clamored up the wooden stairwell. There was a momentary pause, a brief second where time seemed to still. My breath caught with a sharp, quick inhale, and the next moment the door burst open. That's when my heart stopped beating altogether.

Chapter 7

· Taylor ·

"Well, slap me silly and call me Susan." Young Goodman Castillo stood just inside the doorway to my room, and damn, he was shmexy. Uber-shmexy—and rugged. In fact, Shmexy Boy was so good looking, I barely registered him utter the words "leave" and "now" to my erstwhile helper.

Red-faced and eyes wide, Prue mumbled a quick "excuse me" and fled the room, closing the door behind her.

Prickly heat spattered across my skin, and the warm rush of heat that pooled between my thighs just a few minutes before returned with gusto as a pair of familiar green eyes drank me in. Every ounce of air taking up space in my lungs rushed out in a quick whoosh, leaving me breathless and lightheaded. *Those eyes.* Good Lord in heaven, they were striking— and full of pain. What type of torture had he endured? What horrific loss had he suffered that would leave such pain, such torment behind his eyes?

And what beautiful eyes they were. A brilliant shade of emerald with gold flecks rimming the irises like sparks of fire, they burned into my half-naked flesh with startling familiarity.

I know those eyes. I was sure of it. But from where, I had no clue.

I sucked in a shallow breath and concluded I must possess a will of iron, because somehow, I managed to look away. Though, my gaze didn't travel far.

Tall, dark and deliciously tan, this handsome new stranger was a hulking presence in the small room. His broad shoulders spanned nearly the entire doorway. Taut muscle and smooth brown skin peeked out from the open collar of his gray shirt. His dark, baggy pants gathered at the knees and were topped off with a pair of dirt-crusted, leather boots. A brown leather trench coat that looked like it had been caught under a bus and dragged across town completed his outfit. Talk about your retro ensemble. Shmexy Boy looked like he'd flashed in from early colonial America.

But his hair...*Sweet Lord in heaven*...his hair, all messy, black and thick, sent my fingers aching to dive in and tug, despite his ragged and dirty clothing. A few strands of glossy ebony hung over his eyes, framing a strong, handsome face and a set of full, oh-so-kissable lips.

The clamor of heavy footsteps rushing up the stairs drew his attention from me to the nearby entryway. He exhaled a heavy breath and with a shake of his head, raised his hand. The air surrounding the door thickened and skewed for a moment before returning to normal.

I stepped back with a gasp. Had I really just seen what I thought I did? Did he do something to the door? Unsure, I looked to Gabriel, to the door, then back to Gabriel again.

The heavy footfalls ceased and a heavy pounding rattled my skull as Goody Godbert attacked the other side of the door with her fist. "Open this door at once, Goodman Castillo. Ye cannot be alone with my charge behind a closed door. 'Tis highly improper!" The door groaned and shook beneath her heavy beating, but remained closed despite her best efforts otherwise.

I raised a shaky hand. "How did you...did you do something to the door?" He had to have. I'd clearly witnessed the air warp and swell, defying the laws of physics, and stretching the realm of what I believed possible.

He dropped his chin, glancing down at the floor before looking up at me through a set of thick, ebony lashes. A wisp of dark hair fell across his forehead and he shrugged.

I opened my mouth, but I'd be lying if I told you I'd been able to speak. Pretty Boy had stolen my breath away. *Good Lord, he's beautiful.* So beautiful, in fact, he could whammy the entire room with voodoo magic for all I cared. Just as long as he let me look at him. *So pretty.*

The complete absence of sound filled the meager space between us. I no longer registered Goody's frantic pounding or her frantic, masculine voice. In fact, I didn't register anything but the hulking mass of goodness towering a few feet in front of me.

Trapped in our own little world, closed off from everyone and everything as though we were suspended in a sound proof bubble, we stood, lost in each other's eyes.

A strange, magnetic pull clouded my thoughts and kick started my heart. Attraction…that's what the nervous butterfly fluttering in my stomach was, the warm, delicious ache throbbing in my nether regions. Pure physical attraction— potent and powerful. But there was more. The sense of safety and, God, the trust I felt in his presence… It was unreal. And unsettling.

Bad boy was a stranger. Sexy as all get out, but a stranger. I should have been afraid, wary even. But, for reasons unknown to me, I knew without a doubt, I could trust him.

What I didn't know, however, was if I could trust myself. With no memory of my past dealings with men, how was I to know if I could trust my instincts? What if I was some sort of loser magnet?

Taking in the magnificence of the creature in front of me, I quickly decided that I didn't care if he was a loser. And really…since I couldn't remember my past, it didn't matter anyway. Shmexy Boy was scrumdidlyumptious, and I didn't want him to leave.

My tongue darted out of its own volition, moistening my lips, my mind traveling straight to the gutter. Oh yeah, baby. I wanted those full lips of his all over me, that bottom lip between my own as I fisted handfuls of his glorious hair. I wanted to run my hands over the smooth skin encasing the granite hard muscle beneath. And those hands of his…my God, they were enormous, his fingers long. *Oh, God!* The delicious things he'd be able to do with those fingers.

My breath caught, fleeting images of the two of us entwined in a naked embrace in front of a roaring fire, his lips trailing kisses down my neck, bombarded my conscious thoughts. The mental picture… the memory…was so vivid, I felt the ghost of his caress against my flesh even now. Goosebumps pebbled across my exposed skin, despite the fever burning just beneath its surface.

Flushed and a little squirrely, I closed my eyes for a moment, hoping to God I could pull myself together. Fantasizing about Shmexy Boy with him standing right in front of me, although highly enjoyable, probably wasn't the best idea. Until I found out who I was, and where I was, hanky panky was out of the question.

Or at least, it should be out of the question. I bit down on my lower lip. Drinking in the über hotness that was Gabriel Castillo, I wasn't sure I'd be able to resist. The desire I felt for him, the magnetic pull… Well, it was impossible to ignore. And really, I didn't want to ignore him. I wanted to get jiggy with him. Over, and over, and over again.

He came at me fast, his enormous body standing mere centimeters from my own, commanding all of my attention.

Both of us spoke at the same time.

"You saved me last night."

"You're—"

A pained expression distorted the strong lines of his face, and he cupped my cheek.

I gasped as a shock of heat radiated down my jaw-line, a pleasant tingling sensation following shortly thereafter. It was the same wonderful sensation I'd felt last night when he touched me.

Wait, something wasn't right. The man who'd touched me, the Latin savior who'd made me feel safe… He'd abandoned me in the forest when Gabriel showed up, hadn't he? I knit my brows together. Gabriel had a Latin accent, too. Had I imagined another rescuer? Had Gabriel been the only person with me in the forest all along? It was possible, I supposed. Blood loss and shock would definitely cause confusion, and I'd suffered plenty of both.

"You are hurt."

His deep voice drew me back to the here and now. The skin between his brows creased and his eyes darkened as he tenderly ran his thumb across the jagged slash crossing my cheekbone. He dropped his pained gaze from my face, his calloused hand following suit.

White heat burned the flesh beneath his fingertips as they blazed a path down to the cut on my arm. He placed his palm over the wound and a warm rush of heat radiated up and down its length, followed by the same tingling sensation I'd felt in my cheek.

"Forgive me, *Adonia*, for not coming to your aid sooner." He dropped his hand, and my body cried out from the loss. This man, whoever he was, had a magical touch.

Pain and something that looked a lot like regret marred his masculine features for a brief moment, but vanished as quickly as they came.

Punch drunk and dizzy from his presence, it took me a minute to realize he was apologizing. But for what, I had no idea. He'd come to my aid last night, rescued me from that creepy underworld freak. What could he possibly have to apologize for?

I tilted my head back to meet his emerald gaze, warm tears of gratefulness spilling down my cheeks. "You have nothing to apologize for. You stopped that…that thing from…" I broke off, my emotions too raw. Aching for the loss of his touch, I lifted a shaky hand and placed it on the center of his chest where his shirt lay open.

He hissed, his body stiffening under my touch.

I looked up to see he'd closed his eyes, his face contorted as though he were in pain. I pulled my hand away. Had I hurt him somehow? Seemed unlikely. All I did was touch him. "I'm sorry... I didn't mean to..."

He drew a deep breath and opened his eyes, a sea of deep green ensnaring my attention. "There is no need to apologize, *Adonia*. You did nothing wrong. Here," he said and took hold of my wrist, placing my hand back onto his chest. An underlying aura of discomfort radiated off him, though he no longer grimaced.

What happened to him to make him shy away from a simple touch? It had to have been something awful. People didn't react that way for no reason. Had he been beaten? *Oh, God.* My chest squeezed, and I hoped to God that wasn't the case. Who would want to hurt such a wonderful being?

His skin was incredibly smooth and soft, and the same energy that had sparked when he touched my cheek, flared again. The despair and panic pulling me under leveled out before ceasing altogether.

"Whoa." I pulled my hand away and glanced down at it before meeting his eyes once more, a heavy dose of "wow" painted across my features. "Did you... Did you feel that?"

My hand found his chest again, and after a few moments, after he'd grown used to my touch, he closed his eyes and sighed. His body visibly relaxed, the magical force between us radiating a steady stream of peace, comfort and home. I didn't know what the spark was, or how to explain it, but I didn't want it to go away. For the first time since I woke up alone in the woods, I finally felt completely safe.

He opened his eyes, the pain that had filled them moments before morphing into shock and disappointment. "*Cristo.*" Eyes wide, he shook his head and stepped back. "It... It cannot be. I was sure I was wrong. I..." Torn over something, he hesitated before striding over to the window. He placed his hands on either side of the frame and dropped his head with a groan. "*Madre de Dios,*" he muttered under his breath. "Why? Why now? Why can I not have a moment's peace?"

More than a little confused, and if I were being honest, feeling a tad rejected by his strange behavior, I stood crying, half-naked in my shift like a bumbling idiot. What the hell was he talking about? What couldn't be? Didn't he feel the connection between us? Why didn't he want me? I rolled my head toward my shoulder, trying to be sly, and took a whiff. Did I smell? Maybe that damn paste Prue slathered all over me turned him off. *Sheisa!*

Overwhelmed by the massive pile of doo-doo heaped upon me in such a short amount of time, I broke. The floodgates opened, my knees buckled and I sank to the floor as fat tears streamed down my cheeks. Yep. I was a total loser. I didn't know who I was. Didn't know where I was. A hell-beast had attacked me and the one person I felt a connection with didn't want anything to do with me. With my crap luck, a piano was bound to fall out of the sky and flatten me at any moment.

Body shaking with sobs, I was too far gone to put up any kind of protest when a pair of strong hands scooped me up off the floor. He crossed the short distance to the bed, whispering a string of soft words in his native Spanish I didn't understand. The feather mattress sank beneath his heavy weight, and he cradled me against his body, rubbing soothing circles up and down my back with his hand.

"*Lo siento, Adonia.* Forgive me. Please, don't cry."

His thick Latin accent and deep resonant voice wafted over me like a lover's caress, and despite my tears, my nipples puckered to tight buds. The despair eating away at my psyche eased up once again as he held me in his arms. Who was this guy? And why did he affect me so deeply? I'd gone from crying to wanting to drop my panties in two seconds flat.

I swiped away my tears and fought to catch my breath after crying. "What is that you keep calling me? *Adonia?* It's… It's beautiful."

He cracked a smile, and if I'd thought him handsome before, I was wrong. Handsome didn't cut it. Shmexy Boy was drop dead gorgeous, and his smile the most beautiful thing I'd ever seen. His full lips pulled into a wide grin, showcasing a mouthful of perfect white teeth and a set of adorable dimples I wanted to sink my fingers into.

"As are you, my sweet. *Adonia* means beautiful lady."

Blistering heat crawled up my neck and onto my face. I bit my lip and looked down, fighting off the urge to squeal like a girlie girl. *Hot damn! He thinks I'm beautiful!* Really, if I could have gotten away with it, I would have hopped around the room and danced the funky chicken. But my foot hurt and something told me that type of behavior would probably scare him away. So, I squelched my excitement and stayed good and still, relishing the feel of his strong arms holding me close.

He caught my chin between his finger and thumb, lifting my head, forcing me to meet his gaze. Flecks of liquid gold rimmed his irises, fanning the flames of his heated gaze, which cascaded over me like a wisp of hot, molten desire. "Forgive me, my sweet, for bringing you to tears." He tore his eyes away, looked off to the side for a moment, and sighed. Remorse shone clear as day behind his gaze when he faced me once more. "That was not my intention." He raised his hand to my face, the tips of his fingers tracing gentle lines across my cheekbone, over and over as if committing it to memory. His touch stole what little breath I had left. "Do you have a name?"

His eyes never left mine as he waited for my answer. The hand holding my chin? Well, that was another matter altogether. Rough, calloused fingers ghosted along the column of my neck before tracing a back and forth pattern across my collarbone, making me weak in the knees.

My head spun, his rollercoaster of emotions making me dizzy. Honestly, I didn't know whether I was coming or going with this guy. One moment he was hot. The next, stone cold. My touch seemed to cause him agonizing pain one minute, whereas the next he touched me as if it were no big deal. Shmexy Boy had issues. Issues I had no problem overlooking because, damn, he was pretty.

The corner of his mouth pulled up into a sinfully hot grin and he raised an eyebrow. "I'm waiting, *mi dulce*. Do you not have a name?"

Mi dulce? Where have I heard that before?

The quiet bubble we'd been trapped in burst, as the weight of his question pressed down on me. My name. I wanted more than anything to give him an answer. But I couldn't. I didn't know who the hell I was, and if I admitted that to him, he'd probably think I was crazy. Hell, *I* thought I was crazy. The situation sucked ass.

The rhythmic pounding that had magically disappeared for the past several minutes, returned with a vengeance: Goody Godbert's voice crying out from behind the bedroom door.

"Open this door at once or I shall be forced to break it down!"

My eyes flashed wide, and though it pained me to do it, I shuffled off Gabriel's lap and put several feet between us.

The absence of him was both overwhelming and wretched. I fidgeted, smoothing the thin cotton fabric of my shift, over and over. "We should…um…" I motioned toward the door. I'd no doubt whatsoever about Monobrow's ability to take down the heavy door. The woman might have been old as dirt, but she was large, fierce and scared me to death.

Gabriel looked to the floor and shook his head with a sigh. He stood from the bed, the tenderness that graced his masculine features gone, replaced with a mask of cool indifference. "How quickly I forget myself when I am with you. This cannot be. Forgive me, *Adonia*. It will not happen again."

I narrowed my eyes. "What?" *Wait…what?* Not happen again? What did he mean? I most definitely wanted our little moment to repeat itself—and often. He was the only person I'd come across so far that made me feel safe, at ease. Not to mention, he was dead freaking sexy. I needed him, wanted him.

He raised a hand toward the door, and the wooden slab magically flew open. Goody Godbert and another dowdy old woman came stumbling in, anger and disgust swathed across their aging faces.

With a scowl, Monobrow rushed forward and grabbed my chin between her finger and thumb. Eyes wide, she jerked my head to the side, inspecting me at length.

Her plump features twisted and contorted. "The gash on your face…'tis healed." She quickly scrutinized my arm and gasped before looking up in shock, eyebrow raised. "Your arm as well. And the rash…gone. 'Tis a miracle."

My eyes wandered over to Gabriel for a brief moment as I remembered the warm, tingling sensation that crawled over my broken skin. Had he healed me with his touch? Was that even possible?

His expression remained serious, aloof, giving nothing away. The gentle man who'd held me tenderly, gone.

Disappointed, I turned my attention back to Monobrow and shrugged. "Must have been that paste you had Prue slather all over me."

Goody pursed her lips and continued glaring at me with obvious suspicion, but said nothing.

Fidgeting under the uncomfortable weight of her stare, I shifted in place and bit my lip. What did she want from me? Further explanation? "I…uh…I'm a fast healer?"

This, of course, could have been a complete lie. I had no memory of my healing abilities, but would have said anything at that point to get her off my back.

She cast a reproving frown toward me, then Gabriel, and let out a throaty groan, relaying her disgust. "I trust ye both kept to your commandments and refrained from any improprieties."

She eagle-eyed Gabriel with a staggering amount of disdain. "Lechery is a punishable crime, Goodman Castillo. Though, I expect ye know that. Come away now." She raced forward with astonishing speed for a woman of her size and girth, grasped him by the shoulder and with a great heave, ushered him out of the room and into the hallway.

A set of piercing green eyes were the last thing I saw before the heavy door slammed shut behind her.

I took a moment to compose myself and peeled my jaw from the wooden floor below. What the hell had just happened? I glanced down at my hand remembering the delicious electrical spark that flowed between Gabriel and me when we touched. Good God, it had been magical. I didn't know squat about who or where I was, but I knew one thing for certain. I planned on crossing paths with Gabriel Castillo again. Nothing would keep me from him.

Chapter 8

·The Traveler·

Blood, vivid red and hot, trickled down my back, the jagged stone wall tearing into my naked flesh. It hadn't taken long, the span of a breath maybe, for the Fates to sift me back to the cave after the scene at the barn.

I'd known going in, any action I took at the Cobley farm would be deemed forbidden by the Moirai, and worthy of punishment. I just didn't care. To not fight, to sit back and do nothing while evil ran rampant went against my nature, against the very fabric of my being. Not to mention, I didn't do well with people telling me what I could and couldn't do.

Magically pinned to the far wall of the small cave, my legs spread wide, my arms outstretched, I'd been stripped of my powers once again, my shirt torn from my body.

The brilliant light they cast burned my eyes, keeping their celestial forms indistinguishable in the small space. With each clamorous word their brilliance magnified, the heat radiating throughout the space nearly unbearable.

"You were warned, Traveler, to keep to the shadows, to refrain from interfering."

A wisp of light grew from the brilliant orb illuminating the cave, a long spectral arm shifting and curling in on itself as it advanced, closer, and closer.

"You failed to heed our word. And so you must pay...pay with your flesh, with your blood."

The silvery thread of light, now centimeters away, swept across my chest like a mystical dagger.

Crimson droplets of blood trickled down my exposed skin, as the wisp of light split in two. The long arm slithered side to side in the air like a snake with a forked tongue, before striking, peeling away a long strip of flesh from my body.

The spectral arm drew back, the Fates' layered voices echoing off the craggy stone walls. "A pound of flesh, Traveler, for each transgression."

My head flew back, and I cried out, unable to bear the agony in silence. Searing pain knifed through my consciousness as the forked arm struck, over and over, repeatedly tearing strips of flesh from my naked chest.

When the last strip of tissue had been torn from my torso, the luminous snake struck at my arms, my face.

Throat raw and bloody from screaming, my body sagged against the invisible bonds holding me upright. Shock numbed me to the fiery sensation coursing over my flayed body. I was spent, broken.

But deep down, swimming below the agony and despair my body endured, lay anger.

Rage.

Defiance.

My flesh, my blood, meant little to me in the grand scheme of things. I could withstand torture, endure untold amounts of physical pain. But what I couldn't stand, what I couldn't survive, was the knowledge that my soulmate, my other half, was doomed to die because of a heinous curse meant to destroy me. The idea that I was responsible in any way for Taylor's death was more than I could live with.

So torture, punishment, paying with my flesh for interfering? Those things were all fine by me. Bring on the pain, baby. Didn't matter if you flayed the skin from my entire body, burned me to ashes or bled me dry. As long as I had breath in my body I'd fight. Fight for Taylor's life, fight for her freedom from the curse that doomed us both.

Flies swarmed around my raw tissue, swooping and diving over exposed muscle and tendon. Eyes shrouded by my own blood, I couldn't see them, but heard their hungry buzzing, felt them niggling at my ears.

Heat blasted across my flayed torso.

"Foolish mortal. You think we do not hear your thoughts? Sense your defiance? As torture does not affect you, we shall have to take other means to bring you to heel."

Voice shredded and gone, exposed muscles too traumatized to lift my head, I flinched for a brief second before sagging once again against my unseen restraints. What more could they possibly have planned? They'd already burned me alive and flayed the skin from my body. Short of killing me outright, there wasn't much else they could do, much more they could take away.

"That is where you are mistaken, Traveler. There is one thing—or rather, one person, whose life means more to you than your own."

No!

A mangled groan blew past my raw, bloodied lips. Fresh pain lanced across what was left of my grizzled torso as I jerked and thrashed against my invisible bonds.

Taylor. They were going to kill Taylor.

"Indeed, Traveler. We are the Moirai. We hold the life thread of every living mortal in our hands. Should you continue to interfere, should you show yourself to another living soul in this time, we shall cut your precious Taylor's thread of life in two."

Scorching heat blasted against my ravaged body, fire consuming what little was left of me as I cried out Taylor's name with a deafening roar.

Chapter 9

· Taylor ·

I raced down the narrow wooden steps leading to Ingersolls's first floor. Uncomfortable and self-conscious dressed in the cumbersome pilgrim garb, I tugged at the ties to my bonnet or "coif" as Prue had pointed out. Coif, cap, hideous torture device from hell... I didn't care what it was named; I didn't want the damn ugly thing on my head.

Prue, bless her uptight soul, had turned three shades of gray and looked like she might keel over when I tried to leave my room without my hair done up and covered by the annoying scrap of fabric. Loathe to subject myself to any more drama, I'd let her wrestle my long, brown hair into submission. An unattractive bun now rested at the back of my head, covered by the matronly cap, which I fidgeted with as I peered through the doorway to what looked like the dining room.

Spying on the people who'd provided me with medicine and shelter probably wasn't the nicest thing to do. However, I was of the opinion that desperate times called for desperate measures. I didn't know who these people were, or where I was, though I had a few suspicions.

Best I could come up with, I'd managed to land myself in Amish territory. Or maybe in some odd, colonial reenactment village. Regardless, as far as I was concerned, a little surveillance on my part was the best move all around. I needed info, and I needed it bad. Therefore, I did what any resourceful girl with half a brain would do. I hung back and did my best to go unnoticed.

Gabriel, two aging men and the stout and sober Goody Godbert stood in the center of the room around a long wooden table flanked with bench seating. A large brick fireplace took up a good portion of the wall behind them and sported a roaring flame, which heated the sparsely furnished room.

Monobrow flitted back and forth between the fireplace and the men with what looked like an antique tea-kettle in her hands. Two steaming mugs sat on the table in front of the older men, going largely untouched as they threw daggers with their eyes at the handsome young Spaniard standing a few feet away.

Gabriel, clearly angry, pounded his fist against the thick wooden table. Heat blazed behind his viridian eyes, the muscles in his neck straining with frustration. "I have told ye a thousand times, man. I have naught to do with the madness plaguing this village. I was not at Cobley's farm this morning!" He threw his hands up and looked to the ceiling. "*Por el amor de todo que es santo*! I want only to be left alone."

Scorching heat blazed across my skin and my nipples hardened beneath the thick layers of fabric I wore, aching to be touched. The twenty feet between us made no difference; I reacted to him as though he were mere centimeters away. The pure physical chemistry between us was unreal, and oh yeah, I wanted him. Badly.

The shorter of the two older men, the one with gray hair that swept past his shoulders, stepped forward and jabbed a finger toward Gabriel. "Ye lie. Ye have been in our midst, what…a month at most, and look at the calamity that has befallen us. Goody Alston's youngest son died. Jeremiah Whittard's barn burned to the ground, and the ship that carried many a fine Christian soul crashed into the rocky coast killing everyone on board! 'Tis a miracle the woman upstairs is alive! And this morning… The atrocities committed inside Isaiah Cobley's barn. My niece, Abigail, swears she saw you standing amidst a sea of blood. Your presence brings misery, death."

Wheezing and shaky, the man sagged onto the nearby bench with a ragged breath and broke into a coughing fit.

With her stout hands clutching her hideous shawl over her chest, Goody Godbert rushed to his side, but not before treating Gabriel to a vicious scowl. "Please, Reverend. Ye must calm yourself. Ye are not well. Ye—"

The reverend's eyes nearly popped out of their sockets. "Calm myself? Are ye mad, woman?" Still coughing, he choked on his words, his knobby fingers pointing haphazardly toward Gabriel. "There is a monster in our midst! The devil himself plagues this village, bewitching my people, the flock I am charged to bring to our good Lord." He threw his hands up in the air, shaking off the stout woman's attention. "Good heavens, woman! I am beside myself!"

Hmm. I narrowed my eyes and chewed on the inside of my lip. So this was the Reverend Parris I was to meet. Monobrow was right. He didn't look well. A thin layer of sweat covered his ashen skin, which hung loose off his severe bone structure. Dark circles ringed a pair of sunken, ebony eyes.

He was dressed in black from head to toe with a flat, white collar that hung down over his short-waisted, black jacket. Though ailing, he possessed an air of superiority. Or maybe he had a wicked God complex. You know, since he was a man of the cloth and all. I wasn't sure.

Either way, my first impression of the reverend wasn't good. He'd accused Gabriel, the man who'd saved me from the jaws of death and the only person I trusted, of several unsavory acts, including murder. It just didn't jibe.

For starters, I'd come face to face with this so-called devil last night in the woods. I'd also witnessed Gabriel fight the unholy bastard off. No. The man who'd cradled me tenderly in his arms upstairs while I wept wasn't the monster plaguing their village. Thing was, would anyone believe me if I told them? Probably not. I was a stranger, a nobody. I sucked in a quiet breath and continued spying on the heated show.

"'Tis not polite to eavesdrop, ye know."

Every muscle in my body stiffened simultaneously, a bone-cold chill freezing me to my core. I whirled around, prepared to eat crow or come up with some pathetic excuse for my below board behavior, and came face to face with a pair of young girls.

Seated on a bench toward the end of a narrow hallway, I'd completely overlooked the quiet duo when I'd raced down the stairs moments before.

Dressed in the same "Pilgrim Chic" as the rest of the women I'd come across, the older of the two couldn't have been more than twelve. I placed the younger girl somewhere around eight years old, though it was hard to tell given the bulky clothes and bonnet she wore. Both sat rigid in posture on the small bench, with their hands crossed in their laps, eyeing me with frank suspicion.

Just great. Looked like I'd be dealing with a couple of prepubescent haters on top of the judgmental oldies kicking it in the other room.

Aside from Prudence and Gabriel, I'd yet to come across a friendly face.

"Oh," I managed to say as I clutched the fabric over my chest. "You scared the crap out of me. I…uh…" I stuck my thumb out and jabbed it through the air over my shoulder. Killing them with kindness couldn't hurt either, so I plastered a silicone smile across my face and made nice. "I'm new here…and I…didn't want to interrupt." This, of course, was complete bullshit. I was spying and they'd totally caught me. The hell if I was going to admit to it though.

"Ye fancy the warlock, Gabriel, do ye not?" the older girl asked. "I saw the way your breath caught when he spoke to my uncle."

Taken back by the biting label she'd used to describe Gabriel, and surprised someone her age could read me so well, I stood speechless for a moment. Seemed I was incapable of forming simple words, let alone a convincing rebuttal. *Sheisa!*

"Don't worry, Mistress," the younger girl whispered. "Abby and I are good at keeping secrets." She pressed a finger to her petal-pink lips and cried out when the older girl jabbed an elbow into her side. "Abby! Ow! Why did ye—"

The older girl, Abby, raised a brow and pegged her young comrade with a "shut up or I'll pound you" stare. The young girl promptly zipped her trap, and they both dropped their chins, staring at their laps instead of me.

I frowned and turned my focus toward the adults in the other room. I didn't have time to play games, and there was something off about the two girls. They were obviously hiding something, as the younger girl couldn't wait to tell me how good she was at keeping secrets. The vibe they cast was sketchy at best and I knew the fewer dealings I had with them, the better. I placed my hand on the nearby wall and peered into the other room.

The beleaguered minister focused his attention on the aging man at the opposite end of the table. I could only assume this was John Hathorne, the magistrate Goody Godbert spoke of. "He is not to be trusted, John. He is a wraith, a specter in this village. We know not when he comes and goes, nor what he does on that remote plot of land in the woods he calls home." His thin lips pulled into a frown and he shook his head. "And I cannot tell ye the last time I saw his face in church. He's a pagan infidel, a pariah hell bent on bewitching my villagers, a—"

Gabriel, who'd remained stone-faced through the reverend's blistering attack up until that point, sliced his hands through the air. "Enough! I do not attend your bloody monotonous services on the Sabbath because I want to be left alone. That does not make me a pariah."

I eased back against the wall for a moment. *Village? Sabbath? Bewitched villagers?* Christ on a pogo stick. Where was I? I glanced down at my dowdy, colonial outfit and gulped. Maybe the question I should have been asking myself was "when was I?" I shook my head, disgusted with my ridiculous assumption. Afraid I'd miss out on some important piece of information, I sucked in a quick breath and continued my reconnoitering.

Gabriel lunged forward over the edge of the wooden table and got right in Old Man Parris's face. "And if you want to call me a heathen, that's fine. Go right ahead. Just remember, *Reverend*, that this here heathen was the one who carried your precious villager from the depths of the forest and brought her to safety last night after her attack. If I were the monster responsible, she would be dead. *Cristo!*"

A huge lump formed in my throat, a thick layer of cotton coating my tongue. Knowing I'd been at death's door was one thing. Hearing the truth uttered from someone else's lips was another matter altogether. I fought back the onslaught of tears threatening to spill, eternally thankful I'd been giving a second chance at life.

Gabriel pulled back and swiped a hand through his thick ebony hair. Frustration billowed off his large frame in waves, thickening the air with an undeniable tension as he traipsed back and forth. He stopped his mad pacing just in front of the hearth, swore under his breath and pegged the older men with a look that said "listen up, and listen up good."

"I came here today for one purpose: to plead with ye to open your eyes. A dark cloud hovers over your village." He raised a hand toward Parris. "*Cristo…* Ye know this to be true, Reverend. While you incite chaos and entertain ridiculous accusations of witchcraft, a plague of evil thirsting for blood circles, lying in wait." He stepped forward and jabbed a finger through the air. "Ye must listen to me. Go forth and seek out the root of this darkness." He paused.

I stepped back quickly as he glanced in my direction. Had he seen me? Did he know I was listening? Good God, those eyes of his. So intense. So full of pain. *Crappity.* And witchcraft? Innocent people had been accused of witchcraft? I'd landed in the middle of some freak loony town. I bit my lip and waited a bit before peering around the doorway once more.

Gabriel slapped a heavy fist onto the table. "Seek out the evil lurking in your midst before it has a chance to strike again. For I assure you, darkness such as this never grows tired."

Parris stood up with a ragged intake of breath and eyed Gabriel with a mixture of shock and horror. He cast Hathorne a frightened glance before focusing on Gabriel once more. "John, you are witness to this man's confession. Gabriel Castillo admits freely to knowing the dark one's mind and when he will attack. Such knowledge is proof this man is in league with the devil!"

Gabriel threw his hands up in disgust and shook his head. "Foolish, foolish man. I am no more a devil than you."

"How dare you imply I have an alliance with the dark one," Parris roared.

Gabriel stepped forward with his palms upturned. "*Por favor, padre.* Please. You must listen. I am trying to help you, trying to open your eyes. I—"

"Away with you, Satan." The reverend, who'd stepped back the moment Gabriel moved closer, pulled a silver cross from beneath his shirt. Brandishing it in front of him like a weapon, he waved the cross back and forth in front of him like a mad man. "We are strong in the Lord here, foul beast. Be gone, minion of hell!"

Holy hell. Parris was a drama king of epic proportions. All I needed was a bag of popcorn and a diet soda and I would have been set. The reality playing out before me was like a made-for-TV movie. Chock full of drama.

Gabriel let out an aggravated huff, stepped back and threw his hand up. "*Idiota.* I warn you, there is evil lurking in your midst. You are surrounded by pure bedlam! And what do you do about it? Nothing. You've curled your tail between your legs and allowed a couple of ridiculous little girls to foster chaos and hysteria. You are fools. All of you."

A loud gasp drew my attention from Gabriel. I peered over my shoulder to see the older of the two girls standing with fists clenched and jaw rigid, burning a hole into the wall in front of her. No joke, if it were at all possible, I wouldn't have been surprised to see steam rise up from her ears. Little girl was ticked but good.

She muttered something under her breath I couldn't make out and sat down as quickly as she'd stood.

I clutched my neck and drew in a quick breath. Seriously?

Witchcraft? Did these people really believe in that crap? And had I heard him correctly? Children were the ones accusing these women?

Icy dread slithered around my gut as I cast a quick glance over my shoulder at the two young girls seated on the bench a few feet away.

"Don't worry, Mistress. Abby and I are good at keeping secrets."

The metallic taste of copper filled my mouth as I chomped away at the inside of my lip. Good Lord. Could it be? Were the preteen girls sitting a scant three feet from me, the girls Gabriel had been talking about? His earlier reference to "ridiculous girls" had sent the older child into a full on tizzy.

Brown eyes, blank and void of warmth bore into the side of my face. My stomach rolled, a combination of hunger and apprehension. I swiped my sticky hands across the folds of my ugly wool skirt and tried to catch my breath. *No, thank you.* I wasn't even going to entertain the possibility. Regardless of their involvement, those two were up to no good. I felt it deep down in my bones.

What I *was* going to do was try and piece together the clusterfuck situation at hand and figure a way to extricate myself from it. From what I could tell, the skinny was this: some type of dark force or demon had taken up residence just outside the small town, was itchy to embark on a killing spree, and lucky me, I was his intended first course. Clueless to its existence, the townsfolk had been entrenched in a shit storm all of their own. Ignorant, stubborn, and just really damn gullible, they'd allowed a handful of bratty children to rouse a full on brouhaha, resulting in pointed fingers and accusations of witchcraft.

I gritted my teeth and shook my head. "Fools." Gabriel was right. The people in this village were a couple clowns short of a three-ring circus.

Parris and his priggish parishioners were idiots. Their refusal to open their eyes had left the demon perfect opportunity to roam free and attack me, which in turn, pissed me the hell off. I wanted to scream or smack something, but the only thing in reach was the wall, and dammit, I wasn't a fan of bloody knuckles.

Gabriel's rich accent pulled me back to the drama unfolding in the dining area.

He jabbed a finger toward Parris. "The women ye have accused are no more witches than you, Reverend. 'Tis madness, holding them captive. Cruel."

Haunting pain flashed behind his emerald eyes, a large crease forming above them. He groaned low in his throat and the pained expression disappeared with a shake of his head. "Stop this insanity and set them free." He stepped forward and thrust a finger in Parris's direction. "The darkness will return, and with it, it will bring misery and death."

The muscles in his jaw flexed and rippled as he gnashed his teeth together. With a curse, he whipped a knit cap from his coat pocket. "I have said all I can on the matter and will take my leave." He pulled the cap over his thick mane of hair, then thrust his hand forward and pointed to both of the men. "Let it be known I tried to warn ye. Your ignorance will only result in turmoil." He dropped his hand and strode toward the door with an impressive swagger, stopping just beneath the doorway.

My heart nearly stopped as he cast the two men an icy glare, cold enough to freeze hell a thousand times over. "And for the last time, stay off my land."

The moment he closed the door behind him, the minister collapsed onto the wooden bench, coughing and wheezing.

Holy snot rockets. What the hell had I just witnessed? Had the reverend really referred to Gabriel as a minion of hell? I had to admit the man was a bit intimidating what with his enormous size and "I'll pound your ass into the dirt" aura, but the devil's lackey? No, I didn't think so. After the amazing connection we shared upstairs, my gut told me Gabriel was a good guy. Possibly the only good guy I'd come across since I landed in this crazy place.

Reverend Pasty Face was off his freaking rocker. *Criminy.* I'd landed in the middle of some bizarro religious cult.

I closed my eyes and shook my head. *Jesus, Mary and Joseph. I've gotta get out of here.*

"And what do ye think ye are doing?"

"Holy dooley!" Surprised, I staggered back, lost my footing and promptly fell on my ass. *Real smooth.* So caught up in the drama I'd just witnessed, I hadn't heard Monobrow creep up on me until she was right in my face. "Holy Shintock." I crossed myself and let out a nervous laugh. "You scared me." I hauled myself up and swept my hands across the thick layers of my gray, woolen skirt. "I...I..."

Monobrow shook her head in obvious disapproval. Mistrust shone clear as day behind her stormy eyes. "I know what ye were doing. Save your breath, Mistress." She grabbed hold of my wrist and gave a hearty yank. "Come now. There is much to discuss."

✳✳✳✳✳✳✳✳✳✳✳✳✳

Thoroughly confused, I held up my hands and shook my head. "Wait, wait, wait... You think I'm who?"

Monobrow glared at me, her steel gray eyes cold and calculating. "Good Lord in heaven, Mistress. Have ye not listened to a word the reverend has said? Your name is Faythe Ellwood. We thought ye dead these past two weeks. The ship on which you journeyed to us, smashed upon the rocky coast. There were no survivors." She eyed me good and slow from head to foot. "Or, so we thought." The left side of her unibrow shot up, and she shook her head yet again. "I must say, we thought ye would be farther along in your years." She leaned forward, eyebrow raised. "How old are ye, Mistress?"

Crap. I had no idea. Why'd she have to ask such a loaded question? I felt young, but that didn't mean squat. There were no mirrors in this Podunk cabin, so I had zero clue as to what I looked like. Was I old?

My stomach rolled. *Good God!* I *was* old! That's why I couldn't remember anything. I was ancient and senile and... *Wait,* Monobrow had said she thought I'd be further along in my years.

Maybe I wasn't as old as I thought. Maybe…

"Cease your whining, Mistress," Monobrow snapped.

Whining? I'd been whining? How embarrassing.

She grumbled something beneath her breath and shook her head. "Ye match the description of the woman who was to be my apprentice, so ye must be her. Ye must be Faythe Ellwood."

Holy freaking frijoles. I slumped down onto the nearby bench and rested my face in my hands. Faythe Ellwood. The name felt as foreign to me as the clothes I wore and the house I sat in. Could it be? Had I really journeyed across the ocean and survived a shipwreck? I couldn't remember the last time I'd heard of a ship sinking. Then again, I couldn't remember shit, so who was I to balk at their theory? Regardless of whether or not they were right about my identity, I couldn't put a stop to the warning bells clanging inside my head. I knew, deep down in my gut, I was not this woman, Faythe. I knew it with crystal clarity.

But I wasn't about to share that little tidbit with them. Hell no. These people were different, odd. Scratch that. They were whacked out and crazy. Religious zealots. It was obvious they didn't conform to society by the way they dressed, their antiquated manner of speech and the ease in which they accused people of consorting with the devil. Nope, these whackos were likely to banish me from their rigid, backwoods society if I rocked the boat, and then where would I be?

Alone again. In the woods with no food, no shelter and no way of discovering who I was or how to get home. No. Until I could come up with some concrete answers to who I was and how I got here, the smartest thing to do would be to assume the role of their long lost Faythe Ellwood. What that meant for my future, God only knew.

I dug the heels of my hands into my eyes and gave them a good rub before blowing out a deep breath. "Alrighty then. You must be right. I don't remember a thing, but the name feels…familiar," I lied. *Crappity!* My skills in the fibbing department were seriously lacking. They'd be onto me in a heartbeat.

The Reverend Parris, who'd finally managed to get his coughing under control, cleared his throat with a grumble and burned a hole into the side of my face with an odd, intense stare that made my skin crawl and my stomach turn. "I must confess, Mistress Ellwood. We feared ye dead this past fortnight. Ye are a miracle come to aid us with your fine healing skills during these dark, miserable times. Pray tell us; where have ye been these past two weeks?"

His question hit me like a two-ton boulder, knocking the wind right out of me. I opened my mouth, and surprise, surprise...no words came out. What the hell was I going to tell him? I didn't have a clue where I was, let alone where I'd come from. Lying was out of the question, as it required some knowledge of where I was, and I had none. *Criminy!*

I felt my lower lip quiver seconds before the tears started falling. I covered my mouth, stifling a sob. The jig was up. My ass was grass. Unable to answer the simplest of questions, they would for sure boot me from their priggish, holier-than-thou community, or worse, accuse me of cavorting with the devil.

Goody Godbert made a "tsk" sound and sighed. "Did I not tell ye, Reverend? The girl has forgotten herself." She prattled on, ignoring the minister's "humph" sounds and questioning stare. "A direct result, I must say, from the bloody wound at the back of her head. No doubt inflicted upon her by this so-called evil Goodman Castillo referred to."

A loud gasp blew past my lips, my mouth dropping open in shock. "So-called evil?" I slapped my hands onto the table and leaned forward. "Seriously? You don't believe me?" I searched their faces, shocked to find a heavy helping of "girlfriend's got a head injury, don't listen to a word she says" written all over them. "I'm not crazy. There's a giant, skeletal freak roaming the woods and it tried to eat me."

An image flashed behind my eyes. "Wait!" I sat rigid in my seat, the hair on the back of my neck standing on end. "I wasn't alone. There was a woman in the woods with me, chanting something I couldn't make out. She had dark skin and hair and she wore a gray dress. She escaped. Is she—"

Goody sucked in a deep breath, a thin sheen of sweat coating her suddenly pale face.

"Tituba," Hathorne mumbled, disbelief lacing his somber voice.

Parris's eyes grew wide. "Im-impossible," Parris said. "The witch sits rotting in jail as we speak. 'Tis impossible for you to have seen her."

Witch? In jail?

Clearly, I'd heard them wrong. I leaned forward and narrowed my brows in disbelief. "I'm sorry. Did you say…witch?" He couldn't be serious. Yeah, I'd taken a hard knock to the head, but I wasn't delusional. I knew what I saw.

The reverend pursed his lips and sucked in a deep breath through his nose. Lifting his hands so that they sat in front of his body, he tapped the tips of his fingers together and proceeded to ignore my last question altogether. "Will her mind heal, Goody?" He glanced over toward the stout woman, uncertainty tainting his already darkened eyes. "Will she remember herself?"

I crossed my arms over my chest with a huff, pissed at the ease with which he'd blown me off. *Crazy ass bastard.* I knew what I saw: a giant fugly monster with daggers for teeth and wicked razor claws. I also knew this Tituba woman, whoever she was, had been with me in the woods. I'd witnessed the monster dump her unconscious body onto the ground in front of me. I was sure of it. Why they chose to ignore this, to ignore me, I'd no clue. My only hope was that wherever she was, she was safe and unharmed.

Monobrow mashed her lips together and shrugged. "I know not, good sir. If it is the Lord's will, with time I suppose."

"Uh…hello! I'm sitting right here, thank you." *Good grief! Will she heal or won't she? Where has she been?* I felt a bit like an old appliance. Will she work? What should we do with her? With my luck, they'd pack me up and give me away.

My eyes widened. Wait, given the accusations of witchcraft, maybe braving the woods on my own wasn't such a bad thing. At least I knew where I stood with the creepy fog and hungry demon. These people gave me the willies.

The reverend swiped a hand across his face before setting it in his lap. "'Tis of no great consequence where ye have been I suppose. Ye are a miracle, child. Handed over to us from the brink of death by the Lord himself. Truly, mistress, ye are heaven sent."

Fine healing skills? Heaven sent? Okay... Talk about laying it on thick. Ol' Reverend Pasty Face possessed an arsenal of flowery words with which to kiss ass, and he wielded them with deadly accuracy. My guess? His entire congregation hung on his every word. Still, I'd managed to dodge a bullet. The matter of my whereabouts for the past two weeks had been swept under the rug, and for that I was eternally thankful.

The issue of my profession was another matter altogether. One look at the reverend and my gut told me to ignore the aging windbag and run for the hills. I was no healer. Or if I was, I certainly had no memory of it. Still, fleeing the crazy Quaker Oats wannabe and his pious followers would get me nowhere fast. The circumstances I found myself in were shitty and left me few choices. If I wanted answers, I'd need to play along.

Nervous, I cast a quick glance at Monobrow and John Hathorne, who had yet to utter more than one word. Rigid in posture, the old man stood like a statue at the end of the table, his brown eyes boring down on me with an expression that looked like a cross between constipation and something an awful lot like, *eww*, lust. He licked his lower lip, one corner pulling up into a lecherous smile.

My stomach rolled. Seriously? The town magistrate was not only ancient, saggy, and mute, but a dirty old man as well? I bit the inside of my lip and averted my gaze. Too much eye contact might give grandpa the wrong idea, and he didn't stand an ice cube's chance in hell.

Creeped out on a multitude of levels, I squared my shoulders and remained firm in my resolve. Information was key, and these people were going to give it to me one way or the other. I'd flirt with Old Man Hathorne if I had to, but that was as far as he'd ever get.

I slapped on a mask of concern, which wasn't hard given all that I'd heard and witnessed. With a deep breath, I focused on the good reverend, doing my best to ignore his sweaty pallor. The poor man looked as though he might keel over at any moment.

"I'm so sorry. I couldn't help but overhear your earlier conversation with uh…Goodman Castillo. My attack last night, it was the first, correct?"

Lucky me. I'd received a two-for-one Package O' Fun. Along with waking up alone and wounded in the forest, I got to play monster nip to a vicious beast who'd wanted to bleed me dry.

I wasn't about to mention the witchcraft issue. That was a fat bag of crazy all unto itself, and I didn't want them pointing fingers at me. With no memory, and no explanation as to my whereabouts, I was an easy target.

I stared at the sober trio in front of me, my question lingering in the air, like a storm cloud ready to unleash hell.

The Reverend, Monobrow and Hathorne cast sober glances at one another, but remained silent. Why were they not answering me? What were they afraid of? Ignoring the giant pink elephant in the room wouldn't make it go away.

I leaned forward, focusing on Parris. "Reverend?"

With a sigh, he swiped a shaky hand over his face and treated me to a single nod. "The Devil himself plagues our village, Mistress Ellwood. Your skirmish last night in the woods with the devil beast is the first we have encountered. No doubt a byproduct of the evil witchery running rampant throughout our small community."

Unsure of what to say, I sat in silence as he continued.

If it were possible to pale to the point of becoming translucent, Parris nearly succeeded as he sat staring over my head, lower lip quivering. Why wouldn't he look me in the eye? Shame? Embarrassment? "A fortnight ago, my...my daughter, Betty, and my niece, Abigail...they...they were discovered in the woods with my slave, Tituba, dancing and conjuring spirits. Since that time, they have been...wrong." Overcome with another fit of coughs, he sat wheezing and unable to speak further.

I narrowed my eyes. So, something was up with his daughter Betty and niece Abigail. Shame and embarrassment it was. A minister's daughter caught playing hocus-pocus was no small thing. No wonder he—

Wait. Abigail? Ding, ding, ding! Lightbulb moment. *Abby!* The girl in the hallway was his niece? That meant the younger girl, the one possessing a stockpile of secrets was most likely Parris's daughter, Betty. What exactly was wrong with them? Aside from a predilection for mischief, which, for minister's children was probably standard fare, they'd seemed fine enough to me, albeit a tad odd. But to be fair, everyone I'd come across in this strange place struck me as odd. Odd was becoming strangely familiar and less and less shocking as time went on.

Hathorne glanced over toward the still coughing Parris and stepped forward. "From the time the children were discovered, all manner of chaos has overcome our quiet village." His voice was deep, resonant.

I cast a hesitant glance toward the reverend, whose ashen skin had turned a sickly shade of green.

Confused, I whipped my head back and forth between the two, searching their eyes, hoping they'd open up and continue. "I'm sorry, chaos?" No joke, from the sound of his voice and the grim expression he wore, you'd have thought the town had turned into some type of spiritual war zone, with demons and witches zapping and hexing each other from their respective houses.

Hathorne gave a single nod. "Indeed, Mistress Ellwood. Isaiah Alston passed in his sleep. He was but six months old. Jeremiah Whittard's barn burned to the ground, taking with it all he had stored for winter. And five days past, one of William Sigger's oxen dropped dead."

Unease settled in my gut and the temperature in the room plummeted several degrees even though the fire in the hearth raged on. The instances of "witchcraft-created chaos" he referred to were none other than unfortunate occurrences. They were things that, although untimely and horribly unfortunate, could happen to anyone, and certainly not caused by dark evil woo woo. The fact they believed witchcraft to be the cause of such normal, everyday happenings disturbed me deeply.

Disbelief still swirled in my head. Hathorne piped in again, this time leveling me with his words.

"Lest ye do not believe us; just this morning, a blanket of fog enveloped Isaiah Cobley's farm, and unleashed a malignant scourge. Isaiah's daughter, Constance, was attacked; his livestock slaughtered." He paused for a moment, glancing briefly toward Parris, his eyes darkening, his expression growing more somber, if that were at all possible. "The reverend's niece, young Abigail, witnessed Goodman Castillo standing amidst the carnage."

His words hit me like a punch to the gut, and I winced, shock and disbelief wreaking havoc on my emotions. It couldn't be. I refused to believe it. Gabriel, the man who'd saved me, the man who held me in his arms, who'd caressed me tenderly just a short time before, he couldn't be a murdering psychopath. He just couldn't. If that were the case, he would have let me die in the woods last night, let the demon savage me until there was nothing left.

No. Abigail was mistaken.

Despite the chill in the room, beads of sweat formed beneath the reverend's hairline. He let out a wild moan and shook his head. "My daughter and niece suffer, Mistress. They suffer most cruelly." His shoulders slumped forward, and he heaved a sigh, his entire frame shaking. "A dark specter haunts my good niece, my precious daughter, Betty. They…they have been bewitched, Mistress."

I drew back, my brows rising. "Bewitched?" Really, I wasn't

sure why I was shocked by his words. I'd heard nothing but talk of witchcraft and demons since I woke in this strange place. And having come face to face with the ugly gray beast in the woods last night, I wasn't in any place to cast judgment, point fingers or accuse others of insanity. If these people were crazy, I was an absolute nutter myself.

I ran my hand along the wooden surface of the table, my fingers memorizing each dip, each groove in the smooth wood. How does one act when bewitched? Images of blank-faced, mindless automatons uttering the words "must kill, must kill" in a monotone cadence quickly came to mind. I frowned. The girls I'd come across a bit ago, although fairly antisocial and a bit shifty, seemed okay to me. Not robotic in the least.

My confusion must have shown because Parris threw me a bone.

"Betty and Abigail both have been plagued with terrible fits. Their bodies shake and convulse, then slacken moments later. Their skin… It turns deathly pale and cold before they lose consciousness, falling into a deathlike sleep." The reverend gripped the edge of the table as though it were his lifeline. "At first we thought them ill, but then came the visions."

My brows shot up. "Visions?" Good grief. Seemed no matter where I turned, I was bombarded with weird, otherworldly crap. Giant flesh-eating demons, witches and now visions? Fate had slapped my ass smack in the middle of a really bad horror movie. The only difference was, my troubles wouldn't be over in one hundred and twenty minutes, and there wasn't a snack bar anywhere in sight. I needed to get the hell away before I became demon fodder or worse, before someone accused *me* of witchcraft and burned my ass at the stake.

Hathorne piped in from across the table, a large crease forming across his already wrinkled brow. "Aye, mistress. Visions of some of the women folk, hovering over them while they slept, sticking them with pins and flying about at night on a pole."

Okay, so, the situation they were relaying to me was really no laughing matter. It truly wasn't. These people were deeply disturbed, and on many levels. Even knowing this deep down, I couldn't stop the snicker that emerged at the mention of someone flying about at night on a freaking pole. Positive they wouldn't appreciate my snickering, I expertly disguised it with a coughing fit of my own.

Goody Godbert rounded the wooden table and gave me a few hard raps on the upper back.

Lunatics. Simpleminded lunatics surrounded me at every turn. Witches flying around on poles? Visions of townsfolk sticking girls with pins like voodoo dolls? Did the leaders in this village possess any type of brain? Why would they buy into such bunk?

I sipped down some water that had been thrust under my nose and managed to get my sputtering under control.

Monobrow extended a hand toward Goodman Hathorne. "I think we can save the rest of this conversation for another time. Please, John. If you'd be so good as to escort the reverend home? He has not yet fully recovered from that which has plagued him this past fortnight." She whacked me on the back once more, then gave my shoulders a good shake. "Mistress Ellwood here must rest, eat and regain her strength. For tomorrow, she, Mistress Loveguard and I have rounds to make. "

Say what? I did a double take, eyes wide. *Rounds?* That sounded awfully medical. Short of applying a Bandaid and showing a little compassion, I had zero skills in the healing arts. At least none that I could recall, anyway. *Damn this stupid memory loss!*

My little ruse was about to end before it even started.

Chapter 10

· Gabriel ·

With a deep breath, I pulled the butt of my musket onto my shoulder and gripped the barrel with my left hand. The doe, foraging for food, had yet to sense my presence and continued grazing. Quietly, I drew back the hammer and fingered the trigger. "Yes. Just a moment longer, my sweet…"

A heavy gust of wind blew through the forest, rocking the bulky, wooden limbs above and sending a family of ravens screeching from branch to branch.

The doe startled, having picked up my scent on the breeze, and met my gaze for a brief moment. Fear and self-preservation shone clear as day in her glossy eyes before she bounded deeper into the forest and out of my line of sight.

"*Mierda!*" I dropped the musket to my side, eyeing the weapon with a frown. It was just as well. I much preferred stunning my prey with magic to ripping its flesh into oblivion with a musket ball. That particular pleasure I preferred to save for my enemies, of which, it seemed, I had plenty.

I blew out an aggravated sigh. "Spineless, selfish bastards." The village was filled with incompetent idiots, incapable of looking past the end of their own nose to see the truth. "*Espero que se pudran en el infierno.* I hope they rot in hell!"

I closed my eyes and groaned as images from yesterday's encounter with the reverend and the stoic magistrate flashed behind my eyelids. "*Bastardo!*" Why wouldn't Parris open his eyes? The darkness plaguing Salem Village grew larger and more deadly by the hour. The strange fog, the demon… *Cristo!* The attacks would continue should the man refuse to pull his head from between his feeble legs.

Away with you, Satan.

The aging reverend's caustic words rang in my ears, sending my blood boiling. *Idiota!* Such a close-minded fool. I despised his type—stubborn and intolerant, blind to anyone but his or her own kind. Religious zealots were nothing more than incendiaries—highly explosive and hell bent on causing trouble.

I swore under my breath as the reverend's pious face flashed behind my eyes. *Foolish, puritanical windbag.*

I'd come to the colonies seeking peace and respite—a new beginning. Instead, I found this brave new world teeming with the same unrelenting, hate-filled bastards I longed to escape.

With my jaw clenched, I closed my eyes and let the frustration flowing through my veins fester and grow. Strong emotion fueled magic like kindling fed fire, and I sifted deeper into the forest, reappearing a mere foot behind the frightened doe which had escaped me earlier. She cried out, a high-pitched keening that tore at my gut as I stunned her with my magic.

Dropping to my knees, I stroked the soft fur behind her ear and pulled my hunting knife from its sheath. "*Lo siento, mi amiga.* I am so very sorry. But I must eat, my friend. So, I thank you for your gift of nourishment."

Warm blood splattered across my face and hands as the knife sank deep into her tan coat, draining her life's essence in one swift plunge. Darkness seized me, and memories I'd struggled to forget pulled me under, the crimson spattering from my kill catapulting me back to another time.

The crack of the whip echoed off the dark, dungeon walls, ringing in my ears long after the sting of contact had passed. I bit down on the inside of my cheek to muffle my pain, warm, coppery blood coating my tongue. *My suffering was beyond bearable. Though, I would never give Ivanov the satisfaction of knowing just how badly he had hurt me. He may have broken my body, but he would never break my spirit. Defiance was all I had left, and I clung to it like stink on shit.*

The pungent scent of blood and urine permeated the damp chamber, swirling through my nose and sickening my empty stomach. I refused to eat the molding bread and maggot infested meat they threw at me, so I withered into nothing, much to their dismay. When my body grew too weak to support itself, cruel hands would force the rotting food down my throat, keeping me alive against my will.

Beads of warm, salty sweat burned my eyes and loosened my tenuous grasp on the enchanted chains holding me prisoner. I closed my eyes and concentrated, willing my arms to stay in place despite the heavy drag of the thick metal links and begging my weakened body to stay still. After the first few floggings, I'd learned to push past the pain, endure the agony in silence and above all else, remain standing.

I had discovered quickly the horrors that would await me should I drop to my knees during Ivanov's punishments. Along with an extra fifty lashes, the enchanted shackles that bound each of my wrists would be pulled taut, stretching my arms wide until my body gave way and my shoulders dislocated. Ivanov would then leave me to suffer for countless hours before sending his healer to snap my joints back into place.

Once he had brought out a device known as the "Spanish Tickler:" a four-pronged, metal claw used for ripping flesh. I remember well the sick, satisfied grin he wore as he flayed the skin from my abdomen. Unable to suppress my cries of agony, I'd called out, praying for him to take my life, to put an end to my suffering. How foolish I'd been. The depraved bastard reveled in my misery, drew pleasure from my pain.

Unfortunately for him, the damage that device wracked on my flesh proved too grievous. I failed to heal after a week's time, and he was forced to damage me by other means when I faltered.

With a loud hiss, the whip wrapped around my neck like a bloody leather snake hell bent on choking the life from me. "Count, you *miserable Spanish mongrel." Ivanov's deep, Romani voice paused for a moment. His large, seventeen stone frame rounded into my line of vision, his angular face twitching with anticipation, with excitement. "Or should we try something more creative this morning? What say you to fire, Gabriel?"*

Adrenaline rushed through my weak frame, the room spinning as I shook my head. Choking, I sucked in a stream of precious air as the whip released my neck. "Dieciocho…"

Burning pain sliced through my entire being as the leather burrowed into my bloody tissue. "In English, you worthless sack of flesh!"

"Nineteen!"

Crack.

"Twenty!"

Hot, rancid breath wafted across my ear moments later.

"One lash, you grimy leech, for each year of my son's life you stole."

With a growl he slammed his heavy boot into the back of my knees, and I dropped, my bare flesh scraping across the jagged stones. Blood from my open wounds seeped onto the filthy waste-encrusted floor around me.

Warm spit splattered across my cheek. "It sickens me that you draw breath, while Stefan is no more. There was no body to bury. Nothing left of him but ash, carried away by the wind. I spit on you, you son of a bitch!"

Before I had time to register what was happening, a boot came at me out of the corner of my eye and blackness swallowed me whole.

A cool breeze blew across my face, carrying away with it the painful echoes of my past. I gnashed my teeth together with a groan and hefted the doe over my shoulders.

"*Nunca jamás.* Never again." Bitterness and shame whirled within me like a growing tempest, dark rage and hate battling each other for the last vestiges of decency to which I clung. Any goodness left in me had been beaten out of my body, bled out onto the dank prison floor in which I'd been held.

"*Mierda!*" It would be so easy to give into the plague of hate festering in my gut, to become the very monster Ivanov and Nadya claimed me to be. The urge to lash out and destroy overwhelmed me at times, grew stronger every day.

"God help me!" I shook my head, disgusted with myself, and what I'd become.

The Reverend Parris was right. I was a specter, a shadow, cursed to endure life with darkness and misery traveling daily in my wake. Those who crossed my path were condemned, tainted…cursed to know only misery and torment.

Channeling my anger, I sifted once again, appearing alongside my only friend in this strange new place: Erasmo, my Andalusian.

Gray, with a long neck, massive chest and strong legs, Erasmo was a magnificent beast and my pride and joy. Unwavering and loyal, he had been my companion for a great many years, and the only possession I brought with me to the new world aside from the clothes on my back.

After draping the doe over the front of my saddle, I gathered his reigns, which I had tied to the base of a fallen hemlock, and slid into the worn, leather seat. "Come then, my good friend." I ran a hand over his smooth, muscular flank. "Let us journey home."

Erasmo, needing no further prompting, eased forward with a smooth gait, the forest swallowing us whole as we journeyed toward my new dwelling.

Home. With its abundant wildlife, vast acreage of untouched land and air of promise, Massachusetts Bay Colony was a far cry from Seville, the disease-ravaged, demon-infested home of my youth.

From the new saplings sprouting between their larger, ancient brethren, to the multitude of ferns and lush underbrush, to the newborn fawns struggling to keep up behind their surefooted mothers, new life surrounded me at every turn.

A bitter laugh escaped my lips before I could stop it. So much about my life had changed, and in such a short period of time. My journey across the ocean had been a rebirth of sorts. The cocky, self-assured Gabriel Castillo of my youth was no more. That poor bastard died beneath Ivanov's rotting villa a year before, and with him, his foolish boyhood hopes and dreams. Peace and tranquility were a fool's folly. Love, a fairytale.

My thoughts traveled back to her. *Adonia*, the woman I'd rescued just two nights before. The female whose touch…

A shudder ripped through me and a dull ache permeated every corner of my chest. The memory of her tiny hand, her soft skin resting just above my heart, lingered, so fresh I could almost feel it still.

Cristo… I gnashed my teeth together and groaned, refusing to give in to what I knew to be true. What I feared the most.

"You will find love, Gabriel. You will find your soulmate and suffer a multitude of agony when she is ripped from your bosom. Your other half shall be torn from the life she knows, endure untold agony and persecution before fate finally steals her away. From that day forward, misery shall be your constant companion until the moment your heart beats no more."

"No." I closed my eyes, willing the Fates to look the other way, to slay me and spare her innocent life. Why should she, an innocent, suffer for my sins?

I looked upward, the dark clouds looming overhead a perfect match to my blackened soul. With my arms outstretched, I lashed out in defiance, bucking fate, taunting it. "I will not let this happen. Do you hear me? You may have my soul, and may it burn for all eternity, but you will not take hers!"

A violent gust of wind whipped through the trees, scaring away the few birds brave enough to remain in my presence. Bright light flashed just overhead, followed by the clack of rolling thunder. Fat drops of rain filtered through the trees, dampening the forest floor.

The Fates had witnessed my outburst and had given me my answer. They cared not for the cries of a pissant mortal and would do as they pleased.

I urged Erasmo forward, trying my best to put the angelic, brown-eyed beauty out of my mind and failing miserably. *Those eyes.* A deep, rich brown with flecks of gold rimming the irises, *Adonia's* gaze was easily the most beautiful I'd ever had the chance to behold. But it was not only the beauty of her eyes that captivated me. No. It was the level of trust those burnished orbs of hers held that arrested my attention, held me captive. Who was she? Why would she withhold her name from me? And why would she look upon me with such utter faith and confidence? Why could she not see me for what I really was, the harbinger of death?

I shook my head, ignoring the rapid thrumming of my heart and the familiar ache growing deep in my gut. It didn't matter how pale and soft her skin appeared. Or how her long, luxurious, mahogany locks tempted me. Her high cheekbones, petite nose and full pouty lips that begged to be ravaged would not sway my resolve. Nor would the swollen appendage in my breeches.

Regardless of how great my desire for this strange and exotic new woman was, I would not give into temptation. Even if it meant living out the rest of my days pathetic and alone. I'd seen enough bloodshed and death, most of it by my own hand, to last a thousand lifetimes and had earned my lot in life. But not her. Not *Adonia.* I would not damn her to die.

Icy rain pelted my face and temporarily marred my vision as Erasmo broke through a familiar copse of trees. Dread, both nauseating and repugnant, slithered through my gut, heightening my senses, warning me something was amiss. "*Madre de Dios.*" Could I not make it through one day without darkness befalling me?

Evil had passed through this place, and the forest still shuddered in its wake. The scourge that lingered throughout the space left its mark behind. A magical imprint of sorts, which cast an ominous glow invisible to the innocent eye. A mark not even the rain could wash away.

Though he couldn't see the lingering stamp of evil, Erasmo sensed its presence, took a hesitant step back and whipped his head to the side, eyeing me with trepidation.

Lightning flashed again, this time striking a large hemlock several hundred feet in the distance. The tree burst into a sea of bright yellow and red, the falling rain dousing the roaring fire with an eerie hiss.

Erasmo stepped back again and blew a heavy breath before whinnying.

I clutched the reins and steadied him. "'Tis all right, my friend. The abomination that passed through here is gone." Though, how long the creature would stay away, I didn't know. I'd sent it back to its place of origin, banished it to hell. Whether or not it would stay there remained to be seen.

I sucked in a quick breath, alert, eyes scanning the surrounding area. Innocence was a luxury I'd never known. As a warlock and a member of one of the most powerful covens in Europe, my formative years had been spent watching my father and cousins battle demons, banish ghosts and slay undead creatures of the night. I'd never known a world without bloodshed, or a moment's peace. I'd been weaned on stories of battling vampires, cut my teeth on the wooden grip of a stake.

But this new demon stalking the forest…I sighed and shook my head. Never had I seen anything like it, and that, of course, made me nervous. Magical creatures were not easy to kill. Most had a fatal weakness, a flaw, which, when exposed, could be exploited and used against them. Discovering that weakness before the creature returned was my number one priority. That and revealing the source of the demon's harbinger: the mystical fog that had consumed my woodland home.

Yes, I was certain the evil would return, and with it, it would bring a world of panic, hysteria and carnage. I surveyed the damage done to the forest surrounding me and gritted my teeth.

Salem Village was on the cusp of complete and total devastation. For I knew something the all-powerful Reverend Parris did not. The tainted mist, the evil that seeped, lurked in the shadows lying in wait, appeared only when summoned with dark magic. The madness plaguing Salem Village was wrought upon them by one of their own supposedly God-fearing parishioners. A traitor lay in their midst.

Chapter 11

· Taylor ·

"Are ye quite done, Mistress Ellwood?"

Monobrow's manly voice filtered down onto the back of my neck from the second story window above. The god-awful wailing that tore at my heartstrings just moments before had finally ceased. Thank heavens for small mercies.

A fresh wave of nausea rolled through my stomach, and I squeezed my eyes shut, wishing the nasty feeling would just go away already. *Oh, God. Not again.* I shook my head and waved her off. If Monobrow wanted to watch me puke, that was her prerogative, but I really wished she wouldn't.

Unable to stave off the inevitable, I doubled over and played yet another round of "Shout for Hughie," the acidic contents of my gut burning my throat and mouth as they splattered across the dirt floor beneath my feet.

Once the retching subsided, I staggered backward, my back hitting the side of the simple two-story house. Sweaty and weak, I clutched my chest, the rapid pounding of my heart ringing in my ears as I sank to a heap on the ground.

Too tired to move, I stared off into the distance, blackened storm clouds and vivid blue warping and skewing into the dark tree line below. The whirling vertigo continued until I closed my eyes and focused on my erratic breathing. *Deep breaths, girl. C'mon. In through the nose, and out through the mouth. Criminy!* When was the world going to stop spinning? And when was my luck going to turn?

My thoughts traveled back to the vomit-inspiring scene upstairs. I gagged once more, reaffirming my earlier suspicions that I was most certainly *not* a healer.

We'd arrived at Mr. Wyberg's property by way of horse drawn cart, having come directly from Ingersolls Ordinary. Thinking back, if the crude method of travel hadn't clued me in to the fact I was no longer kicking it in the twenty-first century, the large hunks of salted meat pulled from cold storage beneath the kitchen floor before breakfast and lunch should have sparked some questions. That and the blaring absence of a shower or running water of any kind. I'd been forced to sponge bathe, which didn't lend itself to feeling entirely clean. Especially if you'd been forced to pee in a crude outhouse with nothing but a handful of leaves to clean up with. My ass could soak in bleach for a week after that nasty experience and still not feel completely clean.

Hard as it was to get past the crudeness of daily life with these new people, I kept my lips zipped and followed along as best I could. We arrived at Wyberg's house after he'd summoned us in hopes that we might "ease the terrible ache in his digit." After an entire day filled with talk of witchcraft, demons and the like, I was all for a bit of distraction to keep my head clear.

Wyberg's home, much like Ingersolls Ordinary, was simplistic and resembled a large square box with a steep, pitched roof, central chimney, and board and batten door. Grandpa Wyberg kicked it old school, much like the rest of the village.

Once inside, his wife—wrinkled, frail and no bigger than a minute—had ushered us upstairs, sniping the entire way about her husband's "whining" and "stubborn disposition." According to her, Wyberg had rebuffed her every attempt to doctor his throbbing appendage, stating idle hands were the devil's tools. He had a pasture to plough, and come hell or high water, he'd complete his task.

Giving no care to whether or not her ailing husband lay sleeping or awake, she barreled into their room and wasted no time in ripping the afflicted man a new asshole.

"Help has arrived, ye old fool! Not that you will accept it. Stubborn as an ox, ye are. May the devil take ye, for I am done with ye!" She spun on her heels and quickly fled the stagnant room.

With silver hair, a square chin and a burly disposition, Old Man Wyberg was a ghastly sight. He sat propped up against a large wooden headboard, his bloated two hundred pound frame covered with red, feverish skin. His dingy nightshirt was soaked through with sweat and open at the neck revealing a staggering amount of white, furry chest hair.

Upon seeing Goody Godbert, Prue and me, his large frame sagged with relief. He offered up a weak smile despite the pain that shone clear as day in his eyes. "Praise be to God in heaven. Ye have come to help." He pointed a shaky hand toward the lump at the foot of his bed covered in frayed blankets and faded bedding. "'Tis me toe, Goody Godbert. My heifer, Matilda, caught a terrible fright when I last milked her and crushed me foot in a fit of temper. Bloody devil beast, she is. Not only did she damage me, she gave no milk!"

He shook his head and mumbled a string of heated words under his breath before eyeing us with outright despair. "Is there aught that can be done for it? The blasted appendage has given me fits these three days past. I made to slide out of bed this morning and found I could not bear any weight upon it." He cast an embarrassed glance toward the foot in question and averted his gaze. "It pains me to say, but I must confess, Goody. The bloody thing smarts something awful."

I cast a sideways glance at Prue and rolled my eyes. *Men!* When it came down to it, they were all the same. No matter their size, strength or position, they were all big babies.

Prue slapped a hand over her mouth to smother a giggle and then cleared her throat when Goody Godbert shot her a sour look that clearly said "zip it!"

"Aye, good sir," Godbert drawled as she rounded the bed. "I expect it does. Now then, let us see what can be done for your—"

Prue gasped at the same moment I cried out.

"Bugger me!" Maybe the man wasn't acting like a baby after all.

Goody Godbert blanched. "Mistress Ellwood! How dare ye speak such vile words in our presence. Hold your tongue, child, before you upset our patient further."

She focused on Prue. "Go downstairs, Prudence, and fetch me some boiling water. We need to clean the wound."

After Prue had left the room, Monobrow faced me once again and raised a brow. "The wound is not as grave as ye think."

I jerked my head back in confusion. *Not as grave as...* Seriously? Was she not seeing what I was seeing?

"But…" Grimacing at the gruesome sight in front of me, I pointed to the man's rotting foot and shook my head. Swollen three times their normal size, black, green and oozing a thick stream of pus, the first three digits on his right foot no longer resembled toes, but fat, rotting sausages that needed to be thrown away.

A deep, red line traveled up his leg from the festering wound, and I knew right away there was nothing we could do for the man here. Wyberg needed to get his aging butt to a hospital where they could administer some top-notch surgical care and a fat round of antibiotics. Hell, looking at the man's deteriorating flesh, amputation might even be called for.

I narrowed my eyes and glanced from Wyberg, who sat sweating and silent, to Monobrow, who focused all her attention on her patient's oozing toes. "This man has blood poisoning. He needs ER care. Stat!"

Monobrow's head shot up and she mouthed the word "stat," confusion marring her pudgy face. She shook her head and blasted me with a look of hatred, making me wonder why she'd bothered to bring me along on her medical jaunt in the first place.

"I will thank ye not to diagnose my charge, Mistress Ellwood. I have been healing good Christian folk long before you drew your first breath. I think I know a bit more than you on the matter. And as to your talk of a ER, I know not what that is."

What the... I looked to Wyberg, who'd turned a pale shade of green the moment I'd uttered the words "blood" and "poisoning," then back to Monobrow again. Seriously? Was she kidding me? How the hell did she not know what an emergency room was?

I made a show with my hands. "Intensive Care Unit" I barked. "You know...a special place with with doctors and nurses and antibiotics."

Monobrow stared at me as though I'd grown three heads. "Are ye done spouting nonsense, child? There is work to be done." She inclined her head toward the wicker basket she'd brought in with her. "Fetch ye a bit of boneset, Mistress, and brew Mr. Wyberg some tea. We must bring his fever down."

Was the woman high? She really thought some tea would make it all better? The man's foot was falling off and the thin red line crawling up his leg spelled certain doom unless he received a fat round of penicillin. I threw up my arms. "Are you insane? If we don't get that man some antibiotics, and quick, he'll kick the bucket."

"Enough of this nonsense." Monobrow braced her hands on her hips and leaned forward, swiping at me through the air with her fat fingers. "The man cannot walk, let alone kick a bucket about. Now do as I have said, and brew some tea."

"No," I roared. "The man needs hospital care or he's going to die."

I drew up alongside the bed, ignoring the rank odor emanating from the sweaty patient, and got right in his face. "Are you listening to me, Mr. Wyberg? If you don't get yourself some antibiotics, you'll die."

Grandpa turned three shades of pale and whimpered.

"Blasphemer!" Monobrow glared at me with one eyebrow raised, suspicion swathed across her plump face. "Only our good Lord possesses the knowledge of each man's days. Such talk is wicked and smacks of witchcraft."

Old man Wyberg crossed himself and whimpered some more.

Goody Godbert placed a hand on her hip and eyed me fiercely. "Well then? Let us have it. Are ye a witch? Ye were alone in the woods with Gabriel Castillo, and again back at Ingersolls. Did he bedevil you?"

I threw my hands up in exasperation. Was she serious? Bedeviled? I narrowed my eyes and shook my head. "Lady, you are off your rocker."

Irritated, she mashed her lips together and growled through clenched teeth. "Enough of your confusing gibberish. Ye have not answered my question, Mistress." She thrust a stout limb toward the ailing Wyberg. "Have ye sold your soul to the devil to gain knowledge of this man's death? Have ye any power? Are you in league with the warlock?"

Jesus, Mary and Joseph! The woman had more screws loose than an Ikea showroom. "No! I have not sold my soul to the devil. Are you crazy?" My gut instinct told me she was a nutter. You know the saying: if it looks like a duck and squawks like a duck, it probably is a duck. Yeah, Monobrow was a freaking loon.

Doing my best to ignore the look of disgust Monobrow beamed my way, I paced back and forth, swiping at my face with my hands. What had I gotten myself into? What kind of people spoke in Olde English, wore pioneer clothing, treated a pulverized foot with tea and didn't know what hospitals were? I may not have been able to remember shit from shinola, but I knew I wasn't in Kansas anymore, that was for darn certain. Just where the hell was I then?

Tired of wearing a hole in the floor, I stopped in front of the window, my mouth drying up like the Sahara as I peered out at the uncultivated farmland below. The meager scene did nothing to boost my confidence, and instead succeeded in scaring the bejeesus out of me.

There were no tractors, no modern day farming or irrigation equipment of any kind. On the contrary, a half starved set of brown oxen shuffled about in a pen alongside the somewhat dilapidated barn standing kitty corner to the house. An odd looking contraption that I could only guess was some sort of archaic plough lay on the ground in front of the barn next to the pen.

I looked to the sky. Aside from a huge set of blackened storm clouds hovering over the horizon, it was clear. There were no white smudges left behind by jets, no airplanes of any kind dancing across the cerulean sky. *Shit.*

My breathing hitched as panic wormed its way through my stomach and chest. What if... No. I shook my head. It wasn't possible. I circled the room, soaking up my primitive surroundings. No telephones. No light switches. Hell, no electricity. Could my earlier speculation have been right? Should I have been asking myself "when was I" instead of "where was I"?

Shaking, I stepped forward. "Mono..." I caught myself and with a shake of my head, started over. "I mean, Goody? Can I ask you a question?" I bit down on my lower lip, dreading her answer should she decide to respond.

Monobrow, evidently satisfied I wasn't "in league" with the devil, at least for the moment, anyway, looked up from inspecting Wyberg's toe and growled nice and low. "Ye talk too much. That is for certain. Still, if it will silence ye, then fine."

I sucked in a quick breath and fingered the strings at my chin holding my coif in place. The damn things were choking me to death right along with my frazzled nerves. There was no sense in putting off the inevitable, so I manned up and opened my mouth. *Here we go.* "What...uh...year is it?"

She looked up and shook her head with a sigh. "Good heavens, child. You really have damaged your head." She let out an exasperated sigh. "It is the year of our Lord, sixteen hundred and ninety-two."

The house could have exploded into a million itty-bitty pieces all around me, and I would not have been more shocked or surprised. I'd anticipated her answer, somehow knew deep down in my gut I was no longer kicking it in the twenty-first century. But still, hearing the stout woman utter the words "sixteen ninety-two" threw me for a freaking loop. The air in the room thinned out and felt sparse. Or maybe it was just that I was no longer breathing.

Beads of sticky sweat coated my face, hands and neck, and the floor shook beneath my feet.

"Holy Shitake!" An earthquake? On top of everything else? Really? What did the cosmos have in store for me next? Martian attack? A horde of ravenous, flesh-eating mutant bugs?

Dizzy and off balance, I lurched to the side, desperately fighting to keep my shit together. And yeah, I finally realized the earth wasn't shaking…I was. An embarrassing, squeaky whimper escaped my lips before I could stop it, hot tears welling in my eyes. "Oh, my God. Somebody slap me, please, and wake me up from this nightmare."

Sharp, stinging pain lit up the side of my face, yanking me out of my panicked stupor.

Shocked, I clutched my cheek and whirled around to see a horror-stricken Prue standing next to me, a kettle of boiling water in one hand, and her already pale skin bordering on translucent.

"You slapped me!" I gasped.

Her blue eyes darted about the room, avoiding my heated stare. "Aye, Mistress. I did."

"What the hell for?" The skin where she'd walloped me smarted like a bitch. To be honest, there wasn't much on my body at that point that didn't hurt or ache. I was a right wretched mess.

Prue blanched. "I…I…I know not what to say, Mistress Ellwood. Ye asked someone to slap ye, and seeing as Goody Godbert was busy with her patient, I felt obligated to help." She shook her head, worry leaking out from behind her pale blue eyes. Chewing on her bottom lip, she turned and set the kettle down onto a nearby table and faced me once again. "Have I offended thee?"

My jaw dropped a bit and my eyes narrowed. *Have I offended thee?* Irritated, I wanted to grab her by the shoulders, give her a good shake and shout, "Yes! Thou hast offended me greatly, beeyotch!"

Since when did people take phrases like "slap me" and "pinch me" literally?

Oh, wait... How quickly I'd forgotten. I was no longer kicking it in my own time zone, but in the year sixteen ninety-two. *Crap.* Realizing Prue was the only friendly face in a village full of repressed, judgmental weirdoes, I kept my snappy comeback to my damn self. I needed her on my side.

Nauseated and still somewhat dizzy, I blew out a ragged breath and pegged her with a hard stare. "Jiminy Christmas, girl. You've got a wicked right hook." I rubbed at my cheek some more and shook my head. "No. You didn't offend me. Just, *sheesh*. Don't do it again. No matter what I say." *Criminy!*

Monobrow, paying no attention to my nervous breakdown and subsequent boxing match with Knock 'em Out Prue, stood hunched over Wyberg's toe, inspecting it at length. With a loud "hmmm" she reached out and poked at the discolored tip. A thick spurt of yellowish-green goo burst from the wound.

All it took was one look at the funky pus pouring forth from his foot and I was toast. Between the knowledge I'd somehow traveled back in time, and the funk oozing out of Wyberg's rotting sausage, I lost it, tossing my cookies right there for all to see.

"Merciful heavens," Prue gasped.

I glanced her way between retches to see her hand over her mouth, a horrid gagging sound coming from her throat.

"I...I think I might be..." She sprinted toward the far side of the room and shoved her head out the window, having found a better spot to hurl her breakfast than I did.

Too shocked and nauseated to move, I remained just as I was, coughing up nasty bits of what they referred to as dinner—salted meat and pickled eggs—onto my borrowed shoes.

"Oh, for the love of all that is good and right." With a scowl, Monobrow rounded the bed and ushered me, mid spew, to the door. "Good grief, ladies. You shall need stronger stomachs, the both of ye, if you are to follow in my footsteps." She hunched over to meet my gaze, utter disappointment flashing in her eyes as I gagged again. "Outside with ye then. I will not have you vomiting on my patient's floor." She shoved me toward the door. "Out!"

Too stunned to protest, I did as she said and got the hell out.

Cool droplets of rain sprinkled across my forehead, bringing me back to the here and now. The disturbing images plaguing me faded away as I opened my eyes, once again staring off into the distant forest. In the short time I'd closed my eyes, the blackened storm clouds hovering off in the distance had torn through the sky, eating up every last speck of blue.

"Sixteen ninety-two." I shook my head as I whispered. As if somehow, uttering the words on the sly would make them less true. Ha! The reality…my reality, was straight out of the *Twilight Zone*. I couldn't remember who I was or where I came from. I couldn't recall anyone from my past, and as if that wasn't sucky enough, my unlucky ass somehow got thrown back in time. How? And more importantly, why? Why me? What higher power had I pissed off, and how could I make it right?

I slammed my hands onto the dirt floor in a fit of temper, crumpled into a ball and fell onto my side. "God, help me," I cried. "I just want to go home!" Wherever and whenever that was.

"Psst!"

The rain that just moments before sprinkled down in scattered droplets now pelted the earth in a furious deluge. The sound was oddly comforting despite the fact I was now soaked through and bone cold.

"Psst!"

What is that? Squinting in an effort to keep the rain out of my eyes, I sat up and searched for the source of the nagging sound.

Prudence stood beneath the large wooden doorway of Wyberg's house, the upper half of her body getting soaked in the rain as she waved frantically, signaling for me to get up. "Mistress! Come quickly!"

My drab outfit was bulky and cumbersome when dry. Soaking wet, it weighed about twenty tons. It took a bit of effort, but I managed to heave myself up off the now muddy ground and over to my frantic new friend. "Prue? What are you—"

She grabbed me by the shoulders roughly, her long bony fingers digging into my flesh, as she shook her head in despair. "Oh, Faythe. Ye have got yourself into a right heap of trouble."

Great. Just what I needed: more drama. "First off—ouch! Do you mind?" With a frown, I pulled her vice-like hands from my shoulders and gave them a roll. "Here." I signaled toward the door. "Let me inside so I can dry off and then you can tell me about—"

"No," she shouted. She glanced over her shoulder into the house and then stepped out from beneath the shelter of the doorway into the rain, giving me a hearty shove.

I, in turn, fell on my ass, for the second time in one day. Only this time, I landed in a large puddle of mud. Brown muck splattered across my chest and face and covered my hands.

Clothing wet and weighed down with a thick layer of brown glop, I sat, unable to get up until Prue grabbed me by the wrists and yanked me to my feet. As you can probably imagine, I was none too happy with my violent new friend. First she slapped me, and then she shoved me into a giant mud puddle. Fate was doing a fine job at kicking my ass. It didn't need any extra help from her.

I pointed a muddy finger at her. "Look here, Prue. I—"

She shook her head. "Quickly, Faythe. There is no time. Ye must leave this place at once!"

My head shot back in surprise. Had I heard her right? "Leave? Why?" I scanned the meager farm and bit my lip. Why did she want me to leave? A sick feeling wormed its way around my gut. Aside from Gabriel and Prue, the majority of the villagers had proven themselves to be a bunch of insane crackpots. But, they were all I knew, and the idea of starting over again in yet another strange place really freaked me out.

And really, where the hell would I go? I'd been unceremoniously dumped into the past and didn't have a clue as to my whereabouts. I couldn't very well kick it at the local coffee shop. Those damn places wouldn't exist for over three hundred years. And damn, what I wouldn't give for a large caramel macchiato right about now.

My stomach gurgled in response to the idea of coffee and twentieth century food in general. None too fond of salted meat, pickled anything, I'd choked down a few bites, as I hadn't wanted to be rude, and filled up on ale. Yep, you heard that right, ale. Apparently, it was a crime to wear lacy underwear in 1692, but you could consume fermented liquid made from barley from sun up to sun down, as water supposedly made you sick. No wonder my stomach was off.

Prue's bright blue eyes darkened, appearing wild and frantic. A large crease formed over her brow, and the gentle lines of her face drew taut with worry. Girlfriend had a bee in her bonnet over something and she needed to fess up.

I wiped a glob of mud off my cheek and sighed. "What is going on, Prue?"

She tugged at my arm, pulling me toward the barn. "I warned ye, Mistress, to have care with your words. Goody Godbert took great offense to your earlier outburst with Mr. Wyberg and suspects ye are a witch."

Digging my heels into the ground, I stopped short and yanked my wrist from her steely grip. "What? Are you kidding me?"

The look on her face made it painfully obvious she was not playing around. "Nay, Mistress," she said, manhandling me by the arm once more. "I would never jest about such things. I overheard her speaking to Goody Wyberg. She is convinced you are in league with the devil. What would possess ye to confess knowledge of Wyberg's death, Faythe? Goody Godbert means to turn ye over to John Hathorne and the reverend for questioning."

Suddenly out of breath and unable to fill my lungs, I clutched my chest and bent over, gasping and choking. The rain, which had fallen in a steady shower before, was now flying sideways, pelting the side of my face like tiny razor blades cutting into my skin. "Questioning?" I finally managed.

She gave a single nod and turned her head with a cry as a giant gust of wind blasted us both.

Holding a hand to her forehead to shield her eyes, she shouted over the howling wind. "The last three women taken in for questioning were arrested and charged with witchcraft. All three rot in jail. The first two deny any wrong-doing, while the third, Tituba, confessed to her crimes after being beaten by the Reverend Parris himself."

Oh, snap. I backed away, the few bits of precious air I'd managed to pull into my lungs trickling out like a balloon with a slow leak. They'd beaten Tituba? The woman who'd been attacked along with me? Could I have been mistaken as to what I saw? Could she have been sitting in jail this whole time, my attack and recollection of her a figment of my imagination? It was possible, given the trauma from my head wound. Still, I didn't think so. I both seen and heard her skulking about in the woods. I was certain of it.

I shook my head. *Damn.* She'd confessed to witchcraft? Mouth dry, despite the deluge surrounding me, I paced back and forth through the mud, each shaky leg feeling like a ten-megaton boulder.

"I knew it," I shouted at no one in particular. "I knew this shit would happen!" I'd known all along my strange appearance and lack of memory would be my undoing. It had taken half a day, if even that, for the puritanical hierarchy in this village to slap a label on me: witch.

Sure, I'd traveled hundreds of years back in time. And yeah, I'd unfortunately been on the receiving end of an ass-whooping from a hideous, underworld freak. But did those things make me a witch? Um…no! I didn't ask for any of the crap that had been heaped upon me. Good freaking grief. Apparently, I was not only a danger magnet, but I also had the world's shittiest luck.

Prue closed the gap between us, spun me around and pointed

over my shoulder toward the dirt path we'd come in on. "Listen to me, Faythe. Your only hope is to travel north, up Ye Highway and make your way back into the woods near Boxford."

What the… "Ye Highway? Wait a minute." I rounded on her and threw my hands up. "Are you insane? I almost died in those woods last night. There's a monster running loose. Some strange bizarro fog. I—"

She grasped my upper arms and squeezed. "Faythe, listen to me. Gabriel makes his home in those woods. Ye must go to him. Goody mentioned his name along with yours. After the massacre at the Cobley farm this morning, they are convinced he is a warlock. He is to be brought in for questioning as well."

My heart leapt into my throat. Gabriel? How could they possibly think he was a warlock? My thoughts traveled back to our time at Ingersolls. He had done something to the door, something that kept Monobrow and her minion out of my room. And the wounds on my face and arm… He'd done something to them. Sped up the healing process. Quite a bit of what happened my first night in the woods was fuzzy, but I could have sworn I remembered him barking out a slew of gibberish right before the demon disappeared.

Had Gabriel used magic? Maybe. Though, if I were to venture a guess, I'd say that since my memory was currently on hiatus and I sported a head wound, my recollection of what happened that night was probably a bit skewed. The idea that Gabriel might be a warlock seemed ludicrous. There were no such things as witches and warlocks. At least, I didn't think so. If that theory were correct, then I didn't have a damn clue how to explain the existence of the creature that had tried to eat me. Hell, I didn't know up from down at that point. My world had turned inside out.

I couldn't come to terms with young Abigail's confession that she'd seen Gabriel standing amidst a sea of carnage at Cobley's farm. Common sense told me that, if he were responsible for a mass killing, he'd be covered in blood and guts. There hadn't been a speck of blood on the man. True, he could have cleaned up, washed away the evidence, but I was sure that hadn't been the case. Though sexy as hell, his clothing had been covered in dust, his skin smudged with dirt. The man hadn't bathed. At least, not today anyway.

My head spun from thinking about it, so I closed my eyes and shook my head. Better to shove that particular topic under the rug for another time. And besides, if Gabriel were evil, he would have fed me to the demon the other night, not saved me from its clutches.

I opened my mouth to speak and ended up biting my tongue when Prue grabbed my arm and jerked me forward. My feet barely stayed beneath me as she ran me full tilt into Wyberg's darkened barn and out of the rain.

The stench of beast and manure radiated throughout the space, the leaky roof and subsequent dampened hay compounding the stink. I pinched my nose, praying to God I wouldn't gag. I'd didn't have any cookies left to toss.

Prue ignored my obvious displeasure and ushered me to the back of the barn, stopping in front of the last horse stall. "Wait here," she mumbled and plucked a saddle from its resting place on the wall adjacent to where I stood. Girlfriend had the saddle on Wyberg's chestnut mare faster than I could say "Jiminy Cricket."

My heart hammered against my ribs and I really, really hoped she didn't expect me to climb onto that…horse…thing. It was huge, muscled and scary looking. If I fell off of the hulking mammal I'd break every bone in my body. I liked my bones just how they were—unbroken.

Grasping the horse's reins, she pulled the giant beast from her stall, guiding her toward the entrance to the barn. "This here is Providence. She is a work horse and Wyberg's pride and joy. I overheard him boasting about her after Reverend Parris's service two Sabbath's past."

I stared up at the animal and shuddered. Ten tons of rippling muscle towered over me, a glassy black eye beaming me with a look that promised pain and agony should I try to climb on her back. *Oh, hell no.*

Prue's wild blue eyes bore into me with urgency. "Can ye ride, Faythe?"

The walls of the barn tilted and swayed as all the blood rushed out of my head. A small squeak inked past my lips, the last twenty-four hours flashing behind my eyes. *Crappity.* So, I'd been right. Girlfriend planned on hoisting me onto the gargantuan beast. I was a goner for sure. *Dead woman walking right here.*

I shook my head, my mouth suddenly too dry to speak.

Prue frowned and groaned in disapproval. "Good heavens, Mistress. Exactly where is it that ye have come from that you do not know how to sit on a horse?"

I grimaced. The hell if I knew. The only thing I was certain of at the moment was that there was a slim chance I'd make it to Gabriel's sitting atop that horse. It was sure to sense my fear and buck me off the first chance it got. Hell, it might even trample me where I stood.

"Mistress Lovegaurd! Mistress Ellwood!" Goody Godbert's austere voice rang out over the frenzied storm; panic choked the air from my lungs.

Prue didn't give me a chance to speak and motioned me over to the left side of the horse. "Quickly now, Faythe. There is little time. Grab the reins with your left hand."

Apparently I'd lost my free will along with my memory because I did as she said without question, despite the fact I was terrified. I gestured toward the entrance to the barn, a wretched squirrely sensation dancing in my chest. I really didn't want to do this. "Can't I just walk to Gabriel's house?"

Prue's head shot back, and she eyed me as if I'd uttered complete nonsense. "Nay, Mistress. 'Tis too great a distance for you to travel on foot and go unnoticed. Riding is the only way." She tapped the saddle with her hand. "Women normally ride side saddle, but seeing as ye have never ridden before, you will fair better sitting as a man would." She grasped hold of the stirrup and flailed her other arm. "Hurry, Mistress. Place your foot in the stirrup."

I scrunched my nose. As far as I knew, there were two kinds of stirrups: the kind that hung from a saddle and the type you'd find in a gynecologist's office. I didn't particularly care for either. One brought on visions of my impending doom, while the other made me want to clamp my thighs together and squirm while praying for a warm speculum. Yeesh!

Regardless of my dislike for all things equestrian, I knew Prue expected me to comply. She was, after all, only trying to help. Not to mention, Monobrow was hot on our tail, and I had no idea how long the violent storm would keep her from venturing out of Wyberg's house.

With a loud huff, I shoved my right foot into the awkward contraption and waited for further instruction.

She rolled her eyes and sighed. "The other foot."

I pursed my lips and raised a brow. Really? Did I look like a horse jockey? How was I supposed to know which foot goes where? She'd never specified.

It took a moment, but I finally managed to yank my shoe from the annoying foot trap, chest swelling with pride that I'd managed to stay upright. Rustling my sodden skirting, I worked my left foot into the stirrup and raised a brow. I didn't care if she was trying to help me or not. If she asked me to switch feet again I was going to throttle her.

"Very good, Faythe." She reached up and tapped at the front of the saddle. "The next step requires a bit of strength."

My eyes narrowed. That didn't sound good. Tired and weak from readjusting my fluids earlier, I didn't have an ounce of strength left. I felt like a gelatinous bag of flesh, and I was pretty damn certain if I didn't get some food in me soon, I'd keel over.

"Grasp the saddle with your right hand." She nodded. "Good, Faythe. Next ye must bounce off your right foot, put your weight onto your left foot and pull on the saddle."

Sister say what? Bounce my what, where? Pull up on the saddle?

I stared up at the great beast standing next to me, a tiny whimper escaping. The damn thing was tall. I'd have about as much success climbing onto Providence as I would scaling the barn walls. *Impossible.*

"Prudence! Faythe! Enough of this nonsense? Where are ye?"

Prue's frightened blue eyes went wild as they met mine. Monobrow's voice sounded closer than before. She'd ventured out of the house. *Crap.*

"Enough of this nonsense, Faythe," Prue said with a wild gasp. "Time is against us. Now, grab hold of the saddle."

Surprised by the heaping amount of irritation in her voice, I reached up and grabbed hold of the leather seat.

"Jesus, Prue. I—oof!"

With a loud groan, Prue had grabbed a heaping handful of my ass and heaved me upward, propelling me onto the horse. Holy dooley. She'd put me in the saddle all right, just not how she'd intended. Instead of sitting, I'd ended up lying sideways in the leather seat on my stomach with my arms and legs flailing, and the wind knocked out of me.

Prudence took hold of my right foot and wrenched it up onto the horse. "Sit up, Mistress. Move your body!"

Resisting the urge to give her the stink eye, I did my best to comply. Straining all my major muscles and some I wasn't aware I had, I situated myself in the saddle and sat up, reins in hand. My shoulders slumped forward and I wheezed, completely out of breath. If the amount of effort it took to get me on the damn horse was a sign of things to come, I was in deep shit. Gabriel and I didn't stand a chance.

Prue took the reins and guided Providence and me out of the safety of the barn and into the thick of the storm.

The world had gone dark, the storm snuffing out the sun as if it were a mere candle. Ominous gray clouds ate up the afternoon sky, stretching far off into the distance with no end in sight.

Thunder rolled overhead and I clenched my teeth as the frigid rain bit into my skin. Didn't people normally stay inside during storms? Why the hell was I braving the elements? *Oh yeah... How quickly I forget. My ass somehow ended up in sixteen ninety-two, and the freak villagers who found me think I'm a witch. Life sucks.*

Monobrow's robust form appeared in the distance, rounding behind Wyberg's rain-soaked home.

Moving with all the stealth and agility of an elephant in a room full of bubble wrap, we raced through the mud, stopping at the edge of the property where the dirt path leading to Wyberg's house collided with the larger, more heavily traveled road we'd come in on. The large oak towering over us to our left did little to protect us from the storm.

Prue handed me the reins, her voice muffled beneath the howling wind. "Providence is a good horse, Faythe, but to control her, ye must remember these commands. If ye want her to bear left, pull the reins to the left. If ye want her to bear right, pull to the right. To stop her ye must shout 'Whoa.'"

I swallowed down a fat lump in my throat. How the hell was I going to remember horse commands when I was half frozen and scared out of my mind? And wait... She told me how to stop the horse, but not how to make her move. What the hell was I supposed to do, shout gallop?

I stared down at the willowy girl and was struck hard with another question. Something that, until now, I'd overlooked. "Why are you helping me?" Aside from Gabriel, with whom I had a bizarre unexplainable connection, Prue was the only friendly face out of the small handful of people I'd come across. Girlfriend didn't know me from Adam, and although grateful, I was curious as to her motivation.

Thin brows narrowed over a set of sky blue eyes. "'Tis the oddest thing, Mistress. I feel as though I have known ye before now." She hesitated, large droplets of rain dripping from the edge of her nose.

"I…I cannot explain it. I just know I feel a kinship with ye. A sisterly bond, if ye will."

Warmth spread from my chest in comforting ripples and I smiled for maybe the first time since I'd landed in this godforsaken place. How it happened, I wasn't sure, but it looked like I'd made a friend. And given everything that had gone down, a friend in my back pocket was exactly what I needed.

Goody Godbert's deep, manly voice cut through the frigid, biting wind, its harsh timbre chilling me a thousand times more than the hellish weather. "Mistress Loveguard! Mistress Ellwood! Stop!"

Prue's eyes went wild, her body stiffening. "Quick," she spat and shooed me with her arms. "Travel north up Ye Highway. You will pass Whipple Hill on your right and Hathorne's Hill on your left. Continue on until ye come to Indian Bridge. Cross over the river into the forest."

I narrowed my eyes. She hadn't told me how to make the horse move, or the exact location of Gabriel's home. The forest was huge. His home could be anywhere. "But—"

She made a loud clucking noise with her mouth, slapped the horse on the behind and—

"Ahhhh!"

Providence lurched forward and took off, galloping like a racehorse hell bent on winning the Triple Crown.

Fearing for my life, I wound the reins around my hands and prayed. "Oh, my God! Oh, my God! Oh, my God!" *Please. Please don't let me fall off.*

Fat drops of rain bounced off my face, stinging my eyes as we rocketed up the dirt highway toward Boxford woods. I squinted, unease festering in my gut as I peered off into the distance. Gabriel made his home somewhere deep in the thick of the forest. I chewed on the inside of my lip and wove my fingers into Providence's mane. If luck was on my side and I miraculously made it to Boxford, did I really want to brave the woods again? Even for him?

My nipples hardened to tight buds, and a wanton ache tore through my chest. *Oh, hell yes.* Breathless, my thoughts traveled back to our short but heated meeting at Ingersolls. The spark between us—the attraction—had been intense, wild. God, I wanted him. Wanted his bronzed, Latin hands all over me while I did wicked things to him with my mouth. That caramel skin of his looked sinful, and I wanted nothing more than to dive in for a taste.

I shook my head, surprised at how quickly my thoughts had turned sexual. "Holy crap, girl," I muttered. "You must have been some sort of nympho back in your own time." Despite all the yuck that had happened to me, all I could think about was getting some happy happy with Gabriel. I could almost smell his warm, delicious scent even now—spicy, enticing, and incredibly male.

Bad Boy was beyond shmexy, but it wasn't just sexual attraction drawing me to him. Nope. The moment he'd touched me every molecule in my body simultaneously relaxed, and the panic wreaking havoc on my psyche let up, withered away. It was like my soul took a giant breath and sighed in relief. I'd come home. Simply put, Shmexy Boy was magical. Having tasted his comforting woo woo, I knew I'd never be able to stay away. I craved him, needed more of him. And something told me, if I didn't get what I needed, I'd waste away into nothing.

I focused on the dirt road ahead. The dense clouds overhead had finally broken up, allowing a slice of late afternoon sun to shine through and illuminate the dirt road I traveled down. Somehow, the knowledge I was on my way to see Gabriel made the idea of trekking through the forest again less frightening. Or maybe it was just my overblown sex drive and a serious case of stupid convincing me otherwise. All I could think about was wrapping those tan arms of his around me and snuggling in close.

And really, if I were being honest with myself, I'd take my chances with the demon over Goody Godbert, Parris and the rest of their whacked out brethren any day. My only hope was that Prue wouldn't suffer any backlash for helping me. If she had half a brain, then she'd know to lie. Lie like her life depended on it. Because it did.

Chapter 12

· Taylor ·

Dusk had fallen, shadows of brown and green whirring past my line of vision as Providence tore through the forest. The rain had finally let up; the red foxes, raccoons and other small animals that had taken shelter beneath the trees and bushes cautiously made their way into the open.

Brilliant beams of moonlight light shone down through the patchy clouds above like God's fingers, illuminating the damp earth and misty saplings.

I breathed in deep, enjoying the wondrous smell of pine and fresh air. The large hemlocks, reminiscent of Christmas trees, that had seemed so foreign and frightening two nights ago were majestic and beautiful during the early evening hours, their enormous brown trunks jutting into the sky like organic skyscrapers. A mixture of white pine, oak and conifers riddled the area in a sea of cinnamon and sage, ferns, wood sorrel, hobblebush and various wild flowers shrouding their thick roots.

We'd crossed over the Indian Bridge long ago, veering off onto a narrow, almost invisible trail that led deep into the woods.

Muscles aching and skin tight and itchy from the caked-on mud, it had taken every ounce of willpower I possessed to keep riding when we'd passed a large pond a mile or so back. I would have given my eye-teeth for a bar of soap, my left leg for a loofah. The whole "cleanliness is next to godliness" spiel? Yeah, I totally bought into it. Exfoliation was essential, and my ass needed a Divine scrubbing.

No doubt happy she was free from the drudgery of manual labor, Providence continued running, balls to the wall down the narrow forest path. I was certain if I didn't stop her, she'd keep on running until she collapsed, regardless of her destination.

It was the oddest thing. Aside from the other night, I had no memory of this particular stretch of forest, but couldn't shake the feeling I'd been here before. Somehow, almost instinctively, I knew Gabriel's house stood on the northern side of the gentle sloping hill to my left, amidst a sea of sugar maple and hardwood trees.

Whether déjà vu was working its freaky mojo on me, or the strange familiarity was a result of my recent head trauma, I wasn't sure. Either way, it was no big shock when a small cabin came into view as we rounded the bend in the trail.

Gripping the reins good and tight, I gave them a tug and shouted, "Whoa."

Yeah, my efforts? Let's just say they didn't have the desired effect. Providence showed no signs of slowing, let alone stopping. Beasty Girl kept right on running, much to my freaking dismay.

"Oh, for crying out loud," I muttered. I needed to get off the damn devil beast before she passed Gabriel's home altogether. Not to mention, my hands ached from the death grip I had on the reins and my poor thighs would never be the same. Skinny jeans over a set of bowed legs was a fashion statement I never wanted to make.

I winced, my mind taking in the bigger picture. *Crikey.* Would I ever wear another pair of skinny jeans again, or would I be stuck in these awful puritan duds the rest of my days?

Determined to stop the horse not only for the sake of fashion, but also because we were about to pass what I assumed was Gabriel's cabin, I yanked back on the reins and screamed, "Whoa! Whoa! Whoa!"

Providence skidded to a halt.

I, in turn, screamed like a girly girl and flew arse-over-tit into a large bush with a loud "oof!"

Winded, sore and downright pissed fate kept tossing me into various shrubs and woodland greenery, I rolled out of the brush with a groan and glared up at my trusty steed.

Damn nag!

Looking as though she were thoroughly pleased with the turn of events, Providence threw her head back and whinnied before trotting off to God knew where.

Prized work horse, my ass. Try devil's spawn or minion from hell.

Still grumbling, I hefted myself off the ground for what felt like the fiftieth time in the last thirty-six hours and took a good look at the cabin that sat toward the back end of a small clearing.

Flanked on either side by a spattering of giant sugar maples, the newly built dwelling was single story and sported a pitched roof and central chimney. Although much smaller, it closely resembled the larger houses I'd seen while traveling through Salem Village. A modest outbuilding stood off to the right of the house, a particularly ferocious looking horse wandering about in the small wooden enclosure attached to the structure.

Wyberg's horse looked like a mule in comparison to the large, gray beast tromping about the pen, and a ripple of fear shot through me as I pictured myself racing through the forest at breakneck speeds on its muscular back. *Hell. To. The. No.* You'd have to knock my ass out and hogtie me to the saddle to get me on that walking nightmare. I preferred traveling as God intended: in a car. As it would be a few hundred years before cars made an appearance, walking was now my new favorite mode of transportation. I was all for shapely buns and thighs.

A circular stone fire pit sat toward the back of the property, a roaring fire blazing beneath a large, black kettle, illuminating the area in a sea of yellow and gold. Steam, thick and faintly sweet, billowed up from the enormous pot, making my mouth water and my empty stomach moan and gurgle. The massive chunder episode I'd endured at Wyberg's had left me both dehydrated and ravenous. I was ready to chew on my shoes and throw down muddy water if I had to. Desperate times, baby. Desperate times.

Unable to resist the thick plumes of sweet-smelling vapor, I hobbled over toward the fire pit, salivating like a starving dog. The smell was utterly divine and reminded me of…*mmm, pancakes.*

Oh! Syrup. Maple syrup!

That would explain the odd-looking wooden spouts and buckets I saw hanging from the larger maple trees flanking the cabin. Homeboy was getting his Aunt Jemima on.

It hit me like a ton of bricks. The vision, that is, not the kettle. Warm, delicious heat blazed beneath my skin as a sea of smooth, tan skin and taut muscle danced behind my eyes. We were in front of a fire, splayed out atop a bundle of blankets and furs, nothing but air separating our skin. Hot, sticky liquid drizzled a swirling line down the slope of my belly toward my aching core, Gabriel's warm tongue lapping up the syrup in slow, deliberate strokes.

The flapping of wings overhead flung me back into the here and now. *Holy snot rockets! What was that?*

I swallowed hard, doing my best to squash the lusty fantasy before I lost control altogether.

Lightheaded from hunger and pleasantly warm from the heat of the outdoor flame, I stepped forward, intending to lean over the bubbling cauldron for a hearty whiff when a large hand clamped down on my upper arm and yanked me backward.

I rubbed at the sore spot on my arm, positive I'd have another bruise to add to my growing collection, and stared up at a very angry Gabriel. Where the hell had he come from?

Streaks of crimson and carnage soaked his tattered shirt, the worn fabric clinging to the deep indentations of what was surely a perfectly sculpted chest. Eyes burning a hole into my face, he gripped a wicked, blood-smeared blade in his right hand and sneered at me as though I was a slab of meat and he was a butcher.

"My God." I gasped and covered my mouth. "You're covered in

blood." I stepped forward. "Is it yours? Are you hurt?" What in God's name had he been doing? Painting himself with O-positive?

Hathorne's voice echoed inside my head: *"Lest ye do not believe us; just this morning, a blanket of fog enveloped Isaiah Cobley's farm and unleashed a malignant scourge. Isaiah's daughter, Constance, was attacked; his livestock slaughtered. The Reverend's niece, young Abigail, witnessed Goodman Castillo standing amidst the carnage."*

I swallowed hard, a serious case of the heebie-jeebies worming through my gut, crawling across my skin. I knew in my heart, deep down in my soul, Gabriel was not responsible in any way for the Cobley massacre. But looking at him now, covered in blood and brandishing a wicked blade, he sent unease like ice water rippling through my veins.

My questions went unanswered, enmity and disdain radiating off his large frame in pulsating waves. This was definitely not how I'd envisioned our reunion.

His eyes, normally a vivid sage flecked with sparks of gold, had blackened, now darker than the cast iron pot sitting over the fire to my right. The skin between his brows wrinkled and he shook his head in disgust. "Woman! Have you no sense? Were ye purposely trying to burn yourself?"

I narrowed my eyes. "Burn myself?" I glanced over to the pot, then back to him and shook my head. Treat myself to a hearty snack, ease the ache in my empty stomach? Hell yes. Torch my skin? Not a chance. "No. I—"

He thrust a finger toward the curtain of sugar-scented steam billowing upward into the dusky sky and scowled. "The steam rising off the boiling sap will sear the flesh from your bones." He turned his head then and closed his eyes, pain contorting his face from whatever memory flashed behind his lids. When he spoke again, it was through clenched teeth. "Trust me when I tell you that is not something you wish to experience."

I winced, sick with the thought he'd known the horrific pain of being burned. Despite technology and all of the amazing medical advances made in the future, burns were still some of the most debilitating and agonizing injuries one could attain. Suffering that type of trauma in the seventeenth century had to be nothing short of torture.

My hand twitched as I held it to my side, my mind warring with my body's instinct to touch him, comfort him in some way. Blood soaked and covered in gore, he was still the most perfect creature I'd ever laid eyes on. The only difference was the raw edge he exuded now, an aura of danger and pain that chipped away at the strong lines of his face. He was a warrior, a survivor, balancing on the hair thin line that lay between darkness and light, foot raised and ready to topple into oblivion.

Crap. I was a fool, plain and simple. Not only had I almost seared the flesh from my face, I'd unwittingly dredged up painful memories in the one person whose help I needed most. Seemed I couldn't do anything right. *Idiot!*

Panic set in quickly, a squirrely desperate sensation festering in my chest. This was most definitely not how I'd envisioned our second encounter. My long journey on Providence's back had been chock full of steamy fantasies featuring a half naked Gabriel, singlehandedly beating seven shades of shit out of the crazed Salem villagers with nothing but his bare hands and rippling muscles. After avenging my good name, my dream Gabriel then swooped me into his arms, carried me off into the sunset where he proceeded to give me a tongue lashing of the very best kind—if you know what I mean.

My lusty fantasy Gabriel was worlds apart from the cool, rigid creature standing before me now. Jaw set and features pulled into a grim mask of hatred, he looked nothing like the sensitive man who'd cradled me against his broad chest earlier, and every bit like a mercenary in the middle of a mass killing spree.

Fear should have been the dominant emotion coursing through me, but no, all I felt was overwhelming desire and the desperate urge to rip his blood soaked clothes from his body. The connection, the bond between us, was undeniable, fierce, and nothing short of magical. With dark, messy hair that fell into his eyes, permanently sun-kissed skin, a Latin accent that made my girlie bits flame up and a body built for administering the most wicked of carnal pleasures, Gabriel was the epitome of perfection. He was all I could think about.

I swallowed down the dry lump in my throat and fought to control my breathing. The odd mixture of panic and horny had my head spinning, my panties wet, and my lungs tight and hungry for air.

Maybe touching him would break down the sharp, craggy wall he'd put up. At the very least, I knew it would make me feel better. And hey, you can't help anyone else if you don't help yourself first, right?

The spark between us when our skin met, the irrefutable pull that drew me toward him like a supercharged magnet... He had to feel it as strongly as I did. The electricity arcing throughout the space between us was undeniable, hotter than the steam rising from his boiling kettle.

I raised my hand, my fingers grazing the hard edge of his clenched jaw. My body sagged, my soul crying out in relief. *Home.* Touching Gabriel was like coming home.

He jerked his head back with a hiss and pierced me with a savage "touch me again and I'll kill you" glare. "Why are you here, *Adonia*?"

His words struck me like a wrecking ball. *Wow. Totally not what I was expecting.* I'd envisioned a kiss—hot and heavy, slow and seductive, didn't matter which, either would have sufficed. Hell, I would have even settled for him cupping my cheek while staring longingly into my eyes. But nope, lucky me, I got a hiss and a death stare that suggested he'd rather see me six feet under than anywhere near him.

My hand dropped to my side, a dead weight I couldn't manage. I would have given anything... *anything*, to be somewhere else, anywhere else, at that moment.

Criminy! You'd have thought I burned him. Apparently, my touch was *not* like home to Gabriel. Quite the opposite, actually. Drawing from his less than happy reaction and the look of disgust painted across his hardened features, I'd say it bordered on revulsion, which wasn't really the emotion I'd been going for.

Nausea tore through my empty stomach. Hot tears bubbled up, threatening a deluge, and my chest ached as though Providence had punched holes through it with her enormous hooves. Why did his reaction hurt so damn much? I didn't know him, had only encountered him one other time. His rude behavior should've pissed me off, but instead, it leveled me to the ground.

Rejection blows under the best of circumstances. When you've been thrown back in time, attacked by a demon and are running from a horde of lunatics on a witch hunt… Well, let's just say that getting the shaft takes on a whole new level of suckitude. Where was a damn hole in the ground when I needed one? I was ready to jump in and bury myself.

Lower lip quivering and feeling like a complete loser, I stepped back and stared at my feet, refusing to meet his frosty stare. So much for the lusty fantasies I'd enjoyed earlier. How wrong I'd been to think we shared a connection, to think there was someone in this godforsaken place who'd look out for me, who'd watch my back. Gabriel's cool reception was the cherry on top of the ten-tiered poop cake fate had so lavishly bestowed upon me. In the last thirty-six hours I'd choked down enough shit to fill my bad luck quota for the next two centuries. I'd reached my limit and didn't want any more, thank you very much.

The idea of pleading with Gabriel for help after his bitter brush off gave me the skeeves. Uh, yeah…I'd rather chew on Wyberg's crusty drawers than reveal just how vulnerable and needy I really was.

I bit down hard on the inside of my lip, sharp pain and the coppery tang of blood grounding me, staving off the unshed tears threatening to fall. *To hell with this.* The hell if I'd let him see me cry again. Memory or no memory, I felt certain deep down I was wily—a scrapper. When faced with insurmountable heaps of crap, I might blubber and cry like a Grade-A Sissy, but I'd also persevere.

Nope. I didn't need Gabriel. I didn't need anyone.

Uh,yeah… Somewhere, someone had to be laughing at that little nugget of absurdity. What little sense I possessed had clearly washed away with the earlier rain. There wasn't a person on the planet in need of more help than me at that moment. I closed my eyes, disgusted with myself because I knew with utmost certainty the path I'd just veered onto was headed toward calamity, and I didn't have the sense to stop myself and turn around. *Señora* Stupid had entered the building. Everybody look out!

My arms snaked across my chest, forming makeshift bars of protection. I sucked in a deep breath and looked up, steeling myself against his icy, viridian stare. Pride, combined with a heaping amount of stupidity mashed my lips together, preventing me from sharing my hideous circumstances with him. My conscience, on the other hand, refused to let me walk away without cluing him in to the raging storm headed his way.

"First off, my name is Faythe, not *Adonia*." The idea of him using a pet name when he clearly despised me, made my skin crawl. "Prue sent me." The words flew out of my mouth, harsh and clipped. In other words, I sounded like a bitter, raving bitch. Given how crappy I felt, though, I didn't give a fat rat's arse. Shmexy Boy could go suck it. "Reverend Parris and Goodman Hathorne intend to bring you in for questioning. What with Abigail's testimony of…uh… seeing you in the thick of it at the Cobley farm, they're convinced you're a…uh…" *Just spit it out already, girl!* Eager to be done with the uncomfortable conversation, I squared my shoulders, jutted out my chin and let him have it. "They think you're a warlock."

An embarrassed flush crept up the sides of my face the moment the asinine words left my mouth. Afraid of the disgust I might find in his eyes if I looked him in the face, I played with the still soggy folds of my skirt and shifted in place. Surely he'd think I was as crazy as the rest of the whacked out Salem villagers. I know I did.

Still, I couldn't not warn him about their intentions. Religious zealots were unpredictable, crazy and capable of all kinds of disturbing shit. If my little heads up speech saved him even an ounce of heartache, I'd feel as though I did right by him. Even if he had made me feel like a worthless bag of flesh. What can I say? I might talk a big game, but when it came down to it, I didn't want to see anyone hurt.

Unable to ignore the heat of his stare, my resolve weakened and I looked up.

Features twisted in silent mirth, the corner of his mouth had curled up into a corrupt sneer that suggested he knew something I didn't. Or maybe he thought I was ridiculous. I couldn't tell for sure, but if I had to bet, I'd go with the latter. I felt utterly foolish.

He brushed past me as though I were nothing more than a minor annoyance, his voice tainted with a heaping amount of indifference. "I appreciate your concern, but it is both unnecessary and unwanted." He stopped mid stride and hesitated for a moment, as if he were torn over something. Possibly which cruel word he'd like to slay me with? *Rat bastard!*

With a ragged groan, he dropped his gaze to the ground for a moment before looking up. He pointed his dagger in my direction and pegged me with a set of pity-filled eyes. "I warned the reverend to stay off my land. I will thank ye to do the same."

My body sagged, my knees nearly giving way as the air in my lungs fizzled out in slow motion. His words sliced through the last vestiges of control I clung to. Not only did he not want to see me, he'd kicked me off his land as well. Get gone. You stink. Rack off, you toss pot. Go peddle your heartache somewhere else.

I could have sworn he mumbled something else, but I didn't stick around long enough to find out what it was. Or to witness the look of disgust and pity that was surely swathed across his chiseled features.

Body shaking and legs weak, I hauled ass down the dirt path leading to his house, back into the thick canopy of brown and green. As to where Providence was, I had no clue and didn't care. My only thoughts at that moment were to get away from Gabriel as fast as I could. To hell with everything else.

The sun had faded into the distance long ago, darkness shrouding my vision. I could barely see the path before me, tears falling fast and furious, the pity storm inside me unleashing its fury.

I gasped, a bitter laugh choking past my lips. *So much for reining in my tears.* Seemed all I'd done over the past two days was cry. Or vomit. My emotional range needed a serious overhaul. Maybe once I figured out how to get my ass back home, back into my own time, things would be different. *God, they'd have to be different...better. Because right now, everything blows.*

I didn't see the fallen tree branch until it was too late. A loud snap bounced off the surrounding trees, a blood-curdling scream shredding my vocal chords as my upper body hit the ground first, my left arm taking the brunt of the fall. As you can imagine, everything went downhill from there.

Pain was my new first name. Someone Put Me Out Of My Damn Misery rolling in at a close second.

Searing, mind-numbing, roll-your-eyes-into-the-back-of-your-head pain was all I knew at that moment. I knew my injury was bad before I looked, but nothing, and I mean nothing, could have prepared me for what I found when I finally opened my eyes.

My left hand dangled limp at the wrist. Moonlight peeking in slanted beams through the trees illuminated the steady trickle of blood seeping down my fingers onto the dirt below. My empty stomach gurgled, acidic bile rocketing into my dry mouth as I took in the large piece of wood jutting out from my arm, just above the elbow. Blood pooled at the wound, a dark stain soaking the sleeve of my dress.

But worse than the wooden stake to the arm, worse than the coppery stench choking the air from my lungs, was the odd shift in the fabric on the lower half of my arm. Given the shocking amount of pain radiating up my extremity, it was easy to deduce I'd broken the damn thing. In several places, too, judging from the way my sleeve bunched right and left.

Shit. I was done for. A goner. Old man Wyberg's injury wasn't half as serious as mine and had turned septic in a matter of days. With no medicine to prevent infection, no one to help me set my arm or clean and dress the wounds, I was a walking corpse with one foot in the grave.

Nausea rolled through my stomach, a cool sweat coating my skin. My vision tunneled for a minute, the birds that squawked above sounding as though they were miles away.

With a moan, I rolled onto my back, closed my eyes and focused on my erratic breathing. Last thing I needed to do was faint. Been there, done than, didn't need to dish out a repeat performance. What I needed to do was think. Find a way to stop my bleeding and get back to Prue. She was the only person I trusted to help me, the only person I had left.

A loud, beastly roar slashed through the cool, evening air, sending a shockwave of fear rippling through my weakened frame. *Oh, shit. Not again.* Could I not make it through one day, one hour, even, without someone or something trying to come after me and hurt me? Between the crazed villagers, the skeletal monster roaming the woods and my own freaking clumsiness, it seemed like fate was doing its damndest to end my life. Why? I had no clue.

A wave of thick fog swelled through the trees surrounding me, the icy vapor filling me with dread, choking me with fear. The savage growling grew louder and closer with each passing second, the small reserve of adrenaline remaining in my system spiking.

Black spots danced behind my eyes as I rolled over and pushed off the ground with my right arm. Out. I needed to get the hell out of there, away from the fog and whatever evil it had brought with it.

With no sense of direction, I darted left, veering off the makeshift trail I'd been on, into the trees.

The thin columns of moonlight filtering down through the trees cast an eerie, almost milky glow off the ominous vapor, which thankfully seemed to be thinning out the further I ran.

I glanced over my shoulder, a fresh wave of terror wrenching a garbled scream from my mouth.

The fog was following me.

Thick waves of white vapor rolled forward, billowing through the trees and brush as if it were hungry, and I was its next meal.

Clutching my injured arm to my body, I drew on the last bit of energy I had and burst through the trees with a piercing scream. Unable to stop myself, I tripped on my own feet and stumbled forward, careening into the large pond I'd passed on my way into the forest earlier.

I flailed for several seconds, certain I would drown, icy water flooding my mouth and throat. My feet, which I'd been frantically scissoring, finally made contact with the bottom of the glassy pond. I stood up with a breathy gasp, relieved to find the water only chest deep.

The source of the vicious growling broke through the trees and cried out to the brilliant moon above, thick clouds of fog flanking him on either side.

Just like the previous monster who'd attacked me, this new beast was tall, gray and sported a set of teeth straight out of *Jaws*. But, unlike the previous supernatural monstrosity who had been lithe and skeletal, this new beast sported muscle on top of muscle and a serious amount of girth.

Its hungry gaze focused on me, and it stepped forward toward the water only to stop a second later and let out a high-pitched wail.

A sliver of hope coursed through me, along with a wicked spasm brought about by the cold water. My body shook so violently both from fear and from the cold, I feared I'd bite my tongue off. Could it be? Had I finally had a stroke of luck? The beast seemed afraid of the water. Was I safe as long as I stayed in the confines of the pond?

A strange bubbling sound emerged from the water just to my right, sending the beast on the bank of the pond into a full on riot. Roaring and screaming, it paced back and forth at the lip of the water, swiping at the air with its enormous claws.

The bubbling grew closer. *What the...*

Long, bony ridges that looked like something straight out of *Jurassic Park* jutted up from the water's surface before diving deep once more.

I didn't have a chance to move, didn't have a chance to think, before it struck.

A long, viper-like tail erupted from below, the spiked end lashing through the air with supernatural speed.

The world fell oddly silent as several foot-long barbs embedded deep in my gut. The powerful tail wrenched me from the water and tossed me like a rag doll a mere fifty feet from the demonic nightmare who wanted me dead.

Whatever luck I thought I'd come upon when I fell into the water drizzled away with my life's essence onto the muddy bank of the pond.

Big Gray and Ugly rounded the water toward me at a breakneck pace at the same moment monster number two emerged from the pond.

My time was up.

Darkness tugged at me, the silent void a welcome relief from the pain.

"Gabriel."

Chapter 13

· Gabriel ·

"*Idiota*!" I paced back and forth with dagger in hand, the deer carcass from my earlier kill lying half butchered and spoiling in my barn.

I stopped mid stride, my empty hand tearing through my hair as I let out a ragged exhale. "*Cristo! Qué he hecho?* What have I done?"

I was an ass, a heartless, imbecilic fool. In my quest to push *Adonia* away, to snuff out the cosmic bond binding us together, I'd hurt her, ravaged her tender feelings.

Nadya, Ivanov, Parris... They were all right. I was a monster, worthless and cruel.

Adonia...Faythe... God help me, she was innocent, unaware of the evil affliction cast upon us by my former love. Radiating panic and fear, it was clear she'd come to seek my help as well as warn me of Parris's intentions. Stubborn and just plain foolish, I'd shut her out when I should have listened, snapped at her for standing too close to the fire. *Cristo!* The image of her leaning over the flame sent anxiety racing through my hardened veins even now.

Fear. Shameful and cowardly...fear had been the root of my ridiculous behavior. Afraid she would be burned, I'd savaged her with words, pierced her with a harsh glare. Wary of the curse Nadya had placed upon us, I pushed her away, convinced myself if she stayed away, she would have a chance to live. *Idiota*!

I'd rationalized my actions, deluded myself into believing I was pushing her away to protect her, when really, I was protecting myself. "*Nunca mas.*" I shook my head. Never again. I'd promised myself I would never place my trust in a woman again, never allow myself to be vulnerable, to anyone.

But then, like a shooting star, Faythe had blazedinto my life, illuminating the darkness holding me down, haunting my soul. *Cristo!* Other than the softness of her voice, her gentle, quirky demeanor, I knew nothing of her, and it didn't matter to me in the least. She was the moon, and I was the tide— rising, swelling, drawn into her gravitational pull. Denying the bond between us was futile, foolish. The sense of warmth, compassion and complete peace that overcame me when we touched was nothing short of magical. I'd never experienced anything remotely similar. Not even with Nadya, who I was convinced I'd been in love with.

King Solomon was right when he said a fool is wise in his own eyes. In my quest to outsmart fate, to stay one step ahead, I'd destroyed the one thing I clung to in the darkest recesses of my mind: the possibility of hope. *Adonia* was meant for me. She was my other half, and I'd foolishly pushed her away.

My eyes darted toward my barn and the large buck I'd slain earlier, bitterness coating my tongue. What a fool I had been to think I could distract myself. Visions of Faythe's gentle face—features marred with pain, sorrow darkening her amber eyes—haunted me, refusing to go away no matter what I did.

Anguish seeped from my pores like venom, a deadly poison I'd choked on long enough. With a guttural cry, I launched the dagger in my hand toward a nearby tree, the blade sinking into the woodsy husk as if it were soft flesh rather than cold, hardened wood.

I dropped to my knees and looked to the night sky. A spattering of dark clouds shrouded the moon, drowning out the heavens. "*Ayudame, Dios!* God, help me!"

Drowning under the weight of my feelings, my body sagged, my shoulders rolling forward until I sat hunched over my knees. The ache gnawing at my chest, pressing down on me from every direction, was more than I could bear.

Empty.

I felt barren, as though the last piece of hope I clung to had been torn from my body, ripped from my soul.

I straightened with a groan, the denial in which I'd swathed myself dissipating like the earlier storm. *Cristo!* I'd been such a fool. It mattered not how hard you tried, no man escaped fate.

Blazing heat roared to life beneath my skin as I thought of the mythical trio who held my life, *Adonia's* life, in the palm of their hands. A bitter laugh blew past my lips and I dug my fingers into the ground, scooping up a handful of loose earth. I raised my hand high and let the leaves, pine needles and dirt sift through my fingers. To the Fates, we were nothing more than peons. Specks of dust blown away with the coming breeze—here today, gone tomorrow.

The Moirai cared not that we had been damned, cursed to find one another. They cared not for our suffering, or the fact we were destined to be torn apart. Rigid and unfeeling, they upheld the course of destiny at all costs. Even when destiny had been tampered with by evil.

Clarity grew out of the festering anger in my gut, sharpening my vision and drowning out everything else. When all else fell away, one simple truth remained. Cursed or no, *Adonia* was my *alma gemela*, my life partner, my soulmate. *Mine!*

Shame enveloped me like a second skin, dishonor squeezing the air from my lungs. The mix of emotions festering in my gut were too painful to deny, too powerful to contain. Flames fanned out from the blazing fire pit to my right, a wall of fire and self-hatred encircling me. The more upset I became, the higher the flames grew, bright orange and red tendrils curling and snapping, threatening, promising to burn my shame away if I would only step forward.

A loud hiss blew past my lips and I shook my head, frantic, disgusted. I'd sent my female, my fated love into the wilderness, alone, at night, paying no heed, whatsoever, to the fact that evil lurked in the shadows, lay in wait ready to savage the first soul it came across.

The flames surrounding me exploded, brilliant sparks of yellow, white and red, arcing through the open space, the tiny pinpricks of heat burning my flesh, fueling my resolve. Jaw clenched, I shook my head. Faythe would not be that soul. Not if I had anything to say about it.

I shot up off the ground, the blade I'd thrown earlier magically appearing in my hand as I sprinted toward the wall of trees my *alma gemela* had disappeared into earlier.

Darkness was my enemy, black shadows blanketing the forest and shrouding any trail she might have left behind.

I circled a hand through the air. "*Permissum illic existo lux lucis!*"

A tiny pinpoint of light burst into existence, the flare growing larger by the second until it formed an enormous brilliant orb that cut through the shadows like the blazing sun.

A set of tiny footprints veered off the dirt path leading to the entrance of my home, disappearing into the bracken.

"*Mierda!*"

She could be anywhere.

Lost.

Hurt.

The ache tore at my chest, swelled, panic fueling my determination. With no visible trail and no idea which direction she'd run, I reached out with my magic, with the vain hope I would be able to locate her aura, follow her trail that way.

Everyone had an essence, a life force visible to the supernatural and to those with magic. *Adonia's* essence shone brighter than anyone I'd ever encountered. If she'd been here, I should be able to sense her aura's residual trail.

Body humming with power, I narrowed my eyes and reached out with my magic. The memory of her sweet smile, her fresh, citrus scent flooded my senses as it swirled around me.

There! A faint trail, weak and tainted with sorrow wove deep into the woods to my left.

Heat sparked through my frame and I embraced the mad rush that came with sifting, determined to get to *Adonia* before anyone or anything else.

My quest stopped before it even began. Acute, mind-numbing pain leveled me like a blow to the gut, and I fell forward onto my hands and knees, fear overriding all other emotion.

"Gabriel."

Adonia. Her terror-filled voice lanced my chest and burned my soul. She was in trouble…hurt. I needed to get to her. Now.

Scorching heat enveloped me as I vanished, sifting toward my other half. Her pain, her flickering life force, was a blazing beacon that drew me to her with impossible speed.

Panic swelled, a deep, knifing pain that sliced through my chest as I materialized alongside her limp and bloodied body. *No!* "Adonia. I'm here, *mi dulce.*"

Soaking wet and ghostly pale, she lay silent and immobile on the muddy bank of the pond. Dress shredded from the chest down, blood spurted and gushed from several ragged puncture wounds in her abdomen. A large chunk of wood jutted out from just above her elbow, her precious life's essence soaking the fabric covering her broken arm.

My chest squeezed, my lungs burning and devoid of air. *My fault.* This was my fault.

The thick fog rolling around us, the rotting stench of death, both should have clued me in to the demon's presence. But, distraught as I was, I neither saw nor heard anything outside of my *alma gemela.*

A loud roar cleaved the air. Caught unaware, I was struck hard in the chest by the same type of unholy demon I'd battled two nights before. I crashed into a large hemlock, snapping it in two. Winded and dazed, I watched in horror as the bulky, ashen beast hovered in front of *Adonia's* savaged body. Slicing its large, clawed limbs through the air, it threw its head back and let loose an unearthly wail no doubt meant to frighten the enormous cat-like monster emerging from the water.

Mierda! There were two demons.

Sharp, spiny ridges jutted out from the new creature's red, leathery back, its long, barbed tail whirling behind it like a whip.

The water demon coiled its spine and, with a deafening roar, sprang forward out of the pond. Its viper-like tail arced through the air, the barbed tip missing its intended target by mere centimeters.

My gaze traveled from the ensuing fight to *Adonia's* limp body. Too close. Her body lay in the direct path of their fight. I dove forward and positioned myself between her and the creatures, hands up, body thrumming with magic.

Muscles rippling beneath its granite hide, the gray demon lunged toward its opponent. Growling, it swept its powerful arms forward, intent on crushing the water beast. It missed its mark and stumbled forward toward the lip of the pond when the watery lynx sprang from the ground with an ear-splitting scream.

Sinewy and agile, the monstrous cat struck down a mere foot behind where *Adonia* lay unconscious. Fangs bared, it slashed its deadly barbed tail through the air and growled before lapping at the pool of blood seeping from *Adonia's* body into the mud.

Blind fury barreled through my veins as I shot up off the ground and sifted into the melee.

Lightning, white hot and powerful, sparked from my fingertips, anger fueling my magic. With a battle cry I sliced my arm through the air, the fire bolt blasting from my fingers cutting off its serpentine tail like a mystical sword. The barbed end sailed through the night, landing some fifty feet away with a loud thunk. Thick, black blood oozed from the creatures open wound, burning the ground beneath it like acid.

The fighting had gone on long enough. *Adonia* lay in a large pool of her own blood, skin ashen, breaths shallow. She was running out of time.

Channeling my power, I blasted the injured beast with an energy pulse, rocketing toward the large gray demon who barreled toward us with increasing speed. With a frenzied wail, it caught the water demon in midair and tore it in two with its powerful arms. Casting the annihilated and bloodied corpse aside, it pressed forward, red eyes burning—angry, hungry.

With a war cry, I lunged forward and threw my arms out, bolt after bolt of fire blasting from the tips of my fingers.

The beast staggered backward with a tortured wail. It shook its head, scorch marks riddling its ashen hide, and pressed forward again with a growl.

I narrowed my eyes. *Impossible.* I'd yet to cross a demon my fire couldn't kill.

Jaw clenched, I glanced over to *Adonia* before focusing on the demon once more.

There was no time. Every moment I spent battling the demon, *Adonia*'s life force waned. The gray pallor of her skin suggested I might have been too late already.

Arms raised, I hissed the spell through clenched teeth, sending the beast back to the hell it came from. "*Genitus hinc quod reverto haud magis!*" With a blinding flash of light, the creature was gone, the oppressive fog blanketing the area disappearing along with it.

Within an instant I had her cradled gently in my arms and I was sifting us back to my cabin.

Cold. She was so cold. And her coloring was all wrong. Her normally pale skin bordered on translucent, and her lips had turned a shocking shade of blue. "I will remedy this. You will live, *mi dulce*."

I shook my head, my breaths coming in rapid, uneven pants. *Cristo!* Was she even breathing? There was so much blood—everywhere. My hands and arms felt slick with it; my clothing, her clothing, soaked in crimson.

Fire exploded in the hearth, a pile of blankets and furs appearing with a small flash of light. *Warm. I need to get her warm.* Taking care not to jostle her more than I needed to, I laid her down atop the blankets and pressed my ear to her chest. *Padre en el cielo…Father in heaven, please, let her live!*

There was a flutter, an echo so faint I could barely hear it. But it was there. She was alive. Though, for how much longer, I didn't know. Time was of the essence. I needed to act.

I swept my hand over the length of her body, the torn and muddy clothing she wore disappearing with a pop and a flicker, leaving her naked aside from a few strips of lace covering her breasts and the juncture between her thighs. Injuries aside, her body was a sight to behold. Long and lean with just enough softness around her hips and breasts, she was the epitome of beauty. And now that beauty was marred, she was fighting for her life—because of me.

A loud groan blew past my lips, my head shaking, my chest tightening as I took in the sheer magnitude of her trauma. Her left hand hung from her wrist at an unnatural angle, the extremity swollen ten times its normal size and mottled black and blue. The bones in the lower half of her arm twisted left and right, the broken ends threatening to tear through the bloodied skin encasing them. But worse than the stab wound just above her left elbow, what made my stomach seize up and stole my breath, were the jagged puncture wounds riddling her torso. The jagged spines on the water demon's tail had embedded deep in her flesh and literally ripped her apart from the inside out.

I'd wasted enough time. "Do not fear, *mi dulce.* You are not alone. Two things I vow, by my blood, by my body: Never again will I leave you, and no one, earthly or immortal, shall ever harm you again."

Power, unrestrained and potent, hummed beneath my skin, radiating a soft, warm glow as I raised my hands above *Adonia's* mangled flesh. Ancient words that invoked powerful magic flew past my lips as I channeled everything I had into healing my *alma gemela.*

The blank expression she wore near death faded, her features twisting in pain, soft grunts of agony rumbling in her throat as my magic fought to heal her. But her eyes never opened, and her skin remained the same—a deathly shade of white.

Beads of sweat trickled down my forehead and coated my palms as I redoubled my efforts. I groaned, a horrible knifing pain impaling my gut, stealing my breath away. Her muscle, tissue and flesh and bone slowly knit back together, the agony she'd suffered transferring over to me, becoming my pain, my burden to bear for her.

Once complete, I fell back with a strangled cry, energy sapped and muscles limp. The pain, the suffering she'd endured… *Madre de Dios!* It was nothing short of horrific and entirely my fault. Had I but listened to her, allowed her a small modicum of comfort, a kind word, she would not have fled into the forest, would not be fighting for her life.

Skin a pale shade of ivory and body immobile, she resembled a beautiful marble statue; the shallow rise and fall of her chest barely visible to the naked eye. I'd mended her broken bones, healed her stab wounds and taken away her pain, yet she lay still, dormant, floating in the ether between life and death. *The blood loss…too much.* The idea she would not wake was a possibility I couldn't live with. Something I refused to live with.

I knew what I had to do.

Or, rather, who I needed to call upon.

Chapter 14

·Taylor·

Hushed voices nibbled at my ears, taunting me, pulling me from the deep, coma-like sleep that had fallen over me like a veil, blocking out the world.

Warm. *Mmmm.* I was so warm and comfortable. I nestled further into the softness surrounding me and smiled. It felt like I was floating high above the earth, soft clouds cradling my body, the sun's rays a gentle caress heating me from the inside out. The sensation was euphoric, a total high, and I didn't want to open my eyes for fear it would go away.

Images that made no sense rushed through my head. It was like arriving half an hour late to a movie and trying to catch up to speed with what was going on, except, the pictures were all jumbled and fragmented.

I was dancing, surrounded by a sea of people, neon blue light reflecting off their bodies from the sign that hung over the nearby bar. Fire and Ice.

Wait, I know this place.

The image disappeared as quickly as it came, replaced by yet another I didn't immediately recognize. A bedroom…small, the floor riddled with snack wrappers and an empty cookie tin. Two young women, one blonde and blue-eyed, the other brunette, with hazel eyes and…was that a…yep, a lip ring, sat on the floor, a large antique book open between them. They looked distraught, tired. The pretty blonde turned to me and opened her mouth. "Ta…"

I woke with a loud gasp and sat up, back stiff as a board. The fire blazing just to my left rolled and swayed in my peripheral vision, the shadowed figures standing across from me multiplying and warping in on themselves as my eyesight played tricks on me.

That dream. Those images. They were so vivid, so familiar. So much so, in fact, I'd bet my life they were memories—memories of my life in the future.

Hot tears leaked from the corners of my eyes. Why? Why, when I had the answer to my identity within my grasp, did I have to wake up? What was wrong with me, dammit? Why had my brain locked down bits and pieces of my memory, erased my family, my friends from my mind?

I focused, a large knot on the far wall my only point of reference as the dimly lit room spun circles around me. My stomach rolled. I slammed my lids shut with a pitchy groan and shook my head. The spinning, the dizziness, made it hard to concentrate, hard to remember the dream.

Close. I'd been so close to a breakthrough. Close to finally remembering my true identity and where I came from. I was sure of it. The blonde from my dream had looked right at me and opened her mouth to say my name.

And then I'd woken up.

A strangled cry blew past my lips. "No!" On instinct or out of habit, I wasn't sure which, my hands shot up to my head to grab onto my hair, dismay and frustration fueling my hysteria when I found it was still pulled back into a tight bun, covered by a cap.

Thrashing and whimpering, I tore at the cotton covering and shook my head until I was free of it, my hair falling in wild, damp waves about my shoulders. Dirty, snarling and thrashing, I must have looked like Medusa on PCP.

"Easy, *princesa*."

I stiffened. I didn't recognize the voice. Oh, God. Where was I? Had Parris and his band of idiots tracked me down and taken me in? Was I in jail? Were they going to beat me like they'd beaten Tituba?

A rank, coppery taste pooled in my mouth and I struggled to swallow the fat lump forming in my throat. The man seated to my right was blurred, his features hard to make out. Aside from dark skin and brown hair, the only thing I was certain of, aside from his Latin accent, was his size. He was enormous. A massive presence in the room.

"*Por favor…* Please, *princesa*. You must stop thrashing. You will hurt yourself."

Unfamiliar hands grasped me by the shoulders and I lost it, flailing my arms and legs like a mad woman. If Parris and Hathorne wanted to beat a confession of witchcraft out of me they'd have to stand in line and wait their damn turn. My ass was still recovering from a savage demon smackdown.

A deep, snarling growl filled the air. The hands gripping my shoulders disappeared in an instant, the person torn from where he knelt down beside me. A thunderous crash echoed throughout the small space, two distinct male voices shouting words I couldn't make out.

Light exploded all around me, stinging my already strained vision. Whimpering, I curled up into a ball, buried my face into my knees and prayed for Calgon to hurry its ass up and take me away already.

The two men continued battling one another, loud grunts and curse words blasting back and forth, occasionally accompanied by the sound of broken glass or splitting wood. Whoever owned the cabin was in for a shit ton of cleanup in the near future.

The thrashing and struggling finally abated, the room oddly quiet aside from the men's heavy breathing.

I stilled, heart hammering, breaths coming in quick, gulping pants. Head still spinning, I lifted my head and opened my eyes. Vision clouded, I was barely able to make out the outline of the men. They both stood across the room in a holding pattern of sorts, bent over, postures defensive.

Just great. Demons, men... They all seem to want to fight around me. I was beginning to think I was some sort of magnet for violence and destruction.

There was a brief pause, heavy breaths rebounding off the wooden walls. The tension and anger permeating every inch of space eased up as they stood from their fighting positions, though only a fraction.

What started out as low whispering grew into a heated shouting match. If I were fluent in Spanish, which I highly doubted, I didn't remember any of it now. Most of what they said blew right past me, with exception of a few choice zingers any fool would understand.

"Forgive me, Xan for attacking you. I...I don't know what came over me."

Wait, is that...Gabriel? Am I at Gabriel's? My heart sped at the thought. He'd come for me. Who was Xan? And why was he fighting with him?

The stranger, who I could only assume was Xan, threw his arms up. "*Idiota!* There is nothing to forgive. *Saca la cabeza de tu culo!* Pull your head out of your ass! She is your *alma gemela*, your soulmate. I would have done the same thing were I in your place. Go to her! Comfort her!"

I sucked in a quick breath, confused. My head was fuzzy, yes, but I'd managed to pick up the words "soul" and "mate" clearly enough. What the hell was he talking about?

He belched out another string of heated words and followed them up with a deep, frustrated groan. "I've done all I can, Gabriel. It is your turn now. *Adios*, my friend."

He faded, his hulking body reducing to a small ball of light before disappearing altogether.

What the... I shot up from where I lay and rubbed my eyes furiously before looking again. Nope. I hadn't imagined it. The other man was nowhere in sight. I closed my eyes and shook my head. *Fuck! I did not just see what I thought I saw. I did not just see a man vanish into thin air.*

The solution to my current situation was simple: I'd lost my freaking mind. Demons, time travel, witches and magic—none of those things existed. I'd gone off the deep end, lost my mind, needed a damn check up from the neck up. *Sheisa!* I was a damn nut job!

The lone blurry figure standing at the far side of the room drew closer, bringing with him a familiar woodsy scent I instantly recognized. My body sagged, tranquility rushing through my veins as the scent of pine and rich spices whirled inside my head. Warm breath tickled my cheek. Exquisite heat skimmed my flesh like a ghostly caress. Strong hands cupped the back of my head and shoulders as I was eased onto my back once more.

There was only one person in this Godforsaken stretch of time capable of making me feel safe. I'd been right about the voice.

Gabriel.

My body sagged, and my soul cried out in relief as I burrowed into the mound of soft fur and blankets beneath me. Somehow, some way, he'd heard me in the woods, heard me crying out for him, and come running. He'd come for me. Saved me from the—

I gasped again, body stiffening as the memory of what happened at the pond flooded my mind. Two. There had been two monsters. One large, gray and muscled, the other mottled red, fanged and barbed. Panic fired through my veins, a desperate feeling that sent me weeping as I thrashed in place. Full body sobs shuddered through my frame as the memory of the mist, the terrifying ominous fog, played over in my head. It had chased me through the forest, it—

A zing of electricity pulsed through me as Gabriel's hand swept across my forehead and cupped my cheek. "Easy, *mi dulce*. Shh, you're safe now."

Safe. What with everything that had happened to me over the past two days, I'd been of the mindset I'd never feel safe again.

But when Gabriel touched me, held my face in his palm and breathed out those simple words, "Shh, you're safe now," the panic, the despair choking the life from me, it disappeared, vanished.

The reality of the situation stung like a bitch, bringing on a fresh round of silent tears. I knew Gabriel didn't want me. I knew he was merely doing the honorable thing by caring for me while I was injured. But dammit, damn my stupid, traitorous body. All that knowledge didn't stop me from turning into his hand, relishing the feel of his warm skin against mine, glorying in the strange electricity flowing between us.

I was pathetic, a loser, a whacked out nut job. I didn't care. Fate had balled me up like a piece of paper and sling-shot my ass into a waking nightmare I couldn't escape. So comfort? Yeah, I planned on taking it wherever I could.

A stream of warmth tingled from my cheek downward, the panic bubbling up and boiling in my gut receding to a calm simmer. Vision clouded by unshed tears, I blinked several times, my gaze finally focusing on the one person I wanted to see more than anyone else.

Soft light from the nearby fire reflected off Gabriel's emerald eyes, the tiny gold flecks rimming his irises mimicking an explosion of fireworks. Worry lines marred the perfect skin crossing his forehead, pinching the skin between his eyes. Full, perfect lips mashed into a straight line, and a tic alongside his jaw pulsed with every beat of his heart. Fear, anxiety, uncertainty and, God, something that looked a lot like love, intermingled and shone from behind his glorious eyes, radiated from his entire being. It shook me to my core and stole my very breath away.

With a feather-light touch, he ran his fingers from the top of my head down the length of my face. It was like he was putting it to memory, or caressing his most prized possession. I wasn't sure which, and really didn't care. So long as he touched me, the reason didn't matter. I wanted his hands on me, his arms around me, and I never wanted him to let go.

Palm cupping my cheek, he shook his head, the movement slow, almost infinitesimal. "*Cristo!* You're alive." His voice was strained, raspy. The next thing I knew, his hands were fisting my hair, his lips crushing mine in a savage kiss. The events of the day slipped away with each swipe of his tongue, with each press of his body against mine. It didn't matter I was exhausted. It didn't matter that I'd been through hell. My body sensed his urgency, his need, and responded in kind.

He pulled away and pressed a kiss to my forehead. The urgency I'd sensed just moments before, the unrestrained outpouring of relief and possessiveness, dimmed, his expression growing sober, fierce. He narrowed his eyes and clenched his jaw before dropping his hands with a groan. My skin flushed under the heat of his stare, aching for him to wrap his arms around me, hold me tight and never let me go. "Never. Never again will I allow you to be touched by violence. I will not fail you again."

Wait… Fail me? That couldn't be right. He hadn't failed me. He'd saved me. What the hell was he talking about?

Desperate to touch him, I lifted my hand, placing it atop his. The corner of my mouth turned up and I sucked in a shallow breath. "You didn't fail me, Gabriel. I'm alive because of you."

Anger twisted his features and darkened his eyes as he ripped his hand from beneath mine and pulled away. "In spite of me. You're alive in spite of me. I'm the reason you were attacked in the first place!"

Eyes now functioning at full capacity, I was finally able to get a good look at my surroundings and the utter destruction that lay before me.

Gabriel stood several feet away, pacing back and forth amidst a sea of rubble. The remnants of what was obviously once a table lay smashed and broken in pieces on the dusty floor. Shards of glass from a nearby window riddled the space and crunched beneath his heavy boots as he tromped back and forth.

He glanced at me for a moment and shook his head, pain marring his beautiful face. He dropped his hands, which had been tearing through his disheveled hair and balled them into fists. Chest heaving, he closed his eyes, threw his head back and let out an agonized groan.

A thunderous rattling filled the room as the walls of the cabin shook and swayed. A howling wind came out of nowhere and swept through the room. The debris littering the floor rose up from the ground and began spinning around him like a tornado.

Cowering in place, I sat, unable to move, let alone breathe, and watched in silent awe as radiant, white light burst from beneath his skin, blanketing the room in an ocean of ivory and heat.

He roared a deep, pained sound. Then, to my astonishment, Gabriel, along with the light, faded, drawing into a tiny pin-prick before disappearing altogether.

The destruction from the earlier fight appeared non-existent, the room righted as though it had never seen an altercation.

What the hell just happened? Words that normally came easy to me seemed lacking and inefficient. My brain… It just couldn't seem to wrap itself around what I'd just seen. Gabriel, the only person in this awful place I felt a connection to, the man who'd saved me from the jaws of death a handful of times now, had lit up like a Roman candle and vanished into thin air. What the hell happened to him? Where had he gone?

Warm breath tickled the side of my face. "I am truly sorry, *mi dulce*."

I screamed. My arms shot up reflexively, hitting something hard as I dove to the side.

Huddled into a ball and shivering, I stared up at Gabriel, who knelt a few feet away, rubbing his jaw and grimacing.

I didn't know what to say. And frankly, had I found the words to convey the utter confusion and fear I felt, I wouldn't have been able to spit them out with the way my teeth were chattering. Why was I so damn cold?

I looked down, horror doing the Mexican Hat dance across my shredded psyche. I was naked. Well, nearly naked anyway, and several feet away from the pile of blankets and furs I'd been resting on in front of the fire. While I wasn't overly fond of my pilgrim garb, I had to admit, at that moment, I would have given my eye-teeth for the warmth and coverage they provided.

Gabriel's eyes widened momentarily in understanding. He cleared his throat and with a small flash, I was once again seated in front of the hearth, covered in blankets.

I looked down at myself, then at the fire, and finally at Gabriel, mouth open in shock. "So it's true then. Parris was right. You're a warlock?" My mouth felt dry, like someone had shoved a handful of sawdust down my throat and asked me to swallow. And there was an odd, metallic taste coating my tongue. The sensation and weird after taste were both unpleasant and strange.

My hands skimmed the length of my torso, the pain from the water demon's barbed tail slashing through my skin and muscle tissue still very much at the forefront of my mind. Where were the wounds? I glanced down at my arm, expecting to see a whole lot of broken bone and blood, yet the limb was sound, the tree branch that had embedded itself in my flesh, gone.

I met his eyes with what I was sure was a look of total astonishment. "You…you healed me, then?"

Gabriel gave a single nod and stood from where he was crouched. "With a little help from a friend."

I frowned. He must have been referring to the strange man he'd fought. The other dude I'd heard shouting in Spanish. What was his name?

"Alexandre…Xan…is an old friend."

I stiffened. Had I voiced my thoughts out loud? I raised a brow and craned my head to meet his gaze. "He's a warlock, too? Like you?"

Something flashed in his eyes, surprise maybe? I wasn't sure. He appeared hesitant for a moment, like he didn't want to answer my question, or didn't know how. Whatever it was that bothered him didn't last. The expression faded quickly and was replaced once again with a locked jaw and narrowed brows. "He is like me in a way, yes. Along with magic he is blessed with the gift of healing." He tensed for a moment, raking his gaze up and down the length of my body. He exhaled long and slow as if he'd been holding his breath. "With the extent of your injuries, I thought it best not to take any chances and brought in reinforcements."

I gaped at him for a good long while before dropping my gaze to my lap. Thankfully, he remained silent, allowing me to process everything I'd just learned.

Holy... So if Parris was right about the warlock thing, does that mean he's responsible for the attacks? Oh, God... I stiffened, fear and dread worming their way through my veins. The massacre at the Cobley farm. Had Abigail been telling the truth? Was that Gabriel's doing? Was he capable of such atrocities?

I stared up at my silent rescuer, the grim expression on his face doing nothing to help ease my fears. My heart, my soul, both told me Gabriel would never hurt me, but my head...well, it had other ideas.

Despite the intense connection I felt with him, I really didn't know Gabriel at all. Aside from him coming to my rescue, we'd only shared a few brief encounters, none of which clued me in to what type of man he really was. If I were being honest with myself, I had to admit that he'd been more than a little secretive and even downright evasive at times when I'd questioned him. Now that I'd seen his little disappearing act, I knew why.

Gabriel sighed, a deep, weighted breath that dragged his head and shoulders down. "I know what you are thinking, *Adonia*. I can see your mistrust of me painted across your face. Yes, I am a warlock, but evil...no. And despite what the good reverend and his pious followers think, I am not responsible for the darkness plaguing Salem Village."

I was plenty warm sitting in front of the fire, but that didn't stop the shiver that ran down my spine. My body shook with uncertainty. I wanted so desperately to believe him, to trust him without question. Unfortunately, we don't always get what we want, and doubt, dark and bitter, tickled the back of my mind, refusing to go away.

Gabriel had the perfect opportunity to man up and admit to his magical abilities earlier when I'd tried to warn him of Parris's slanderous accusations. Funny how those accusations turned out to be true. Pretty Boy was chalk full of power, teeming with mystical woo woo. Heat blasted across my cheeks as I thought about our little interlude back at Ingersolls. I'd point blank asked him if he'd done something to the bedroom door to keep Goody out. He'd managed to evade that particular question by charming me with those sexy "I'll eat you up and you'll like it" eyes. Damn sexy bastard.

Lies by omission were still lies when all was said and done. I shook my head, chest hollow, heart aching. How could I trust a liar?

Eyes grim, he cast his hand toward the hearth and snapped his fingers. A large bathing tub appeared out of nowhere, hot steam rising from the heated water. To the side of the tub sat a set of fresh clothing.

A low groan escaped my lips before I'd even realized I'd made a sound.

Gabriel sliced a hand toward the fire and inclined his head toward the steaming bath. "I shall leave you to yourself, then. The warm water should help ease any residual pain you might have, as well as warm you further. I will return shortly with food."

He moved then, took a few hesitant steps toward the front door then stopped. With a sigh, he turned, his expression hesitant again and full of…worry? "A dark evil taunts Salem Village, lurks throughout the woods. You have witnessed its wrath firsthand." Jaw set in stone, his expression turned serious. "I give you my vow. You are safe with me, *mi dulce*. I will do everything in my power to protect you from harm." He shook his head then, his eyes downcast for a brief moment before meeting mine once more. "I will not, however, keep you here against your will. Safe passage shall be provided for you to whatever destination you choose, should you decide to leave."

Sadness and regret seeped out from beneath the mask of strength he wore like armor. "There are many things in this life that I regret, but none so much as keeping the truth from you, *mi dulce*. I cannot live…" He paused, visibly torn. "I refuse to endure…" Obviously struggling with something he wasn't ready to share, he shook his head and sighed. "Trust me. The fewer people who know of my abilities, the better. I did what I thought was best."

The skin between his eyes creased as though he were in pain, and my heart ached for him, for whatever it was he felt he had to hide. "I hope you can forgive me, *Adonia*. I hope you choose to stay." He lifted his hand toward me and opened his mouth as if to say something else, only to drop it to his side and shake his head seconds later. With a groan and a small pop he vanished.

Chapter 15

· Taylor ·

My jaw dropped and I sat dumbstruck, at a complete loss for words. *Holy hell.* My knight in shining pilgrim garb, the champion who'd repeatedly plucked me from the jaws of death was a warlock.

I pinched myself. *Ouch!* Okay, so I was awake. So much for chalking my experience up to being a dream. The small patch of skin I'd twisted stung and burned something awful. I'd definitely pinched myself harder than was necessary. *I'll just add that to my growing number of bumps and bruises.*

I blew out a deep breath and glanced at the bathing tub. Steam wafted up from the heated water, beckoning me to submerge my beaten body in its toasty goodness. *Is that lavender I smell?* Whatever herb he'd placed in the bath smelled both divine and relaxing. Grimy and world weary, the idea of getting clean—really clean—from the skin out, sounded heavenly.

I glanced over my shoulder toward the front door and bit my lip.

Gabriel had given me a choice.

Beyond the splintered wooden slats lay freedom. Freedom, and a handful of monsters who wanted to sink their teeth into me. And let's not forget the strange ominous mist and town full of religious zealots who were certain I was Satan's daughter.

My ass was naked and in the bath before I'd even realized I'd made my decision.

I sank down into the tub with a groan. Relief permeated every cell in my body. The soothing burn of the near boiling water lapping against my flesh melted away the residual tension in my muscles, leaving me nothing more than a gelatinous bag of bones.

No joke, at that moment, Gabriel could have popped in, peeled the flesh from my bones and hacked me to pieces and I wouldn't have cared. The scalding water felt too damn good. I was blissed out, too relaxed, and too damn tired to care.

Besides, deep down, I really didn't believe Gabriel was responsible for the heinous crimes Parris and his posse had accused him of. Capable? Definitely. If Homeboy was able to magically poof himself in and out of existence and bippity boppity boop his destroyed home into rightness with a blink of an eye, then he was surely capable of the type of mayhem wrought upon the Cobley farm.

Thing was, if he was evil like everyone thought, then why did he save me? And twice for that matter. Why not let me die at the monster's hand the first time I'd been attacked? Or the second? It made no sense for a big bad warlock hell bent on annihilation to save a strange wayward girl from harm. Nope, I may not have known much about my sexy savior, but what I did know was that he wasn't evil. I knew it in my bones.

I also knew whatever secret he held onto was eating him alive, destroying him from the inside out. If he didn't share his burden with someone, and soon, he'd implode. The hurt he'd exuded, the absolute look of pain in his eyes when he'd apologized to me had been almost more than I could bear. What had happened to him? What couldn't he endure again?

My thoughts traveled to the reverend and his good buddy, Goodman Hathorne. Both were pious, judgmental and ready to throw someone—anyone—under the bus to obtain resolution for the mayhem plaguing their small town. "Pshh." Taking in the bigger picture, I totally understood Gabriel's reasoning for keeping his abilities secret. If he didn't hide his true nature, he'd be persecuted.

Pleasantly warm from the inside out, and too tired to think about anything further, I snatched up the bar of soap and wash rag that sat nearby and went to work. Layers of dirt, grime and heartache peeled away as I scrubbed myself clean. Skin pink and fresh as a daisy, I sank deeper into the water, resting my head against the wooden lip of the tub. The comforting heat and soft crackling of burning wood from the nearby fire, combined with the warmth from the bath water sapped what little energy I had. My lids grew heavy as I gazed at the roaring flames, hues of bright orange and yellow swaying back and forth in a hypnotic dance. Gabriel's last words wove their way through my subconscious.

I hope you can forgive me, Adonia. I hope you choose to stay.

"Mmmm…stay. Yes. I'll stay." The thought of never gazing into those gorgeous viridian eyes, of never breathing in his delicious spicy scent was unthinkable. I'd become so attached I could smell him even now, all masculine and musky, appealing in every way.

"Good," a deep voice murmured.

My God. This dream feels so real. That voice. That delicious scent. I sank down into the water further. "Mmm…good," I said with a moan. "Gabriel. Yes, he is good."

Warm breath and a soft chuckle tickled my ear. "I am pleased to hear you think so."

Wait…

The intoxicating scent whirling around me, the sound of Gabriel's deep voice… Neither were a dream.

A small gasp escaped my lips as I opened my eyes.

With his hair mussed, linen shirt torn and disheveled, Gabriel stood in front of the hearth gripping a large tray of food. His expression held a mix of astonishment, doubt and relief. The left corner of his mouth turned up for a brief moment, the half smile vanishing as quickly as it appeared. "My apologies for waking you, *mi dulce.*" He lifted the tray toward me. "I thought you might be hungry."

My stomach came to life with a loud gurgle and I groaned as the delicious scent of…

I shot up out of the water. "Oh, my God. Is that…turkey?"

Gabriel's eyes widened for a brief moment, the vivid green I loved so much darkening to deep ebony. A low groan blew past his parted lips and he shifted in place, staring. "Forgive me, *mi dulce*. While I certainly enjoy the view, I cannot help but think you might prefer a bit more…coverage, while you eat."

I froze, a loud gasp blowing past my lips. Completely ravenous, I'd forgotten I was in the bath and now stood in front of my very handsome champion in the nuddy.

I didn't have time to move. Hell, I didn't even have time to blink. Before I knew what had happened, I found myself sitting in front of the fire once again, clothed in a linen shift and covered in furs and blankets. The same odd, dry mouth sensation I'd experienced the first time he'd poofed me from one place to another made its presence known, and I struggled to swallow down the tacky lump lodged in my throat. Magic, like drugs, seemed to come with side effects.

Hesitant, no doubt gauging my reaction to his near proximity, he closed the small gap between us and knelt down, setting the tray on the ground in front of me.

My stomach roared.

Several hunks of fresh roasted turkey lay waiting for me to devour alongside a stack of what looked like cornmeal cakes and a small bowl filled with… Was that…*syrup!*

Every cell in my body simultaneously cried out in anticipation. Heaven help the fool who tried to come between this food and me. *I will cut a bitch.* I dunked a shaky finger into the warm gooey substance sitting alongside the cakes and placed it on my tongue. *Oh, God.* It was like an orgasm in my mouth. Nothing had ever tasted so good. Swirling my tongue around my finger, I closed my eyes and groaned.

Gabriel's quick intake of breath drew me out of my hunger-induced stupor. I peeled my lids open to find him staring at me, his gaze fixed on the finger I was licking clean. Eyes dark and full of desire, he looked hungry—for me.

With his eyes following my every movement, I slowly pulled my finger from my mouth, the connection, the longing I felt for him becoming an almost unbearable ache. Lost in his molten gaze, his intoxicating scent, his rugged beauty, everything about him left me breathless, wanton. As hungry as I was for sustenance, I couldn't deny the new craving bubbling up inside me. The magnetic pull, the electricity arcing between us was powerful, magical. *He* was magical, and I knew, though I couldn't remember anything of my life in the future; I knew I'd never experienced this type of intense, all-consuming connection before.

His gaze darted to the food momentarily before drawing me into its depths once more. "Please, allow me." With deft fingers, he broke apart a small piece of corn cake and swirled it through the syrup. Amber sweetness dripped from his fingers along with the cake as he lifted his hand toward my parted lips.

My body sagged, bare legs sinking further into the soft furs below as though I were a spineless bag of skin. "Oh, my God. So good." I closed my eyes, another "mouthgasm" hitting me as the sweet, yet savory morsel hit my tongue. Weak, tired and hungry, the sugar-covered corn cake was easily the best thing I'd ever eaten. Unable to keep a lid on my emotions, a low, throaty moan erupted from deep within my chest.

I gasped, surprised by the set of warm fingers brushing across my lids as I attempted to open them.

Warm breath caressed my face like a feather light kiss. "No. Keep them closed, *mi dulce*. Let me feed you." The combination of his deep voice and Latin accent floating across my skin like a lover's caress sent a pleasant shiver down the length of my spine. My breath caught, the events of the past two days, the dangers of the outside world falling away. There was only Gabriel, me and a smoldering fire of longing and need I had no intention of dousing.

No more games.

I opened my eyes.

Soft, golden light from the fire cast a warm glow over Gabriel's tawny skin, bursts of gold reflecting off the set of hungry eyes drinking me in.

He opened his mouth to speak, and I quickly placed a finger to his lips. "Shh. It's my turn now."

Eyes focused on the sensual curve of his full bottom lip, I swept a finger through the bowl of syrup in front of me. Warm amber nectar slid down its length as I lifted my hand and gently brought it to his lips. "Taste me."

Fire blazed behind his eyes and he swore, a low, guttural sound. "*Cristo.*"

Blistering white heat enveloped me the moment he took my finger into his mouth. Tongue lapping up every bit of sugar, he grasped my wrist gently and pulled my finger from his mouth with a small pop.

His molten gaze ensnared mine as he turned my wrist and brushed his lips against my palm in a gentle kiss. The feather light pull of his soft lips and warm tongue against the skin on my inner arm were a stark contrast to the rough pads of his fingertips preceding them. Goosebumps rippled across my skin and I fought to breathe, my heart thrumming a staccato beat against my ribcage.

He stopped his delicious torture just above my elbow and looked up, dark eyes filled with desire. "Delicious. And sweet, like honey." The corner of his mouth turned up, and he flashed me a hungry smile. "I cannot help but wonder if the rest of you tastes as good."

The electric current flowing between us surged, lighting my skin on fire from the inside out.

He leaned forward, the soft strands of his ebony hair tickling my skin as he nuzzled the area between my neck and shoulder, inhaling my scent.

The remaining air in my lungs fizzled out in a small whoosh as he ghosted his lips up the length of my neck and hovered, lips mere centimeters from my own. Breathless, dizzy and completely under his spell, I whispered his name. "Gabriel."

It was then that the world I knew ceased to exist.

With his fingers buried in my hair as though he'd never let go, he eased me back onto the soft furs, his lips crashing against mine in a savage kiss meant to claim me.

He was everywhere. Above me. Surrounding me.

Nimble hands kneaded my flesh, fingers tugging, pulling me closer.

I wove my arms around his neck and melted into his embrace as he held me tight.

Not tight enough.

He groaned, his tongue seeking entrance, eager to deepen the kiss. I parted my lips and breathed him in, positive I'd never need air again so long as I had him.

The taste of syrup lingered on his tongue as he explored my mouth, the sweetness combined with his perfection further fueling my desire. I couldn't imagine wanting anyone more than I wanted him. He was everything.

Hands sliding up taut muscle, I buried my fingers in his thick, glorious hair and gave myself over to sensation, blocking out the rest of the world.

Time as I knew it came to a screeching halt.

The total absence of sound permeated the space surrounding us, clarity slicing through the foggy haze shrouding my mind. There was only me and Gabriel—my other half. I might have been lost in a time that wasn't my own, but I'd found my heart, my home, in Gabriel.

I gasped as he pulled his lips from mine, breathing in air I was sure I no longer needed as he paid homage to my neck with his mouth. He trailed his lips across my collarbone, sucking, tasting—

driving me mad.

Afraid this was a dream, I trailed my right hand down his back and held on for dear life, my other hand still fisting a handful of hair. The weight of him pressing against me felt so good, almost indescribable. I never wanted the sensation to end. If I was dreaming, I wanted to stay trapped in this fantasy world forever. I wrapped my legs around his waist, crying out in pleasure as his bulging erection pressed against my core.

Oh, God…

He lifted his head and gazed at me as he ran a hand down the length of my torso.

"*Tan bella.* So beautiful." He tugged at the hem of my shift. "I want to look at you, *mi dulce.* All of you. May I?" His voice was raspy, filled with desire.

Incapable of speech, but unable to deny him anything, I nodded.

The linen shift I wore vanished in an instant.

Oh, yeah. Magic definitely had its perks.

Heat from the nearby fire licked at my already flushed skin as I lay naked in front of Gabriel. Even through the dim lighting I could see his expression held a mix of wonder, appreciation and need. "Exquisite." He swallowed, his breaths coming in shallow pants. He lifted a shaky hand and groaned. "I want you, *mi dulce.* Badly."

Emboldened by his erotic admission, I pressed myself up onto my elbows and reached for his hand. Calloused fingertips brushed against mine sending jolts of liquid heat rocketing up my arm. "Then take me." With my gaze fixed on his, I drew his hand to my breast, certain I would die if he didn't touch me again. "I'm yours."

White light flooded the space as his body crashed against mine, arms and limbs tangled in a passionate dance, as we fought to hold one another tight.

Strong hands slid beneath my back, and he rolled us easily, lifting me so that I sat straddling him.

Fully clothed, Gabriel was a sight to behold. Naked and bathed in firelight, he was magnificent. Awed by his sheer beauty, I took a moment to appreciate his perfection.

Tan skin covered layer upon layer of sculpted muscle. Wide shoulders topped off a bare, sculpted chest, its sinewy perfection no doubt the result of hour upon hour of manual labor.

I leaned forward, tracing my hands along his shoulders toward the center of his chest.

His body jerked beneath my touch, a sharp hiss blowing past his lips.

What the…

"I…I'm sorry." Unsure of what had just happened, I pulled my hand away. "I didn't mean to—"

He pushed up quickly, our chests nearly touching, and pressed a finger to my lips. "Shhh, *mi dulce*. You did nothing wrong." Soft lips nipped at my jaw, sending ripples of pleasure cascading down my neck.

Grasping my wrist, he eased back onto the furs, eyes heavy lidded and full of desire. "Let it go, my sweet and just," he placed my hand around his bulging erection, "feel."

If I thought I'd been breathless before, I was wrong.

Blistering heat enveloped me as I took him in hand, pulsating waves of delicious heat igniting my core.

He was enormous. Long, thick and smooth like silk sheeting over steel, I marveled at the way his body shuddered with each stroke of my hand.

"God in heaven…that feels…"

Darkened eyes watched with rapt desire as I continued stroking, his pleasured expression the most beautiful thing I'd ever seen.

But it wasn't enough. Not by a long shot. His pleasure was mine. I'd discovered my purpose, my reason for being. I understood, finally, the intense connection between us. Gabriel was my other half and I wanted… No, I *needed*, to drive him to the edge of perfect bliss, feel his body clench beneath mine, hear him shout my name as he released. Only then could I be happy, whole.

A loud hiss blew past his lips as I took him into my mouth, power and strength wrapped in pure velvet. His body jerked, every muscle contracting, taut, rigid, as I worked him, up and down, tongue swirling around his magnificent length over and over.

My core ached for his touch, and I rubbed my thighs together in a vain attempt to ease the pressure. I wanted him inside—inside my body, inside my heart, my soul.

His breaths came in shallow, rapid pants as he gripped handfuls of blanket and furs. "*Adonia…I…*"

My gaze locked with his as I cupped his weighty sack, fireworks igniting amidst a sea of deep green. He threw his head back as he released, a loud roar rumbling from deep within his chest. "Faythe!"

Faythe. The name echoed inside my head.

I stilled beneath the warm hands tugging at me, pulling me upward, holding me close. I'd craved my name on his lips, drove him past the edge of bliss to hear him utter the word. I'd succeeded all right, and now lay numb in his satisfied arms, aching to tell him the truth, desperate to give him a name I didn't know, a name I couldn't remember. His pleasured cry was a heavy weight pressing against my chest, the dull ache battling the sensation of his lips against mine, the feel of his strong arms wrapped around me.

My name isn't Faythe.

In the end, sensation and desire won the battle for my attention. My reality, sad and painful as it was, was no match for Gabriel's skilled mouth.

Heat blazed beneath my skin as Gabriel trailed feather light kisses down the length of my neck. Moisture pooled between my thighs and my nipples hardened to tight buds with each sweep of his tongue, each caress of his lips.

I closed my eyes, reveling in the sensation. His touch was pure magic. He was magic, and he was mine.

"*Mi cielo.*" His voice floated across my skin like a lover's touch, soft and gentle. "My *alma gemela*... So beautiful, so sweet." He shifted, his warmth pulling away from me for a moment and returning quickly. Warm breath tickled my ear as he pressed me back onto the blankets, his deep voice undoing me one syllable at a time. "I hunger for you, *mi dulce.*"

I gasped as warm liquid pleasure drizzled over my breasts, down my torso. *The syrup.*

Soft strands of hair tickled my skin as he bent forward and took my breast in his mouth. His tongue, *oh, God, his tongue...* It flicked at my sensitized nub sending shockwaves of ecstasy rippling through my body.

"Delicious," he said before licking at the sugary trail leading to my other breast, treating it to the same glorious attention.

I threw my head back with a moan, unable to leash my cry of ecstasy as his tongue traveled lower, licking the trail of syrup headed straight for...

Heaven.

My back arched up off the soft furs, pure, pleasured bliss exploding from every cell in my body. "Gabriel!"

He groaned, a low, throaty sound that sent ripples of ecstasy fanning across my sensitive core with each vibration.

I was so damn close, ready to explode and we hadn't even done the deed.

"Delicious," he said in between sweeps of his tongue. "Sweet, honeyed perfection."

The delicious torture went on and on, his magical tongue driving me to the brink, sending me to the edge of total body orgasm, then stopping. He was a monster. He was a saint. He was a goddamn tease.

Aching for completion, needing his warmth against me, his flesh inside me, I tugged at his broad shoulders and whimpered. "Please. Please, Gabriel. Come inside. Finish me."

A deep growl tore through his chest and he lunged forward, entering me in one swift movement.

I threw my head back and cried out, the fullness of him a searing sensation that rode the border between pleasure and pain. A sensation I never wanted to end.

He was everywhere.

Surrounding me.

Filling me.

Completing me.

Swept away by an ocean of bliss, I closed my eyes, the rhythmic movement of our joining, the erotic sound of skin slapping against skin sending me rocketing toward completion.

Breaths coming in heavy pants, his tempo increased, strong hips slamming into mine with passion and aggression. Soft fingertips brushed across my cheek before burying themselves in my hair. "Look at me, *Adonia*. Show me your eyes."

Completely under his thrall and helpless but to obey, I opened my lids.

Oh…God.

Dark, passion-filled eyes ensnared mine, his expression reverent, full of love.

He pulled his hand from my hair and grasped mine, lacing our fingers together as he continued to pump in and out.

So close. God, I was so close.

Soft, golden light shone from between our joined hands, the warm luminescence pulsating in undulating waves, its brilliance and delicious heat bathing our joined bodies in a mystical glow.

Cresting, on the edge of what would surely be the most powerful orgasm I'd ever felt, he drew back, teasing me with a long, deliberate stroke before sheathing himself fully once more. Over and over he tortured me, our joined hands, his heated gaze grounding me, the only things keeping me from floating away.

"Our souls have merged, *mi dulce*. Can you...feel it? We are one... now." The muscles in his neck and jaw strained as he fought to maintain control, perilously close to orgasm.

"You are mine, *mi dulce*. My *alma gemela*, my soulmate. My love." He pressed his lips to mine in a heart-stopping kiss that stole my breath away and slammed into me one final time. Connected, mind, body and soul, scorching heat radiating around and through us as we toppled over the edge of bliss into orgasm.

Pulsating waves of pure pleasure rocked my frame, radiant light encasing us in a bubble of ecstasy.

We lay, hearts hammering in unison, arms and legs entwined for an immeasurable amount of time, neither of us moving, neither of us wanting the sensation of finally becoming "one" to end.

He pulled his head back from where it lay nestled between my head and shoulder, smooth strands of hair tickling my sensitized skin. Soft lips brushed a feather light trail up the column of my neck before pressing against my temple in a gentle kiss. Nothing but warmth and love shone behind his luminescent eyes. "This is my promise to you, *mi dulce*. None shall come between us. For I am yours, and you are mine, both in body and soul. And so shall it be for all eternity. I love you."

Chapter *16*

·The Traveler·

I sifted out of the damp forest brush and dropped to my knees in front of a large trough filled with water behind Ingersolls. Scattered clouds blocked out the moon's light, shrouding my naked form in a blanket of darkness.

Water.

The cool liquid burned my new skin and hit the back of my throat like a thousand tiny razor blades cutting into my flesh. Beyond thirsty, I drank anyway, disregarding the leftover pain from my most recent torture session.

Fuck. How long had the Fates tormented me? How long had they kept me locked away in the cave? Hours? Days? I wasn't sure. The pain had been too much, brought back vivid memories from my days spent locked away beneath Ivanov's manor.

Unable to use magic to astral project and transport my essence somewhere else while they laid waste to my body, I'd been forced to remain conscious and intact, to endure every second of mind numbing agony as they stripped the flesh from my body one bloody fucking piece at a time.

I winced at the memory of the sea of flames engulfing me the moment the last piece of skin had been torn from me. The sickly scent of my disintegrating body permeated my nose even now, souring my stomach and choking the air from my lungs. Reduced to nothing but ash and skeleton, the Fates had knit me back together one painful piece at a time only to exact the punishment again, and again, and again. *Goddamn mystical bitches.*

A pound of flesh, Traveler, for each transgression.

The Fates ancient voices echoed inside my head even now, a cacophony of power, aggression and haughty indifference. They thought themselves judge, jury, executioner—above all others.

Fire shall purify you, oh insignificant one, and remind you of your place in this world. You are but a flyspeck on the grand canvas of our universe—easily wiped away, a stain that shall be blotted out forever.

How well I knew my place in this world. Ivanov, Nadya, both had shown me just how insignificant I was. Burned the truth of my reality into my psyche along with my flesh. I was a peon, a pawn in the Cosmos's grand scheme, cursed to give and receive both misery and pain. And after spending three hundred painful years parted from the only woman I ever loved, there was nothing anyone could do to break me. The Fates bloody punishment had been nothing but surplus.

I squeezed my eyes shut and shook my head. *Fuck them.*

This flyspeck was still alive. Cold, naked and riddled with pain, but alive nonetheless. Ivanov and Nadya had taught me how to endure the most horrific of pain. Short of death, I could withstand anything the Fates threw at me. And despite the threat they placed on Taylor's life should I make my presence known again, I planned on doing all I could to ensure she made it home to her life in the future, alive and in one piece. Nothing in my godforsaken life had been more important.

I shoved my head into the wooden trough, the icy water giving way to a new level of clarity as it revived me from my pain induced haze. I surfaced and backed away, resolve warming me from the bone out despite the cool breeze biting into my naked and newly formed flesh. The Fates had overlooked three important facts. Three basic truths I clung to when all else failed. Life was never black and white. Rules were meant to be broken. And loop-holes were a goddamn thing of beauty.

Those bitches didn't want me to reveal myself? Fine. Not a goddamn problem. I'd cloak myself as I watched over Taylor, make sure any action I took appeared as nothing more than a random act of nature.

I would be the fallen tree blocking the path of those hell bent on chasing her, the unseen threat that spooked the lynch mob's horses, keeping them far from wherever she was. I would be a fly on the wall, a ripple on the wind. Unseen yet ever present, I would be chance, the unforeseen occurrence in the Fate's master plan. The chink in their armor, a goddamn thorn in their side.

Starting now.

Raw heat jolted through my frame, energized matter snapping and coiling at the stagnant space surrounding me as I unleashed the mystical force within. Molecules shifted, matter reorganized and within milliseconds I was a wraith, a whisper on the cool breeze wafting over the enormous wooden structure before me—invisible, resolute.

Riding the breeze like a wave, I sifted into the first floor of Ingersolls and went straight for the food storage space in the floor. Starving and weak, I couldn't help Taylor if I couldn't stay on my feet.

I tore into a hunk of meat, telling myself it was a juicy steak and not a salt cured hunk of crap that tasted like someone's old shoe. *Shoe... Fuck. I need clothes.* It took a bit of concentration because I was so damn hungry, but I managed to manifest a T-shirt, some jeans, and a pair of boots. My stomach gurgled, thankful for the food, no matter how shitty it tasted, and I plowed through the rest of the meat and finished off three quarters of a loaf of stale bread.

Satiated but nowhere near satisfied, I chucked the last bite in my hand with a disgusted groan and cast a glance toward the stairs leading to the second floor.

Taylor.

I was standing in her room before I realized I'd even sifted.

I exhaled slow and heavy. *Fuck.* The room was empty.

My pulse hammered as I scanned the spartan space, my skin crawling with dread, with panic. Bedding lay mussed and empty. The tattered jeans and dirt stained yellow tee she wore the night she appeared lay cast aside into a messy heap on the floor, forgotten. Taylor was gone, her intoxicating scent the only thing remaining.

I closed my eyes, the whirling scent of citrus and home feeding my power, narrowing my focus as I sought out her life force with my magic. Didn't matter the distance. So in tune with the essence of her soul, I'd crossed a vast ocean of time and space, traveled back hundreds of years and still found her. I would always find her, always come for her. Until the day I breathed no more.

Fuck, no…

Knuckles rubbing against my chest, I staggered backward with a muffled groan, reality eviscerating my heart with each ragged breath I took.

She was with him.

Shit.

She was with me.

The younger me, from this time, this reality.

The walls surrounding me began to shake and rattle as memories slammed into me, one after the other, each mental picture a constant searing pain reminiscent of someone draining the marrow from my bones.

I breathed through clenched teeth, my hands balled into fists at my side.

I knew how long the Fates had kept me away, knew what day it was now, and would give anything, anything to trade places with him, be in his skin.

Taylor had just survived a near fatal attack.

And we'd just made love for the first time.

I sifted into the night sky, threw my head back and cried out into the inky blackness, a deep thunderous echo the sleeping villagers below would mistake as the sound of an impending storm. An act of nature.

Little did they know I was the storm, a raging tempest filled with jealousy and grief, three hundred years in the making.

Images of Taylor's lithe, naked body writhing beneath mine flooded my mind, blinding me to all else. Her silken skin, the texture of her long luxurious hair beneath my fingers, the erotic sound of her breathless moan as I sheathed myself deep in her warmth; I heard and felt the memory of them as though they'd just happened.

I squeezed my lids shut and shook my head, electric sparks from my magic supercharging the nearby clouds, causing them to rumble.

It was happening right now. He…No…I…*fuck*… He was feasting on her body, savoring the sweet spot between her legs, holding her small frame against his until their hearts beat simultaneously. He was claiming her. His *alma gemela*, his soulmate, his other half.

No!

Lightning exploded from my fingertips, scorching the damp earth below, a vortex of dark clouds forming a deadly spiral around me.

She's mine!

To be jealous of my younger self was absurd. The madness, the utter despair gnawing at my chest was deranged, down right preposterous. It was all those things and more. And yet I couldn't contain the envy bubbling over, or the cyclone of rage surging around me. I was a ticking time bomb ready to explode, a tempest ready to unleash hell.

A surge of dark energy blasted me from below, its malevolence a heavy weight pressing against my already ravaged nerves.

The same ominous mist I'd encountered before both in the woods and at the Cobley farm billowed through the center of the small village like a spectral scourge, a thick blanket shrouding my vision.

"What the…"

"Ego voco thee, creatura of obscurum…"

Angry whispered words cut across the harsh winds whipping around me, their constant repetition demanding my attention. Latin in origin, they were the beginning of a—*shit*—the opening to a summoning spell.

Ego voco thee, creatura of obscurum…I summom thee, creature of the night.

Maniacal laughter floated up from the edge of the mist, a sick, satisfied sound that could only belong to one person: Tituba. Illuminated by a large shaft of moonlight, she looked wild, deranged and deadly. Hands covered with the blood of whatever animal she'd sacrificed in order to carry out her evil plans, she stood just outside the milky vapor, eyes pitch black, a vengeful smile painted across her dark features. Long tendrils of ebony hair floated about her head on an invisible breeze, like Medusa, the stiff fabric of her gray dress billowing out behind her.

Adrenaline surged beneath my skin, pulsing through my veins like molten lava—hot, lethal.

Arms extended out and upward, palms facing the sky, she threw her head back and cried into the night. *"Vindico qui onero mihi…"*

Punish those who oppress me…

A thunderous clack rent the air as a pair of black, monstrous forms burst forth from the ground with deafening shrieks and shot up into the night sky. With a resounding screech, the larger of the two flew toward the forest and out of sight, while the other engaged in a perilous nosedive straight for Tituba. The ground shook beneath the creature's massive weight as it slammed down in front of her, dirt and debris riddling the misty air.

Large, black leathery wings extended, the stygian nightmare threw back a head full of slick red hair and let loose with an ear-splitting scream that threatened to burst my ear drums.

Fuck. An Aerico demon. She'd fucking summoned Aerico demons. Who the hell was this woman, and how did she know how to summon a Greek disease demon? "Shit!" Taylor's life hung in the balance, and... *Dammit,* I didn't have time for psychotic witches and their hideous demon spawn.

Pulling a dagger from the folds of her skirt, Tituba slit a jagged cut from inside her elbow down to her wrist, crimson blood pooling on the ground in front of the shrieking hell beast. "*Ut Ego sino, sic vadum meus hostillis sino.*"

As I suffer, so shall my enemy suffer...

White vapor coiled around Tituba like a deadly snake, and she disappeared into the mist with a baleful laugh.

I narrowed my eyes, muscles coiling, ready to attack. "Not if I have anything to say about it, bitch." This shit had to stop—now. And while I knew I couldn't reveal myself to any living soul during this time, the Fates never said I couldn't take out a demon. Aericos, like all underworld creatures, didn't possess a soul.

I smiled despite the clusterfuck situation breaking out around me. *Loopholes.* Oh yeah, baby. They were a thing of goddamn beauty.

The remaining Aerico jettisoned into the sky. Red eyes blazing, hungry for destruction, it made a beeline straight for Ingersolls, no doubt eager to spread a devastating plague with its diseased ravaged flesh.

Seething with pent up aggression and itching for a fight, I went after the hell beast, fully intending to take care of Tituba after I put down her newest assassins. Her nasty revenge mission was what spawned the ugliness rampant in Salem Village, and what would ultimately take Taylor's life. Bitch was going to pay.

One with the storm spiraling around me, I shot across the sky, enveloping the Aerico seconds before it crashed through the roof of Ingersolls. A whirlwind of power, a tornado filled with pain, I was a weapon, poised, eager to unleash the rage within. The hell if I'd let this mythical dirt bag harm any innocents. Salem Village had seen enough mystical shit to last it a lifetime. It didn't need a pandemic on top of everything else. It was time to kick some fucking ass.

Gale force winds crashed against the two story structure, tree branches, dirt, debris and various tools left carelessly in the open littering the air as I swept the newly summoned Aerico into my whirling vortex and kicked off into the sky.

Magically immobilized in the center of the cyclone, the ebony creature arched, writhed, clawed and lashed out. Storm clouds masking us from view, the sound of rolling thunder drowned out the god awful sound emanating from its hideous mouth as I dumped the demon amidst a cluster of trees in the center of Whipple Hill, just a short distance from Ingersolls.

Power rolling off me in waves, I sifted to the ground just a few feet in front of it, a large ball of energy pulsing between my hands.

Teeming with muscle and powers drawn from the fires of Hell, the demon launched itself off the forest floor with a terrifying wail, its enormous wingspan drowning out the first rays of early morning light. Birds and nearby wildlife scattered as it descended upon me, sword-like claws poised to rip out my jugular.

Cloaking myself with invisibility, I sifted behind its massive form and unleashed the growing energy pulse in my hands. The ball of mystical fire struck the demon hard in the back, blazing a giant hole through its left wing.

Screaming in pain, the Aerico rounded on me and kicked off the ground, frustrated shrieks blasting me when it realized it could no longer fly.

Blackened mouth opening wide, the hell beast screamed, a billowing stream of fire bursting from its muzzle like an underworld flame-thrower.

I sifted out of the way, hovering behind it amidst a clump of trees.

Foolish mortal.

The Aerico's archaic voice echoed in my ears though I knew it hadn't spoken aloud.

I am not so easily defeated. I know you lurk behind me and will bathe in your blood when I rip your head from your—

"That's enough talking," I said as I watched the demon's crimson fall of hair catch on the breeze, its newly decapitated skull rolling through the damp underbrush like a bloody bowling ball.

Pontificating, overbearing, underworld POS. Overconfident and just plain stupid, the damn thing had failed to notice me summon a pair of short swords and was now a heaping dose of fertilizer for the growing trees.

Heat buzzed beneath my fingertips as I blasted the beast with a bolt of electricity, setting its disease ravaged hide on fire. Burning the carcass was the only way to ensure no one came in contact with its tainted remains.

Rage expelled, the winds from my anger-fueled storm slowly receded, my leftover pain and aggression vanishing with them into the obsidian sky.

With the first rays of the early morning sun looming on the horizon, I knew I didn't have much time to locate and destroy the second Aerico before it wreaked bloody havoc on the village, unleashing illness and plague along with a shitload of misery. With paranoia, fear and accusations of witchcraft running rampant, a demon sighting would likely send the villagers over the edge into full-fledged homicidal mania.

Cloaked with invisibility, I sifted into the sky, soft orange and yellow rays casting muted light over the dark horizon. *Where the hell would the Aerico have gone?* I closed my eyes, reaching out with my magic to search for the creature's dark aura, but didn't get far.

Muffled shouts from the village below snared my attention and I sifted along the eastern side of Ingersolls to get a closer look.

Salem Village, which had been a picture of peace and quiet some thirty minutes before, was now a hot bed of chaos and disorder. Muted candlelight riddled the open space as villagers dressed in night clothes flooded the dirt highway in front of Ingersolls. Frightened voices shouted into the night, venom coating their terrified shrieks.

"'Twas the warlock and his new concubine!"

"Lord have mercy on us!"

"The devil himself plagues this village!"

One frightened voice carried above the others, its desperation pulling me from my stupor along with its familiar tone.

Prudence Loveguard.

Eyes wild, Prue thrashed and fought, digging her heels into the ravaged soil. "Stop this madness! I beg of ye! I know not what is wrong!"

Dressed in a linen night dress, bonnet hanging askew, she fought against Goodman Hathorne's steely grip as he dragged her from the warmth and safety of Ingersolls into the heart of chaos.

A mixture of fear and disgust tainted Hathorne's already rigid features as he took hold of Prue by the shoulders and shook her violently. "Cease your struggling, foul creature, for it will do you no good. Your treachery this past day has resulted in grave consequences." He stepped back, eyes suddenly wary, filled with a mixture of fear and contempt.

"Drawn from a fitful sleep by the sound of evil, young Abigail Williams attests to witnessing a dark figure flying across the sky, its baleful screech setting her blood to ice. Goodman Wyberg, a most Godly man, died this evening past, a deadly curse placed upon him by the very witch you helped escape: Mistress Ellwood. What say you, Prudence? Are you in league with the devil? Have you given yourself over to the dark one?"

Gasping for air and barely able to speak, Prue shook her head and whimpered. "'Twas not my doing, good sir. I love our good Lord and cherish his commandments. Please! You must believe me. Mistress Ellwood... She is no witch. I assure you. I know not what is happening!"

"Silence!" All eyes, including mine, moved toward the gruff, austere voice parting the crowd. With her right hand gripping the ends of her shawl against her chest, the left flailing about like a dying fish, a hysterical Goody Godbert emerged from the raucous assembly, pure venom and hatred pouring forth from her large mouth at high volume. Quick as a whip despite her enormous size, she shot past the struggling duo and stopped, her plump, bare feet sinking into the muddy earth below her. Cold eyes filled with judgment and hatred, she drew her arm back and slapped Prue across the face with a loud "thwack!"

"Deceitful child!" she spat. "I cared for you as a daughter. I shared with you the love of our Good Lord, made you my apprentice and taught you all that I know."

She shifted her gaze from Prudence, who was unable to do anything but shake her head and cry, to the growing crowd of frightened villagers drawn toward the chaos like moths to a flame. Lips pulled into a tight line, she shook her head.

"The entire village woke to the sound of unearthly wailing rising up from Whipple Hill. Your willingness to help the witch escape has allowed the devil to walk among us. Ye are not but a liar...a murderer...Satan's mistress. Ye shall rue the day ye gave help to the likes of Mistress Ellwood and her warlock lover." Brows pulled down over a set of cold, gray eyes, she spat at the ground near Prue's feet and sneered. "May God have mercy on your soul!"

"No!" Shaking from head to toe and hysterical, Prue sobbed uncontrollably, barely able to speak. "Goody! Please!" she cried and lunged forward, latching onto the woman's right arm. "Please!"

Goody, in turn, hissed as though Prue's touch had burned her and yanked her limb away, cradling it against her chest.

I pressed my lips together and shook my head as I watched the scene play out. Goody ignored Prue's desperate pleas, gathered up the folds of her wrinkled night dress and turned on her heels, the waiting crowd swallowing her whole.

Godammit. Fat splinters of wood dug into my skin as I punched a jagged hole into the side of Ingersolls. "Smug, sanctimonious bitch." I drew my hand back, fresh droplets of blood trickling down my knuckles and onto the ground below. *Fucking idiot.* Swept away on a wave of chaos and fear, much like the rest of the village, she'd cast a blind judgment against Prue, mercilessly feeding the mob's need for vengeance and so called "Godly justice."

I bit down on the inside of my cheek and shook my head. "Pshh…" Murder was still murder, regardless of whose name you committed it in. These people were certifiable.

"Devil woman!"

I cringed, a fat dose of "what the hell else can go wrong" squeezing my gut.

Reverend Parris's aging voice skipped across my eardrums like a cheese grater, feeding my growing disdain. Much like when Moses parted the Red Sea, the crowd of horrified villagers drew back as he emerged, eyes wide with horror, mouths agape. "Prudence Loveguard! Ye have colluded with the warlock, Gabriel Castillo and his wanton mistress, Faythe Ellwood. The crime of witchcraft is punishable by death. Come first light, ye shall face judgment."

Oh, fuck. The small amount of air remaining in my lungs fizzled out as I listened to the reverend's caustic words. I'd survived the Salem Witch trials three hundred years ago…barely. Anytime someone uttered the words "witchcraft" and "judgment" you could be damn sure someone would hang. Thing was, no one had so much as looked sideways at Prudence the first time around.

Hand balled into a fist, I punched another hole into the side of Ingersolls and swore under my breath. "Dammit!" The Fates, though callous and power hungry, had been right about the consequences that came with sifting time. My presence in this place *was* altering the course of history. In my quest to save Taylor from hanging, my actions, though miniscule, had most likely sent Prudence to her executioner.

The angry mob rallied behind Parris, violent words shouted in frenzied voices.

"Hang the witch!"

"No! Burn her! Ye cannot suffer a witch to live!"

"No!" With a mangled sob, Prue's eyes rolled to the back of her head, her knees giving way as she fell in an unconscious heap on the ground.

Hatred and loathing magnified the deep grooves in Hathorne's aging face as he locked gazes with Parris, the two waging a somber and very silent conversation. With a nod, Hathorne signaled two nearby men to help lift Prue's unconscious body from the dirt. "Escort her to the holding cell with Tituba and the others. When the morning sun rides high in the heavens she will be tried and sentenced for her crimes."

I raised a brow. *Tituba?* Had I heard Hathorne correctly? Tituba… Sitting in jail? A sarcastic laugh blew past my lips as I shook my head. "I don't fucking think so, assholes." I'd witnessed Witchy Woman working her evil mojo firsthand prior to this evening's attack, and I'd seen her roaming the woods more than once over the past few days. Her mystical ass was far from incarcerated. Quite the contrary. She was running amuck, summoning demons and creating mass hysteria in the process.

I ran my hands through my hair and swore. "Fuck!" Felt like I was being pulled in a hundred different directions. I didn't have time for this shit. If I chased after Tituba I risked the Fates wrath. If I sat back and did nothing… *Fuck!* I clenched my jaw and punched another hole into the side of Ingersolls. If I sat on my ass and did nothing, I was still screwed.

The Fates had immobilized me, rendered me useless. I couldn't help Taylor, at least, not directly. And on top of that, I was sure to endure a shit load of guilt for not stopping a murderous witch when I had the chance. I didn't even want to think about what horrors the next few hours held for poor Prudence. "Fucking damned if I do, and damned if I don't."

The crowd surrounding Ingersolls shifted, the majority of the women converging on Ingersolls like a swarm of mosquitos, buzzing with gossip. The men rallied together alongside Parris and Hathorne.

"Evil is upon us, my brothers!" Parris's flinty voice carried over the loud discord, a mask of seriousness and determination etched across his aging face. He raised his arm and gestured toward the dark tree line beyond Ingersolls. "The devil himself lurks in our woods. He has enlisted the help of the warlock, Gabriel Castillo, to carry out his wicked plans."

"Wicked plans, my ass." Fire blazed beneath my skin, my hatred for the pious reverend growing at an exponential rate. In the short time I'd lived in Salem Village, not once had I done anything to draw the man's ire. And while he was right about my being a warlock, he was dead wrong about everything else. I'd sought peace, a quiet life of solitude in the woods, and was persecuted for what they considered my sins. Hell, the only soul in this time who knew of my abilities was Taylor…or Faythe, as I had known her. Sharp, knifing pain slashed through my chest. My honesty, my love for her had led to her demise. I truly was the harbinger of death.

Voice elevated several octaves, the reverend continued on with his frenzied diatribe. "Young Faythe Ellwood, a once goodly woman, has fallen under the warlock's evil spell and has been bewitched to do his bidding." He swept a hand toward the large crowd of angry men, his darkened eyes radiating a challenge. "Who among you has courage? Who among you will stand with me and fight this evil scourge?"

Evil scourge? Evil? Maybe. I was definitely cursed, but a scourge? I'd be lying if I said I wasn't insulted.

Voices rumbled and shouts grew loud as men, one after the other, stepped forward with arms raised.

"I will stand with ye!"

"The power of the Lord shall grant us victory!"

"We must burn them! Purify them by fire!"

Shit. I shook my head in disgust and backed away quickly, each molecule in my body exploding apart as I sifted to the scene of my fight with the Aerico. Always with the fire. Assholes always wanted to burn me.

Whipple Hill was just as I'd left it, the remains of the Aerico demon still burning, black sooty tendrils spiraling up from its blazing carcass. I stared, deep into the heart of the flames, small wisps of brilliant blue arching and writhing beneath a cloud of yellow and orange, mesmerizing and beautiful.

Fire... It had been the bane of my existence, my saving grace when fighting demons, and a necessary evil I'd tolerated since my days spent rotting beneath Ivanov's manor. Whether used against me as punishment, or by me when fighting off an angry hoard of demons, everything, everything, always came back to fire.

Buzzing with power, I lifted my hands, palms up, and coaxed the withering flames into an enormous bonfire, the heat of which scorched my skin and burned the inside of my nose. I needed to warn Taylor and my younger self about the coming mob and Tituba. Things in Salem Village were about to get really ugly, and while I couldn't reveal myself, couldn't fight, the Fates never said my younger self couldn't.

Chapter 17

· Gabriel ·

A growing sense of panic rose in my chest as I lay in front of the hearth next to *Adonia*, arms and legs still entwined. "*Cristo. Que he hecho?*" What have I done?

"Mmmm…" *Adonia* shifted, the velvet skin on her upper thigh brushing against my swollen erection.

Dios mio… I groaned, ready to take her again if she'd have me. My desire for her would never wane. She was the very air I breathed.

Body flush with mine, she brushed her hand up the length of my opposite arm and pressed a kiss against the sensitive skin between my shoulder and neck. "Your native language is beautiful. What did you say?"

Mierda. Nothing got past her.

Now that our souls had merged, lying was out of the question. We were connected, on a primal level—one that would allow her to sense my deception. Still, having barely escaped death just hours before, *Adonia* didn't need the weight of Nadya's hateful curse on her shoulders. No. I would bear the brunt of that particular burden for the both of us, and in turn, do all I could to ensure she'd never suffer because of it.

I buried my face in her damp hair and kissed the top of her head. Distraction, it seemed, was my only option.

Eyes trained on her, I waved my hand in a wide arc above us. "Look up."

She glanced up, her sated, heavy-lidded eyes widening, a soft gasp blowing past her lips as the wooden roof overhead disappeared. "Oh! Oh, my God…" She glanced at me for a brief moment, surprise lighting up her face, then gazed up at the sky. "Beautiful."

I knew, without looking, the marvel she wondered at, having appreciated its beauty daily for the past year.

Lush hues of orange, pink and purple smeared across the sky as the morning sun crested over the horizon. The newly awakened wildlife sang of its beauty, sparrows and warblers chirping a distant melody. Dawn's first blush was breathtaking, yes, but it paled in comparison to the angel lying in my arms. I cupped her cheek, every part of me aching to touch her, cherish her. "*Si fuera possible, mi dulce, te daría del cielo.* Were I able, *mi dulce,* I would give you the heavens and all they contain."

Warmth and love radiated from the depths of her rich, caramel eyes. "It's magical," she said on a whispered breath. Pink lips pulled into a gentle smile, she leaned in close and pressed a soft kiss to my temple. "You're magical, Gabriel. Thank you."

Ghosting her hand up the length of my arm, she squeezed my shoulder before wedging her head into the crook of my neck once more with a sigh. One leg threaded between mine, every inch of her warm, tantalizing body molded against me like a second skin.

I slid my hand up the length of her neck, fingertips brushing her smooth skin, committing every inch, every detail to memory. "What is this?" I asked, a faint surge of power licking at my senses as I ran my fingers along a small patch of flesh behind her ear. Magic. She'd been touched by magic before?

My blood boiled beneath my skin at the thought of another man touching her, let alone another warlock. What was she hiding from me? "*Adonia.* Are you aware you—"

She brushed my hand away. "Uh-uh…" she whispered forcefully, the soft pads of her fingertips trailing a back and forth pattern across my collarbone. "Quit trying to distract me. I want the truth, and I want it now, buddy."

The same fingers that sent a bonfire igniting in my gut just moments before trailed from my shoulder to the center of my chest, drowning all thoughts except for what she was doing. I drew in a ragged breath and stiffened, both from the directness of her question and the demons of my past. *Cristo!* Why? Why did my body have to react that way? And after so long?

I heard her quick intake of breath as she drew her hand back. "Gabriel?"

When I didn't respond immediately, she pressed up onto her elbow and stared down at me, brows creased, eyes that were alight with wonder moments before, now dark with worry. "Did someone…" Her voice broke and she looked down for a moment before continuing. "Did someone…hurt you?"

With my lips pressed together, I turned my head and stared at a random notch in the wood floor, unwilling, unable to meet her penetrating, pity filled gaze. I squeezed my eyes closed, wishing I were doing something, anything other than having this conversation. *Madre de Dios. Adonia* was tenacious. My attempt to distract her from the reality of our situation did little to quell her curiosity. She was strong-willed, direct. Two qualities I greatly admired despite the grief they were about to cause me.

I shook my head and groaned. It seemed no matter how hard I tried, I couldn't escape my past. Perhaps it was a sign. A sign that I couldn't move forward, begin life anew with Faythe, until I let go of the ghosts haunting me. *Dios mio.* How I wanted to rid myself of their daily terror.

I exhaled a heavy breath and stared at the floor once more, unseeing, wishing I could somehow magically erase the horrors of my recent past. Unlike the vast majority, this woman— no, this angel beside me—she accepted me for who I was, magical abilities and all. *Cristo!* Would she still want me after she discovered the truth? That I was nothing more than a murderer, a destroyer of life, a walking curse? I wasn't so sure.

Soft fingers caressed the side of my face, turning my head, drawing my hesitant gaze to hers. "Don't shut me out, Gabriel. Not now. Not after the amazing connection we just shared."

I reached up, catching a strand of her silky hair between my fingers before sweeping her long mane off her shoulder. *Beautiful.* Staring up into her warm caramel gaze, expression taut with concern, I found it hard to deny her anything. I'd relinquish my deepest secrets, divulge the secrets of the universe, offer up my soul if only to take away her worry.

My voice sounded choppy…not my own. "The sins of my past…" my hand found hers and placed it on my chest once more, the sensation no longer dredging up dark memories, "haunt me daily."

She pulled away slightly, her brows knit together in confusion. "What do you mean, sins of your past? Talk to me, Gabriel. Please."

I could deny her nothing. Fear gnawed at my gut as I released the glamour spell I wore like armor, the air surrounding me warping and skewing. A ripple of light descended down the length of my torso revealing the horrors beneath, revealing my true appearance.

Once a vivid red, most of burn scars covering my chest and abdomen had faded, the raised, mottled skin pink in some areas, brown in others. Five jagged ridges traveled from my collarbone to just below my navel, the scarred grooves slashing through the melted skin, as though a miniature rake had been drug down my torso.

I closed my eyes, unwilling to meet the look of shock, the expression of pity she surely wore. Jaw aching, teeth grinding, I patiently waited for the terrified gasp, the pitied sob, positive at any moment she would leave.

But the sounds never came.

Her warm body remained pressed against my own.

Warm, silken lips pressed feather light kisses down the length of one of the jagged scars, each gentle caress soothing away the hurt, easing the residual emotional pain I carried with me wherever I went.

"I wish I had your magic," she whispered between kisses. "I'd wipe the memory of it from you…" Mouth trailing back up my chest, she hovered, mouth achingly close to mine, pure love radiating from behind her luminous chocolate orbs. "I'd take away your pain."

Body shaking with tension, I broke, a ragged gasp blowing past my lips as I fought to pull precious air into my lungs. *Never.* Not once in the short span of my life had I ever experienced such unconditional love. That we'd only just met, that she knew next to nothing of me clearly made no difference to her. She'd given her heart, her soul, freely and the reality of that overwhelmed me.

"Oh, God!" She whimpered, her tiny hand shaking as it flew to her mouth. "Pain." She shook her head, eyes suddenly glossy with unshed tears. "You're in pain and I—"

I was upright in an instant, crushing her against my chest in a tight embrace. "Shhh. Dry your tears, female. I feel no pain." I traced my hands up and down the length of her back in long soothing strokes. I was an idiot, a fool. So focused on myself, my own demons, I'd failed to protect her feelings and had once again caused her to cry. *Damned selfish bastard.*

Her body trembled beneath my arms. "But you—"

Releasing my hold on her, I sat back and cupped her face in my hands. "You slay me with your words, *mi dulce.*"

Brows furrowed, she opened her mouth to speak, but was cut short when I silenced her with a kiss. "No one," I said, pulling away slightly, "has ever spoken to me with such tenderness, has ever shown me such unconditional love before." My heart squeezed as I pressed another kiss to her forehead and pulled away. "And though I crave your affection, your love, your inner light…" I sighed. "*Alma gemela* or no, I know I am wholly undeserving of it." *Cristo.* How I ached to deserve her, to be something more, something better than I was.

"Undeserving?" She cocked her head to the side, her soft features masked with unease. "Seriously? I can't think of anyone more deserving of—"

"I took the life of my closest friend."

I sat, rigid, muscles tensing as I awaited her response. The truth I'd held onto for so long lingered in the air between us like an impenetrable wall. And though I knew I'd likely driven the most important woman in my life away with the truth of my past, it felt as though a heavy boulder had been lifted from my chest. The reality I'd been choking on for the past year finally cleared, allowing me to breathe fully.

Silence permeated the space between us, her expression blank, frustratingly void of any emotion that might give aid to what she was thinking. Did she fear me? Did I disgust her? The truth of what I'd done certainly disgusted me. *Cristo!* Did she regret our lovemaking? The idea left me feeling hollow, empty.

Bitterness coated the back of my throat, the same whirlpool of self-hatred and disgrace that choked the life from me daily crashing against me with an ocean of shame. Ivanov and Nadya had been right. I was an abomination, a monster incapable of giving or receiving love. Self indulgent and greedy, I'd broken down, given in to my desire for *Adonia*, paid no heed to the end result, and in turn, damned her for all eternity.

I raised an impatient brow, frustrated not only by her lack of response, but by the lack of emotion she wore. I bared my soul to her, revealed my darkest secret and she sat, stone-faced and silent. I leaned forward, eyes narrowed. "Have you nothing to say?"

"Seriously?" Frustration laced her voice as she crossed her arms over her chest. She eyed me with frank aggravation and heaved an irritated sigh. "I mean, really? Are you shittin' me? Am I not allowed at least a minute to think, to process what you've told me?"

I gave her a single nod, inwardly cursing my impatience on the matter. She was right, of course. The weight of my revelation was enormous. Of course she would need time to acclimate, to process. I eased back, unease whirling in my gut, as I stared into her heated gaze. *What is she thinking? Is she afraid? She appears irritated, more angry than fearful.* The muscles in my jaw ached from clenching, but I remained silent, hopeful.

The lines creasing her forehead relaxed and she gave a small exhale before shaking her head. "The past is just that, Gabriel. The past. I don't care what you did way back when. I care about the man in front of me now."

Surely my ears had deceived me. Had she just confessed she did not care I murdered my best friend? "You… You do not fear me then? I do not disgust you?"

Lips pressed into a thin line, eyes narrowed, she leaned forward and struck me hard in the shoulder, the blow causing me little pain, but her, very obviously a great deal. "Ouch!" She flapped her hand through the air before bringing the injured extremity to her lips. "*Sheisa* that smarts!" Anger blasted from behind her darkened eyes as she treated me to another scowl and shook her head. "Men! I swear. You're all useless as tits on a bull!"

I raised a brow. "Tits on a—"

"Clueless!" She grasped onto the sides of my face with each hand and gave me a good shake. "Your brain… It's oozed out your ears." Visibly frustrated, she threw her hands in the air and growled. "First, you drop a bomb on me and expect me to respond instantaneously. Then, when I tell you how I feel, you don't believe me. Criminy!"

Words escaped me. Shaken by the fact she had remained silent, and confused as to what armament had to do with anything, I raised a brow in question but remained silent, surveying her with great appreciation. Chest heaving, hair wild and eyes blazing with anger, she was glorious, a goddess in her own right.

The lines creasing her forehead receded, the muted light from the nearby fire bathing her gentle features in a soft glow of light. "I know you, Gabriel." She reached up and cupped my cheek. "It doesn't matter we've only just met. I've touched your soul, felt it wrapped around me and witnessed firsthand its goodness. If you murdered your friend, then something compelled you to do so. I'm certain there's more to what happened than what you're telling me."

Jaw clenched, I stared at her in disbelief, unsure of what I'd done to deserve the love and trust of such a radiant human being. I turned my gaze toward the hearth, avoiding her outpouring of utter trust and faith. *Dios mio.* She was too much. More than I deserved.

"Oh, no you don't," she snapped and took my face in her hands once again. "I see what you're doing. You're shutting down, tuning out, losing yourself in that gorgeous head of yours. Don't shut me out, Gabriel. Ease your burden and get it off your chest. Share with me."

I breathed in deeply and sighed, impressed with her persistence, and torn because I knew the answers she sought would destroy everything.

Jaw set, her gaze unwavering, she trembled, her silken skin pebbled with goose flesh despite the warmth radiating from the fire. Fear and uncertainty were no doubt waging a war inside her mind, but she hid the silent battle well, her shivering the only visible sign.

I snapped my fingers, and with a pop she was once again covered in a linen shift, a thick wool blanket wrapped around her shoulders. Grasping a handful of hair at the nape of her neck, I pulled her close and pressed a kiss to the top of her head, breathing in her heady citrus scent. "I can deny you nothing." I let my hand drift forward, my thumb gently pulling across her cheekbone. "It will be easier for me to show you, I think." I shook my head, grimacing. "I promise you, *mi dulce*, you will not like the answers you innocently seek."

She raised a thin brow and pursed her lips. "I think I'll take my chances. Start talking."

Cristo! Where to begin? Burying my fingers in her silken hair, I grasped either side of her head, closed my eyes and established a connection, merging my thoughts, my memories, my entire consciousness with hers. Her quick intake of breath was the last thing I remembered before we traveled deep into the dark recesses of my memory, to a place I'd sworn I'd never return.

Chapter 18

· Gabriel ·

Teeming with fear and hatred, the cool, night breeze provided little relief to the blaze of fury boiling beneath my skin. I gritted my teeth, muscles tensing as I sifted into the gardens at the Reales Alcázares. "Damn, drunken fool."

With only a crescent moon to illuminate its beauty, the lush green of the garden lay dark, muted and disturbingly cool. The heavy scent of citrus from the nearby orange trees lingered in the air, going largely unnoticed as I sifted in a zigzag pattern throughout the lush courtyard.

Cloaked with invisibility and relying on the element of surprise, I used telepathy to call out to my oldest friend, my brother in arms. "Stefan!" Mierda. Where was he? With the Lamashtu demon running loose throughout Seville, a drunken romp in the capital's garden with his current tramp was not only ill-timed, but highly inappropriate. Every able-bodied warlock was needed to destroy the Mesopotamian night demon before a plague of epic proportions spread throughout the city.

Seven evil entities in one, the Lamashtu had scattered itself throughout the city, seducing men with her unholy beauty and cursing her prey with an incurable, highly contagious disease.

Unable to locate the Lamashtu's host body, the majority of the coven had spent the past several days euthanizing her pestilent, decaying victims before they contaminated anyone. The majority, that is, except Stefan. Unable to cope with the savage murder of his childhood sweetheart by a rogue vampire, most of his days were spent drinking, his nights, drowning his sorrows with meaningless trysts.

A soft giggle floated across the courtyard, drawing my attention toward a large stone fountain. There! "Stefan! Enough of this nonsense!" I sifted closer, a wisp of gauzy white fabric floating like a feather on the night air before disappearing from sight with a small pop.

"Mierda!" This was my fault. Had I kept better watch over him, prevented him from drowning his sorrows in cheap spirits, his family and I would be hunting the Lamashtu, as opposed to tracking down his drunken ass.

A low groan reverberated off the ancient stone walls of the palace courtyard, a deep voice, tainted with the effects of alcohol echoing throughout the space. "Ina…my love."

"No!" I stood frozen in place momentarily, each of Stefan's drunken words a dagger plunging deep into my chest. "Ina…" The host body for the Lamashtu. Cristo! A deep ache tore through my gut, reality bearing down on me with jagged teeth. The odds my inebriated friend would both find and seduce the very creature the coven had been tearing the city apart for were well beyond the frame of what I thought possible. Life, while never this easy, was most definitely always this cruel.

"The Moirai." I clenched my fists and groaned. The Fates had a hand in this. Of that, there was no doubt. But why? Seville was crawling with demons, with evil undead. What purpose did it serve the ancient trio in the grand scheme of things to destroy one of the city's champions?

Eerie laughter tickled the back of my neck, the abundant trees doing little to stifle its muted sound from carrying across the intricately cut topiary maze. Body thrumming with power, I sifted to the Patio del Crucero and took a knee. Fingers scraping against rough stone, I opened myself up and willed my senses to locate my endangered friend.

"Come. Come, *mi amor*…"

My body seized, each muscle hardening to granite as the Lamashtu's traitorous plea echoed from below the ancient stone pavement I knelt on. Madre de Dios! The bitch had lured him to the ancient baths beneath the courtyard.

Preparing to sift once again, the sound of Nadya's irritated voice anchored me in place. "Have you found him yet?" My chest squeezed, both from the sight of my love and from the knowledge her brother had been willingly lured to what was sure to be a watery grave by the Lamashtu.

Her father, Ivanov, materialized alongside her, grim faced, sword in hand. "Time is of the essence, Gabriel. The Lamashtu has struck in several places this night. Have you found my wayward son?"

"Idiota!" Nadya spat. "Bastardo!" Fire blazed behind her dark eyes, her long, ebony hair a wild mass of curls flowing down her back and over her shoulders. The sleeve of her black gown was torn at the shoulder, smooth patches of ivory visible with each upward sweep of her arm. "A demon terrorizes our great city, and my brother, drunken fool that he is, chooses to go whoring. When I find him I—"

Anguish whirled in my chest, the dull ache chipping away at me with each beat of my heart. "Bite your tongue, female. Your beloved brother is in grave peril." Bitterness coated the back of my tongue as I stood from where I knelt. Bathed in soft beams of moonlight, the balcony and flat archway of the palace gateway loomed over us like an enormous spectral shadow, oppressive and unforgiving. Dios mio… How would I tell them it was too late?

Ivanov shot forward, sword raised, his expression full of apprehension and disbelief. It was then that I knew he sensed something was terribly wrong. He shook his head, his resonant voice cracking as he spoke his son's name. "Stefan?" Like me, he dropped to his knee, metal clanging against stone tile as he reached out with his magic in search of his only son.

"No," he mumbled, head shaking in disbelief. The muffled words he spoke grew louder as they ran together, morphing into a tormented cry that tore at my gut. Face racked with pain, breaths coming in ragged pants, he threw his head back and screamed into the night sky. "My son! No!" Brilliant beams of light engulfed his enormous body, and with a small pop he disappeared.

Ivanov's anguished cry had confirmed my fear. It was too late. We were too late. Shock, disbelief—they dulled my senses, clouded my thoughts. I stared at the shadowed structure in front of me, disbelief chiseling away at me like the darkened grooves of the stone archway. How had this happened? Stefan had been fighting beside me, beside his father, since we were young boys. He perceived evil better than any warlock in our coven. How had he fallen into the Lamashtu's web of lies so easily?

Despite my efforts to snuff its reality from my head, the truth of the situation rang clear. Had Stefan been thinking clearly, had he been sober, he never would have succumbed to the Lamashtu's siren call. "Chinga!" I spat on the ground. "Damn this life!"

Sharp nails dug into the flesh on my arms as Nadya shook me hard, her high-pitched screams a faint echo in the vacuum of grief swallowing me whole.

"Gabriel!"

Hot, stinging pain blazed across my cheek, the burn drawing me from the dark pit I'd begun spiraling into.

Ebony eyes wild, she laced her fingers between my own, her powerful magic surging in pulses from her life force to mine. "Stefan needs us. Let us go!"

Moisture clung to the air inside the underground bathing chamber, cool and crisp. The muted glow from scattered torches lining the walls reflected off the bathing pool, the disturbed water sloshing over the lip of the large basin. Shadows loomed against the dim cavernous walls, two dark wraiths writhing in time with Ivanov's tortured chanting.

Trapped inside a ball of energy, the Lamashtu's host body, Ina, hovered above the bathing pool, screeching and writhing as she struggled to free herself. Ungodly beautiful, with flaming red hair, green eyes and alabaster skin that glowed beneath her sheer, white gown, it was easy to see how so many succumbed to her lure. If the remaining six entities she'd scattered throughout Seville were as unearthly beautiful as she, the city would fall within the next few days, a plague of epic proportions decimating everything and everyone.

Ivanov's chanting grew louder and more frenzied, brilliant sparks igniting from his fingertips, bolt after bolt of energy encasing the demon and drawing forth its evil spawn.

Nadya, who had been chanting a cloaking spell, shrouding the battle between us and the Lamashtu from the inhabitants of the palace, rounded on her father. Voice unwavering, she laid a hand on his shoulder, channeling her energy into him as he repeatedly shouted the spell that would bind the Lamashtu to the underworld for all eternity.

I rushed toward Stefan who lay thrashing on the cold stone floor, tortured groans cutting through his father's shouts with ease. Nausea tore through my gut as I knelt alongside his deteriorating frame. Large, festering boils covered every inch of visible skin, a fine spray of blood coating the nearby tile with each labored cough he choked out.

"I am a fool," he wheezed moments before a large seizure overtook him.

Wanting to ease my friend's pain, I lifted a hand to cast a spell when he jerked, sifting several feet away.

"Don't touch me! I am unclean, tainted."

His black, shoulder length hair hung in ragged strands over his face, slices of once tan skin now a deathly ashen gray peeking through. "Forgive me, my friend, my iniquities. I have not been whole since Analucia died."

A high-pitched shriek drew my attention from Stefan toward the center of the pool. The Lamashtu hung frozen in midair, back arched, long hair billowing about its head like a crimson cloud. Bright, luminescent orbs, six in all, rocketed from the ceiling like falling stars aimed straight for the demon's chest. An explosion of fire burst from the demon's body as each entity bound to its evil host, the magical bubble she floated in now engulfed in a sea of flames.

I closed my eyes and pressed my lips together, willing the sick, retching sound coming from Stefan's direction to cease. I turned, my gut seizing as a pool of blood spilled forth from his rotting lips. He didn't have long…the sputtering, the choked gurgling noises he emitted a precursor to imminent death.

I raised a hand. "Let me ease your pain, brother. Let me—"

Dark, frightened eyes burned themselves into my memory as he sifted away, disappearing with a terrified, "No!"

Nadya's voice sounded inside my head, her tone biting, urgent. "Find him, Gabriel. Ease his pain, or all will be lost."

With a single nod I opened my senses, easily homing in on my dying friend's waning life force. Heat blazed beneath the surface of my skin as I sifted to the top of La Giralda, Seville cathedral's towering minaret.

Weak and unable to carry his own weight, I found Stefan slumped beneath one of the arched windows, bleeding from the mouth, breaths coming in quick, shallow pants. Body trembling, face twisted as though he was in grave pain, he held my gaze, eyes pleading. "Remember your vow, my friend."

"No!" Anger whipped through me and I threw my arm out, blasting a hole in the tower wall with my magic. "Do not ask that of me."

Struggling to pull air into his lungs, Stefan shook his head, the movement so slight it was barely visible. Resignation tainted his once vibrant voice. "You…must, Gabriel. I…hold you to your… promise."

I stumbled sideways with a ragged groan, my shoulder hitting the lip of one of the carved out notches in the tower wall. Looking down on Seville from the lofty bell tower, the city appeared peaceful, the muted glow from the sun's early morning rays creating an air of serenity. Dawn was fast approaching, the sound of footsteps and movement clanging from down below.

Too much. I slammed my fist against the stone wall, bones crunching, skin tearing with each repeated blow. What he asked... It was too much. I knew what I'd promised years ago. I remembered our youthful pact. I also remembered I'd never intended to keep my vow.

I tore my gaze from the city below, the sight of Stefan's rapidly deteriorating flesh eating away at my gut. "I will not end your life, Stefan. Do not ask this of me. I..." I shook my head, heartbroken, ashamed. "I cannot."

A large tremor ripped through him, his once strong, muscular frame having languished into a feeble sack of bones. "You...are my truest friend, Gabriel, and...a good man. I will make this...easy for you." With a labored groan, he sifted atop the ledge of one of the large openings on the tower wall.

I lunged forward. "Stefan! No!"

"The moment my body...hits the pavement the disease will spread. There are people...milling about already. Are you willing to—" He doubled over with a groan. "Ahh! Dios en el cielo!" He gripped the edge of the open window, the rotting flesh of his hand leaving behind a bloody smear. He glanced from his hand to the stain which magically burst into flames, thus eradicating the possibility of contamination, before letting his eyes fall on me once more. "Would you risk contaminating innocents? Spreading this plague?"

I stood, anchored in place, mouth open, words hanging on the tip of my tongue, yet unable to speak. Cristo. I was weak, a coward. I reached out, pleading with him though I knew it would do no good, though I knew, deep down, he was right.

"Please, Stefan. Do not do this."

Ebony eyes bore down on me, his expression one of trust, one of complete forgiveness. "Watch over my father and sister. Tell them I am sorry…for…for everything." He glanced down at the street below before meeting my gaze one final time, muted rays of orange and yellow from the newly risen sun illuminating his sorrow, his resignation. "Forgive me, my friend."

"Nooooo!" Time felt as though it had slowed immeasurably. I lunged forward the same moment he leapt from the window, fire exploding from my fingertips like bolts of lightning.

Stefan's once powerful, healthy body exploded in a ball of flames, disintegrating to ash that carried away on the morning breeze.

"Gabriel, no!" Laced with hysteria, Nadya's voice ripped away the last shred of sanity I clung to in that moment. "Murderer! What have you done?"

Adonia fell back with a loud gasp as I severed our mental connection, her eyes closed, her face twisted in pain as she shook her head.

I sat for a moment, hands still lifted in front of me from where I'd held her, unable to move, unable to breathe. It was as I had feared. She thought me a monster, like everyone else.

I dropped my arms and sat back, a familiar bitter ache gnawing at my gut. "You were warned, *Adonia*. The truth regarding my past is not easy to swallow."

Disgust chewed at my innards, eating me from the inside out. Betrayed, beaten and tired, I had allowed Ivanov and Nadya's hatred to seep into my psyche. I'd cast away the truth of what had happened and lost myself in their hatred of me.

I would doubt myself no more. "Though I will never forgive myself for spilling his blood, I would not act differently if given the chance. I kept my vow to Stefan, prevented him from harming innocents. If taking his life in order to save the lives of countless others makes me a monster," I glared at her, resolute in my conviction, "then so be it."

She groaned, still visibly frustrated. "Goddammit, Gabriel. I don't think you're a monster. Quit assuming you know how I feel."

Lips smashed together, anger radiating from behind glossy, unshed tears, *Adonia* was a sight to behold. She lunged forward and repeatedly jabbed me in the chest with her finger. "I get that you've been through hell and back, so I'm prepared to cut you some slack. But seriously... You need to quit being so freaking impatient with me. Give me a chance to work through all of this before I respond and don't assume I'll think the worst of you. That's just not going to happen."

I opened my mouth to speak and was silenced, a pair of warm, nimble fingers smashing my lips closed.

"Uh uh." She shook her head and frowned. "You've done enough talking, thank you very much." Scowling, she ripped her hand away and sat back on her heels, shaking her head at me as though I were a child who needed scolding. "It's time to let go, Gabriel. Time to forgive yourself for Stefan's death. You admitted yourself, you wouldn't change what happened. Had you not acted as you did, countless others would have suffered. There was nothing else you could have done."

No longer able to contain the emotions inside, I exploded off the sea of blankets, arms slicing through the air. "*Estas loca?* Are you mad? Of course I could have done something!" Shame rippled through my veins like ice water. "I knew Stefan despaired after the death of Analucia. I knew he was fast spiraling into a black abyss and failed to watch over him properly. I could have done something... bound his powers, kept him from sifting."

Fire engulfed the side of my face where *Adonia*'s hand met my skin. Eyes alight with fire, body trembling with anger, she was no longer seated across from me, but rather pressed against me bodily, her face a hair's breadth from mine.

"Enough!" she growled through her teeth. "I'm going to speak now, and if you open your mouth, interrupt, or try to protest in any way I won't hesitate to light up the side of your face again. You feel me?"

Ferocious female. The lioness had unsheathed her sharp claws and she was nothing short of magnificent.

Satisfied she had made her point, she drew me back onto the pile of blankets and furs in front of the hearth before straddling my lap.

Placing a palm against the side of my face, she peered into my eyes, her expression resolute, serious. "Believe me when I tell you, Gabriel, what happened to Stefan was unfortunate." She shook her head, her brows creased. "But, it wasn't your fault."

Her brow raised when I opened my mouth, and I quickly shut it again, careful to avoid her wrath.

"Stefan chose his path, however unfortunate, and in doing so, placed himself in harm's way. If you'd held a bottle to his lips and forced him to drink I'd say yes, you had a hand in his demise. We both know that wasn't the case." Her expression softened then, her soft fingers threading through my hair, the pleasant sensation eating away at the numbness plaguing me. "Hurting or no, Stefan made a string of bad choices. His actions, and his actions alone, led to his death. He killed himself, Gabriel, and left you to clean up the mess."

Chapter 19

· Taylor ·

With my head resting on his shoulder, I gently massaged the taut muscles in Gabriel's back. Legs circling his waist and crossed at the ankle, I'd wrapped myself around him like a pretzel.

He held me tightly, squeezing my frame against his chest as if he'd never let go.

After witnessing firsthand the trauma Gabriel had endured with his closest friend, I was sure there wasn't a person on the planet who needed comforting more. I was also sure he hadn't revealed the entire story. I'd yet to learn how he came to be riddled with scars. It didn't make sense to me. He'd healed me after my demon attack. I'd sported broken bones, had been covered in puncture wounds and bleeding out. Yet, here I sat, perfectly whole as though nothing had ever happened. What had prevented him from magically healing? Why had he not healed himself?

I slid my fingers up the length of his back, threading them through his glorious hair. Pulling away from his delicious warmth would be painful, but his needs came before mine, and I knew he had more to share. I pressed a kiss to the crook of his neck and pulled back so I could see his face.

Tired. His expression, his eyes, they both exuded a heaping amount of exhaustion. But the tension in his jaw, the stiffness in his muscles, they'd receded, and I was sure it was because he'd finally opened up. The pain, the haunted aura that normally radiated from behind his eyes had lessened, and for that I was thankful. Wasn't there an expression, or maybe it was an old saying that went something like "the truth shall set you free"? My memory was still fuzzy, but the words, regardless of where I'd heard them, made a lot of sense.

"There's more you need to tell me, Gabriel." I trailed my hand down the length of his neck, over his shoulder, and let it come to rest on his chest. A spark of something, a painful memory maybe, flashed behind his eyes for a split second. He blinked and it was gone as quickly as it came. "Who did this to you, Gabriel? Who tortured you?"

Still seated on his lap, I felt his body stiffen beneath mine, the muscles in his neck bulging with strain. With eyes closed, features drawn into a pained expression, he shook his head. "No, *mi dulce*. The burden of that truth is too much to bear. You do not want to know."

I wrapped my arms around him once more and squeezed, my heart breaking for him all over again. *My God… What type of person would inflict such heinous torture on another human being? And why was he so intent on keeping the truth of their identity from me?*

A flash of long, dark hair and ebony eyes danced behind my eyes. I gasped, the truth of what happened to him smothering me as though I'd been caught beneath a landslide. My lungs seized up and I fought to breathe. *No…* I shook my head, hot tears sliding down my cheeks. *She wouldn't have. She… She couldn't have.* "Nadya," I said on a whispered breath.

Gabriel's body stiffened, silently confirming my suspicion.

"My God," I whispered. I pulled back and ran a finger down the jagged length of one of his raised scars, a firestorm of bitterness and rage welling inside my chest. "Nadya and her father did this to you," I met his gaze with my own, "didn't they?"

Jaw clenched, lips smashed together, he averted his eyes, refusing to meet my gaze.

I didn't need a confession from him to know I was right. Nadya and Ivanov were responsible for the crapload of baggage strapped to his back. I knew it. I knew it with every fiber of my being. "Show me."

He stared at me, a mixture of shock and horror blaring from behind his eyes. "No!"

Body shaking with anger, I bit down on the inside of my lip until I tasted blood. He needed this. He needed to show me, to get this burden off his chest. Witnessing his horrific past firsthand would most likely kill me, but I'd do anything, take anything upon myself to make him whole.

Unable to contain my emotions, I clamped onto either side of his head with a mangled sob. "Show me!"

Warm hands gripped my wrists and yanked them away, holding them between us. "You do not know what you ask, female." He shook his head once. "No."

My quest to remain strong, supportive and brave died the moment he uttered the word "no." My body sagged and I fell forward, the top of my head resting in the indentation just below his throat. How? How could anyone who claimed to love another, hurt them in such a manner? And how…how was he able to remain so stalwart? I would have caved under the weight of his burdens long ago, but he…he soldiered on. He was…amazing.

I clenched my hands into fists and pounded them against his naked shoulders. "I'll kill her," I managed to say in between sobs. "I'll kill the both of them."

"*Adonia*." Gabriel took hold of my wrists, effectively putting an end to my frantic pounding. Shifting both my wrists into one hand, he placed a finger beneath my chin and lifted my head, forcing me to meet his gaze. "Look at me, *mi dulce*."

He opened his mouth to say something else and I cut him off. "I don't care who she is. I don't care how powerful she is. That bitch and her father are going to suffer. Take me to her. Poof us…sift us… Do whatever the hell it is you do. Just take me to her." The flaring panic combined with the giant lump in my throat muffled my voice, making my words high-pitched and near incomprehensible "She needs to die, Gabriel. She needs to..." My head fell forward as I cried, so overcome with emotion I could no longer speak.

Strong arms wrapped around me and held me close. "Shhh, *mi dulce.*" He buried a hand in my hair and pressed a kiss to the top of my head. "It is over, my sweet. It is—"

"No." I lifted my head, blasting him with the full weight of my emotion. "It's not over. Nadya, Ivanov... They need to pay for what they did. They need to—"

"They are dead, *Adonia.*"

He stared at me silent and grimfaced, patiently waiting as I fought to grasp the reality of what he said.

With eyes narrowed, I shook my head. "Dead? You—"

He cut me off with a labored groan and grasped each side of my head. His masculine scent whirled inside my nose as he pressed his forehead to mine. "I spilled their blood, just as I did Stefan's. See for yourself."

Darkness pulled me under, Gabriel's memories a powerful riptide I couldn't escape. In the vision that followed, his thoughts became mine. His pain, my pain. We were one body, suffering from the same broken heart, reliving the same horrific memories in excruciating detail.

My body sagged against the jagged stone wall as the metal door to my chamber closed with a loud bang. The enchanted metal cuffs binding my wrists and ankles dug into my flesh, the unforgiving length of chain stretching my arms and legs outward still drawn painfully taut.

I kept my head down, my eyes closed, my breathing shallow.

Today's punishment had been much like the previous day's. The previous day's like the day before it. Whether by flogging, fire or torture device, Ivanov always found a way to unleash his pent up rage, a way to break me. Or so he thought.

Having endured a year's worth of captivity, of pain and suffering at his hand, I'd grown accustomed to his erratic mood swings. He was always enraged, always angry with me for killing Stefan, but there were the days when his rage took on a life of its own. In the beginning, it was on those days I found myself wishing for death, praying for the end to come swiftly. Usually unconscious or too wounded to move, the charmed shackles that bound my powers and kept me prisoner would be removed while Ivanov's faceless minions cleansed my bloodied body and magically knit me back together.

Today had been one of those days.

I smiled inwardly for I knew something Ivanov did not.

I'd learned how to separate my mind from my body, how to temporarily block out the pain.

I had formed a plan.

The thick, metal door swung open with a loud creak. I didn't need to open my eyes to know who had entered. The same two servants who always attended to me after my punishments swept across the bloodied stone floor, the hoods from their flowing brown robes drawn over their heads, concealing their true identity.

Biting pain flared through my skull as a large hand gripped my hair and yanked my head up.

"The swine still breathes."

A low growl tore across the dank space. "Damn traitorous pig. Remove his shackles."

Careful not to move or make a sound, I continued hanging limp against my bindings while the servant who'd yanked my hair unlocked the metal cuffs binding my wrists.

The right side of my face hit the dirty stone floor, breaking my fall the moment both wrists were released. I relished the pain. Soon I would be free.

The servant left me in a tangled heap as he unlocked the cuffs about my ankles, then dragged me toward the center of the chamber. Hot, stale breath wafted over my face as he positioned me on my back.

"Why does the master insist upon healing him? Why not let him die?"

Evil laughter filled the dim space, fueling my silent rage. "Death is too good for this traitor." Warm spittle slid down my face from where the servant had sprayed me with obvious disgust. "He must live if he is to suffer."

The sound of water being squeezed from a cloth echoed throughout the space as the men knelt beside me, preparing for the healing ritual.

Astral projection relied upon focus as opposed to pure magical power, for which I was greatly thankful. With my powers no longer bound by the enchanted cuffs, I projected my conscious self high above the chamber floor and looked down upon the gruesome scene.

My body lay ravaged and lifeless on the filthy stone floor, deep jagged tears from Ivanov's latest torture device raking a bloody trail down my newly burned torso.

The servants knelt over a shallow silver basin alongside me, chanting in Latin as they tossed various herbs and the like into the healing potion.

It was now, or never.

Heat scorched through me as I re-entered my body, a year's worth of pent up rage and aggression showering my captors in a sea of flames.

I sifted off the floor with a deafening roar, a phoenix rising from its ashes.

Magic fueled by pure hatred; I focused on Ivanov's life force and sifted out of the dungeon, paying no heed to the tormented shrieks of my burning captors. As I had suffered, so would my enemies.

The scent of tobacco and chocolate hung thick in the air as I neared the heavy wooden door leading into the library. My stomach churned; the familiar scent that had been such a comfort to me a short year ago now filled me with revulsion and hatred.

Some things, it seemed, never changed.

After a long day the two still enjoyed spending a quiet evening in *the library: Ivanov with his pipe and a book, Nadya with her violin and hot cocoa. How many nights had I spent with them, lounging on the velvety chaise, reading, basking in the relaxing sound of Nadya's skillful playing?*

Too many to recount.

The music I'd once found so relaxing now grated on my senses and sparked my fury.

Time after time I'd been told I was a monster, a murderer, had the truth of my evil ways beaten into me with brutality and without mercy. Yet, there they sat in all their finery, sipping liquid chocolate and reveling in the written word as if nothing were amiss, as if they hadn't burned the flesh from my chest, then scored the melted remnants with an iron talon just a few hours before.

If I were a monster, then Ivanov and Nadya were the spawn of Satan himself.

Blind with fury, I sifted into the study, heat rolling off my naked form in waves.

Seated behind a large, mahogany desk, his hulking frame bent over an enormous tome, Ivanov had no chance to react. Rendering him immobile with my magic, I wrapped my arms around his head, grasped him by the chin and ~snap~!

His body slumped forward onto the desk, his head twisted at an unnatural angle, an expression of shock forever painted across his malevolent face.

Nadya's horrified gasp blistered across my skin.

"Father! No!"

Ivory gown hung low across her heaving chest, Nadya stood frozen in place for the briefest of moments, as if time itself had ceased moving forward. Her playing interrupted, her arms hung loose at her sides, her hands still gripping her violin and bow. The shattered expression she wore, so full of grief, so full of pain, reminded me, for a split second, of the woman I had once loved.

Time, as I had learned over the past year, was fleeting, as was love. Her pained expression vanished in an instant, hatred and disdain taking up their familiar posts behind her ebony eyes.

"Murderer!" Jaw clenched, she lunged forward with a vengeful cry. "You will pay—"

I threw my hand up and shouted, "Existo etiam!"

With a strangled gasp, she froze mid-step, body stiffening beneath my binding spell.

With a flick of my wrist she floated forward as I rounded the desk, her bound and immobile frame inches from my own.

She glared down her nose at me and hissed. "You cannot bind me for long, swine. You are weak. Your powers will give way, and when they do I will end you." Her delicate lips pulled up into a haughty sneer. "Let me assure you, lover, you will suffer greatly before your heart gives way."

I raised a brow and barked out a quick, manic laugh. "Always so sure of yourself, my love." I plucked the bow from her frozen hand and trailed the tip along her middle as I circled her slowly.

Hatred burned the side of my face as I came to stand in front of her once more, her glare haughty, indifferent.

"Let me assure you," I said, caressing the tip of the bow along the line of her bosom, "I will suffer no more by your hand." I lifted my arm, positioning the tip of the bow over her heart like a dagger. "And as for my heart giving way..." With a grunt I drove the makeshift sword through her chest, a muffled gasp the only sound escaping her shocked lips "I do believe it is yours that will cease beating first."

Nearly spent, and unable to look upon her any longer, I lifted my hand, releasing the spell the bound her immobile. Her body fell limp to the floor, blood from the wound pooling around her, staining her ivory gown. I sifted to the door, then turned and lifted my hands, showering the room in a sea of crimson and orange. "May the fire you so loved to cleanse me with, purify your soul, lover. Otherwise I fear you may rot in hell."

I turned, my body disappearing as I prepared to sift, when I heard her shout.

"Ego vomica vos!"

Brows narrowed, my gaze followed her voice, the flames circling the room nearly smothering her.

Blood spewed forth from her lips, as she lay crumpled and broken. Her breathing had grown shallow, her voice weak. With a ragged inhalation, she rolled her head to the side and stared up at me, vengeance clouding her vision, even as she drew her last breath. "I curse you, Gabriel Castillo. In this life you shall know naught but pain and suffering. You will find love, Gabriel. You will find your soulmate, and—"

"No!"

Gabriel yanked his hands from my head and pulled away with a ragged cry as he fought to catch his breath.

Dizzy, I fell back onto my rump and clutched my head. "Oh, God. I…" *Too much.* The horrors, the atrocities he'd suffered at Ivanov's and Nadya's hands had been too much. And though I valued human life, I wasn't sorry he'd ended theirs. Hell, I was angry I hadn't had the chance to inflict a little pain before killing them myself.

Especially Nadya. The evil pushing out from behind those cold, black eyes of hers made my skin crawl. What kind of person cursed someone with their dying breath? *An evil person,* I thought. A chill swept through me, and I wished to God I could put the bloody picture of Nadya's last moments out of my mind. Gabriel had been right; the truth of his past was a terrible burden to bear. But bear it, I would.

Muscles a bit stiff and more than a little sore, I rubbed at my neck and shoulders, hoping to ease the ache. I cast a pleading glance at Gabriel who sat staring at the floor wearing a pained expression. *Not good.* Sharing was supposed to make him feel better, not worse. I leaned forward and ran a hand down the length of his arm. "Hey. Why did you pull away? What did Nadya curse you with?"

He looked up then, his eyes full of sadness and something that looked an awful lot like guilt. "I am sorry, *mi dulce*. I—"

Scorching heat blasted from the hearth as the burning timbers exploded into what looked like a wall of fire.

"Get back!" Gabriel shot forward and placed his body in front of mine, shielding me from the growing sea of flames.

"What is it? What's happening?" I cried, terrified, but unable to look away. Long sweeping tendrils of yellow and orange swept across the front of the hearth, the majority of the wall soon blanketed in fire.

Only, the wall wasn't burning. It was the oddest thing. The flames, though projecting heat, didn't actually burn.

"What the…" I gasped as an image of the woman who'd been attacked with me in the woods burst forth from the flames. *Tituba…* She stood at the outskirts of Salem Village, from what I could tell, chanting a slew of words I couldn't make out. What was she… "Holy shit!" I clutched Gabriel's shoulders, my fingernails digging into his naked flesh.

Two winged creatures had exploded up from beneath the ground in front of Tituba with an earsplitting, ungodly wail.

Heart pounding, I covered my ears and hid my face behind Gabriel's back. "What is that? What the hell is going on?" With the oppressive heat blasting from the wall of fire, it felt like I'd landed myself a front row seat to a horror movie in hell.

Sensing my extreme fear, Gabriel reached back, grasped my thigh and squeezed. "There is no need to be afraid, *mi dulce*. It is a message."

I peeked up from behind the safety of his shoulder as a new picture burst forward out of the flames. "A message? From who? I don't…"

Another image burst forth, again of Tituba. I narrowed my eyes in confusion. *Wait a minute. This can't be right. I just saw her…* Face gaunt and tired, she was laying on the ground in what looked like a small cell, her black dress and cream colored apron both a filthy shade of gray from the thick coating of dirt covering her. Was she in…jail? From her haggard appearance, it looked as though she'd been there for quite some time. The conflicting images confused the hell out of me and made no sense. Where exactly was Tituba and what the hell was she up to?

Tituba's image faded, another picture bursting forth with crystal clarity. I gasped, the small amount of air I'd managed to breathe in, escaping in one great whoosh. "Prue?" I pushed off Gabriel's shoulders and stood on shaky feet. My heart clenched at the vision of the frenzied mob pointing and shouting; my stomach seized when I read Parris' lips.

I tore my gaze from the fiery message to Gabriel who sat grimfaced.

My only friend in this time had just been accused of witchcraft and was due to stand trial come first light. All because she'd helped me escape.

I glanced over my shoulder to the soft beam of light cascading into the room from the nearby window and dropped to my knees with my hand over my mouth. How long had the sun been up? Were we too late? Had they already tried Prue?

With nausea whirling in my gut, I cast a pleading glance toward Gabriel before shooting up off the floor. "We can't let this happen. We have to rescue Prue. Now!"

Chapter 20

·Taylor·

Riddled with guilt over Prue's senseless capture, I exploded out the front door of Gabriel's cabin, paying no heed to his shouts of warning.

Cool morning air bit into my skin as I barreled toward the tree line, the early morning sun casting a warm glow against the lush, green canopy.

Prue was in trouble because of me and I had to get to her. It was one thing for me to run from a pack of crazies who thought me a witch. Self-preservation was an innate quality most humans shared. It was a whole other thing to sit back and do nothing while your only friend suffered because of you. Yeah, I was afraid of Parris and his whacked out posse. But I was also scared for Prue. Girlfriend had been there for me, had helped me escape when Goody meant to hand me over to Parris and Hathorne, and I knew I'd never be able to live with myself if I didn't reciprocate. My only hope was that I wasn't too late.

Paying little attention to where I was going, I barreled into Gabriel, who'd materialized in front of me, with a loud, "Oof!"

Holding me against his chest, he took the brunt of the fall as we skidded through piles of damp earth, maple leaves and pine needles.

"*Estas loca?*" he shouted and quickly rolled me off of him.

I shot up onto my feet and cast a quick glance at the narrow trail just outside of his property before meeting his angry gaze.

With a scowl, he sifted from the ground and positioned himself a few feet in front of me. Arms crossed over his naked chest, he blocked my escape and shot me a glare that said "Go ahead, girlfriend. Try and get past me. We'll see what happens."

"Are you mad?" he shouted. "The moment you set foot in Salem Village you will be captured."

"I don't care!" I shot forward, ducking and weaving, trying everything I could to get past him and failing miserably. Why couldn't he understand? I had to do this. I had to help Prue.

Hysterical, I rushed him. Hands balled into fists, I pounded away at his shoulders as fat tears streamed down my face. "Get out of my way! Please!"

With a shake of his head, he barked out a string of words I couldn't understand and grasped my shoulders. Dark eyes bore down on me, his heated gaze and worried expression almost more than I could bear. "I will not let you do this, *Adonia*." He crushed me to him, his powerful arms snaking around my torso. Warm breath brushed across my neck as he spoke through gritted teeth. "Carelessly throwing yourself into the lion's den will not save your friend."

I braced my hands against his chest and pushed, struggling to free myself from his iron grasp. "Let me go, Gabriel! Please! I…I can't sit back and watch her go to jail" My stomach clenched. "Or worse yet, hang because she dared to befriend me."

Groaning, he loosened his hold. Shifting one hand about my waist, the other cupped my cheek as he held my gaze. "Have you completely forgotten the events that transpired last night? Evil lurks throughout these woods, *Adonia*. You experienced the sharpness of its teeth firsthand."

A chill shot up the length of my spine as I remembered my terrorized jaunt through the forest. So worried about Prue, so caught up in the moment, I'd temporarily blocked out my hellish experience with the demons at the pond. What the hell was going on with my head? Why was it so damn eager to block out crucial information?

Gabriel gently brushed his thumb across my cheekbone, the soothing sensation warming me from the inside out. "The devil lurking in the woods is not my only concern, *Adonia*. Religious zealots are dangerous." He narrowed his brows, his expression gravely serious. "You must understand this: the reverend, the magistrate—both are looking for someone, anyone, to shoulder the blame for the chaos plaguing their village. If there is any hope of helping your friend we must move forward with caution."

I sucked in a quick breath and swiped at my tear stained cheek. "W-we? You mean, you'll help me?"

His face fell for a moment as he drew back, the flash of pain swallowed quickly and replaced with tenderness. Forehead creased, he shook his head. "You are my *alma gemela, mi dulce*. My soulmate. Your pain is mine. Of course I will help you."

Momentarily stunned, I stood with my mouth open, once again at a loss for words. How quickly I'd abandoned our connection, denied the depth of his feelings. Overwhelmed with emotion, I'd jumped to conclusions, mistook his interference with indifference and assumed the worst. For someone who sported the name Faythe, it seemed as though I had none.

I glanced up at him through my lashes, lower lip quivering in shame. "Forgive me?"

Gabriel pulled me against his chest once more and squeezed as a fresh round of tears sprang forth. His warm breath fanned over the top of my head, sending a ripple of warmth zinging through my panicked frame. "*Te quiero mucho, Adonia*. I will always help you, Faythe. I love you."

****

Cloaked with invisibility, we sifted into the heart of Salem Village—the eye of the storm.

The gruesome scene laid out in front of me choked the air from my lungs. My chest ached, a god-awful hollow feeling, as though someone had burned a hole clean through it. My hands shot up to my mouth, my knees gave out, and I crumpled to the ground. "No!"

We were too late.

A large mob had formed in front of the town meeting house. Men, women, children…all hurled angry shouts of condemnation and hatred toward a very dead Prudence.

The makeshift scaffolding that had been erected was tall, providing a full view of the barbaric proceedings to those viewing. Not that I needed another look. The image of Prue hanging, small tendrils of hair fanning up from her snapped neck with the early morning breeze would forever be burned into my memory.

Parris's aging voice carried over the melee, shredding the last vestiges of my sanity with each biting word. "Evil walks amongst us!"

My body sagged, my entire frame sinking into the dirt. "No no no no…"

Strong hands swept me off the ground and held me tight as time came to a screeching halt, the reality of what had happened slowly sinking in.

Prudence, my only friend, my only ally in this time aside from Gabriel, was dead.

Dead because of me.

I shook my head, tears blinding me to all else as a guttural cry worked its way up from deep within my chest. *Dead. Dead. She's dead because of me.*

Out of my mind with guilt, I thrashed against his steely grip, too far gone with grief to comprehend my efforts were in vain. I wanted to scream. I wanted to cry. I wanted to run. But most of all, I wanted to hurt those that hurt Prue. Why? Why had they taken the life of an innocent woman?

With a deep breath, I closed my eyes and let loose a tortured wail.

Gabriel's large hand clamped down on my mouth, muffling my scream as he sifted us further away from the angry crowd.

He whispered into my ear, the words barely registering.

"You must control your grief, *mi dulce.* If you allow it to consume you, if you succumb to it, you will only draw attention to us." He shifted, turning us to face the army of villagers and pointed toward the scaffolding. The reverend and Goodman Hathorne stood with their focus on the heated congregation, drawing their ire, fueling their discontent. But Goody Godbert... She stood off to the side, brows drawn together, a scowl slashed across her face as she scanned the noisy crowd. But for what, I wasn't sure. Had she heard me scream? Would that have even been possible over the noise of the crowd?

As if she heard my thoughts, Monobrow snapped her head in our direction, her blistering gaze boring into my invisible skin as though she actually saw me. Impossible. Gabriel had cloaked us. I narrowed my eyes in disbelief. "She... She can't see us, right? She couldn't possibly—"

A low growl erupted from Gabriel's chest, his muscles coiling, stiffening beneath my touch. He spoke through clenched teeth. "Evil walks amongst the villagers indeed." He turned his head to the side and spat. "*Idiotas!* They cradle it to their very bosom."

I shook my head, completely confused by what he said. "What do you—"

Parris's voice boomed over the crowd's unrest. "Parishioners! Good people of Salem Village! The Lord has prevailed this morning!"

Flanked by Goodman Hathorne and Goody Godbert, who continued casting heated glances in our direction, Parris stood atop the scaffolding, arms raised, eyes wild. He swept an arm toward Prue's dangling body. "Prudence Loveguard, Satan's newest foot soldier, has been freed from her bondage, the evil plaguing her soul, released." He turned on the crowd, eyes dark, and expression grave. "Let us not grow complacent! Our work has only just begun. Evil walks amongst us yet and must be stamped out!"

The mob roared. Raised arms, hands beating against an unseen enemy, riddled the crowded space.

"Burn them!"

"Hang them!"

"No! They must drown! Drown the warlock and his wanton lover!"

What little air remained in my lungs fizzled out like a dying balloon. Swept up in a whirlwind of fury and fear, the people of Salem had senselessly murdered a beloved villager and were now gunning for Gabriel and me.

I clutched my chest, gasping for breaths that refused to come. "It's over. They…they…she…" The world spun around me as I tried, and subsequently failed, to get the words out. "Dead! Oh, God, Gabriel! Prue…she's…dead, and they're…" Panic flooded my system, and my heart felt like it was about to explode out of my chest. I covered my face with my hands and curled into the safety of Gabriel's embrace with a desperate sob. "We're next!"

With a groan, he turned me around and beamed me with a heated stare. Strong arms crushed my chest against his. "I will destroy Salem and everyone in it before I see you hurt!"

I whimpered underneath his angered gaze, crumpled beneath the weight of all that had happened over the past few days. "I can't take this anymore, Gabriel." Demon attacks, accusations of witchcraft, and now Prue's death. It was all too much, and it all centered around me. My presence in this place had created a cataclysmic snowball effect of pure chaos—an unholy mess. I'd no clue how I'd traveled back in time. But I was certain of one thing: the past was trying desperately to purge itself of my unwanted presence.

I pushed at his chest, trying to break free. "Let me go. Let them have me." I stared up at him, teary eyed. "Before another innocent life is lost."

Rage ignited behind Gabriel's eyes. With a groan, he sifted us to the edge of the small clearing in front of his home.

With one hand behind my head, the other at my waist, he pinned me against a nearby tree with an animal like growl.

"Jamas!" He pressed a savage kiss to my lips and threaded his fingers through my hair as though he'd never let go. Body flush with mine, he ground his hips against me. He groaned and freed my mouth from his savage attack to whisper in my ear, throatily. "Wretched curse be damned! Never. I will never live without you."

Rough bark bit into my skin through the thick layers of my woolen dress, grating at my back. *Curse? What was he talking about? Could that be what Nadya—*

"Oh, God…Gabriel."

Warm hands tugged at the bodice of my dress while he kissed a trail down the length of my neck to my chest. His warm breath wisped across the moisture left behind from his kisses, fanning my growing passion. My nipples tightened to stiff buds, crying out for his touch.

"You are mine, *mi dulce.*"

I arched my back, craving the madness he brought about with his lips and hands, while secretly cursing the hideous dress I wore and its fifty billion impossible to work buttons.

So familiar. This felt so… I sucked in a quick breath. The fantasy I'd had my first morning here…rough tree bark scraping my back… Gabriel's mouth on my breasts…his enormous erection grinding against my girlie bits—I was living it out…in the flesh. Which meant…*Oh, God.* My dream wasn't just a fantasy, it was a memory. *Holy…*

A low moan escaped as he gently sucked at the flesh below my collarbone, tiny sparks of electricity zinging through my heated frame like fireworks on the verge of exploding. *So good.* Desire swept through me, the combination of licking, sucking and pulling driving me wild with need.

More. Numb with grief, overwhelmed by my situation, I needed to feel, to forget, even if only for a moment. I wove my fingers into his hair at his neck and held him closer. More. *Criminy.* I needed more.

All it took was another tug, and the buttons holding my bodice closed exploded from the annoying fabric keeping us apart. *Halleluiah!* It was all I could to do breathe, let alone think straight as he palmed my left breast, sucking the now diamond hard nipple into his mouth.

I threw my head back and cried out, the heat from his mouth combined with the delicious grinding of his hips sending shockwaves of pleasure to my aching core.

He grasped a handful of hair and pulled, forcing me to meet his hungry gaze. "Do not take your eyes from me, *Adonia.*"

Nimble hands navigated the thick layers of wool and cotton separating us, both swiftly and with ease. Warm, calloused fingers grasped my ass, lifting my feet from the ground. I snaked my legs around his waist and moaned in pleasure at the sensation of his swollen cock pressing against my very aroused core.

Finally! No more cumbersome wool clothing acting as a barrier between us. Just warm skin against skin.

Hot.

Slick.

Ready.

I wasn't sure what kind of lovemaking this was, or if you could even call what we were doing making love. All I knew was that I needed him, to live, to breathe, and without him, I'd be lost forever.

"Your body," he rasped, the tip of his cock pressing against my entrance, "is mine."

I bucked against him, willing him with my mind, with my body to continue. "Please, Gabriel…"

He impaled me in one swift movement, the exquisite sensation, the sheer fullness of him causing my eyes to roll back into my head.

With his forehead pressed against mine, he rammed into me with hard, driving thrusts, each one sending me closer and closer to the edge.

He slid his hand up so that it rested over my heart, the other still gripping my ass. "Your heart," he said through clenched teeth, "your soul, all of you…is mine, Faythe."

He pulled back good and slow, his breaths coming in shallow pants.

Faythe. My vision tunneled, and the sound of our frenzied lovemaking faded as that word, that name, echoed inside my head and tore at my heart. He'd claimed me with his words, uttered the name with total adoration—and it killed me. My name wasn't Faythe and I needed to tell him.

"Gabriel, I—"

He silenced me with his lips, his kiss jumbling my thoughts. I moaned, low in my throat. I needed to tell him something. What was it?

He slid the hand that rested over my heart between us and fingered my core as he drove himself home one final time. "You are mine. *Para siempre.* Always."

We peaked together, crying out as we rode wave after wave of perfect pleasure.

He cupped my face after gently setting me to my feet, ghosting his lips across mine, softly, sweetly. "*Te quiero mucho, Adonia.* I love you very much."

"Mmmm." I laid my hands over his, reveling in the love and affection shining from his eyes. "Gabriel," I whispered, and squeezed his hands. "I lo—"

My body stiffened, my gaze darting over his shoulder as an unearthly wail sliced through the air.

Thick clouds of mist sliced through the quiet forest, billowing toward us at an alarming rate of speed. From within its milky depths another deep, baleful cry rang out, chilling me to the bone. My body stiffened, the air seeping from my lungs. *Another demon!*

Gabriel didn't speak, just wrapped me in his arms and sifted me to just inside the door of his cabin. Body humming with magical energy, he pressed a kiss to my forehead, backed out the door and waved a hand across his body.

The air surrounding the cabin warped for a brief moment, a ripple of light flashing bright and fading quickly.

I stepped forward, eyes narrowed. "Gabriel?"

Jaw clenched, features drawn tight, he closed his eyes for a brief moment before meeting my gaze once more. "Forgive me, *Adonia*. This madness must end, and it must end now." His body shimmered into nothing as he sifted away, his last words floating across the gentle breeze "You will be safe inside my home."

"No!" I lunged for the door and bounced off a whole lot of nothing. I flew backward as though someone had kicked me hard in the gut and tumbled ass over tea-kettle across the floor. Grunting in pain, because that shit really hurt, I rolled over and glared out the open door. "Goddammit, Gabriel! What have you done?"

The hell if he's going to keep me here while he goes off to fight. I scrambled off the floor and flew at the open door once more, garnering the same results.

Gabriel had charmed the house. Nothing got in. Nothing got out. Including me.

Goddammit! I was trapped.

Gooseflesh pebbled across my skin, a sick feeling of dread drowning out the warmth, the comfort I'd felt in Gabriel's arms just moments before. The ungodly screeching grew faint, Gabriel no doubt drawing the demon away from the cabin, as well as the village. But the fog… The fog grew thicker, engulfing the cabin and surrounding forest in a clear, opaque vapor. *What the…*

I couldn't see him through the mist, but I heard Erasmo, Gabriel's mighty Andalusian, bucking and running throughout his pen, no doubt agitated by the evil lurking about. *Shit.* I swallowed hard and sucked in a quick breath. That horse was hell on wheels. If it was scared, I was in deep doo doo.

A thin sheen of sweat coated my skin as I paced back and forth. I wiped my sticky hands against the rough fabric of my skirt and prayed my earlier meal wouldn't make reappearance. I was damn tired of vomiting.

Gabriel…

My hand shot up to my mouth and I shook my head, whimpering. Gabriel was God knew where, alone, fighting yet another demon. What the hell was going on? Salem, it seemed, had turned into some sort of amusement park for monsters and demons, where innocent villagers were served up as fast food. Why? Why were they here, and why on earth had Tituba summoned them?

I ran a hand through my hair and chewed at the inside of my lip until I tasted blood. If anything happened to Gabriel… My gut twisted, a horrible ache tearing through my middle. Breathless, I grabbed my chest and bent forward. "Oh, God," I sobbed. "I don't think I can live without him."

"Well then, Mistress. I suppose then 'tis time ye die."

Body tensing, I whirled around to see Tituba standing just outside the front door.

Dark hair fanned out behind her, along with the ends of her ivory shawl and her brown dress, as though a fierce wind blew across her slight frame. Fire blazed behind her ebony eyes, an unnatural glow radiating from her dark skin. Powerful. She looked powerful, otherworldly, and altogether different from the image of her in the jail cell I'd seen just a short time ago.

Chanting a slew of words I couldn't make out, she circled her hand in front of her. The air surrounding the home rippled once more with the release of Gabriel's spell, and she crossed through the entrance into the cabin. "'Let us have some fun, shall we?"

I shuffled backward, stumbling over a bench and crash landing onto my ass. Terrified, I continued scrambling backward on my hands and feet like a crab.

Something was off, and it wasn't just the fact that a deranged lunatic with mystical powers was gunning for me. The Tituba stalking toward me with hate-filled eyes looked nothing like the image of the woman I'd seen in the fiery image earlier. That woman had been gaunt, filthy and wearing a black dress. She'd appeared entirely incapable of the mayhem the woman before me was bringing. Gabriel's words from earlier rang in my ears as Tituba stalked forward, her movements slow and precise.

Evil walks amongst the villagers, indeed. They cradle it to their very bosom.

Images and voices flashed rapid fire in my ears and behind my eyes, my subconscious desperately trying to bring a hidden truth to light. I blinked, the images continuing to play as though stuck on some type of automatic loop.

Parris's horror stricken face after I'd revealed I'd seen Tituba in the woods the night of my attack. *"Im-impossible,"* Parris said. *"The witch sits rotting in jail as we speak. 'Tis impossible for you to have seen her..."*

Tituba slicing her arm open in front of the demon she'd just summoned...

Goody Godbert, roaring in pain and cradling what appeared to be an injured arm against her shawl covered chest immediately after Prue had grabbed her...

Shawl-covered...

I stiffened and my hands shot to my mouth as I sucked in a ragged breath. The Tituba from the vision I'd seen wore a black dress and no shawl. The Tituba standing before me wore a shawl I'd seen many times over the course of the few days I'd been here. It couldn't be? Could it? "G-Goody?"

A wicked laugh blew past her lips. With a snap of her fingers, the glamour she wore rippled away. Dark skin became light. Raven hair faded to gray. Her slender frame expanded exponentially.

"Oh. My. God." *Jiminy freaking Cricket!* I'd been right.

Goody Godbert stood just a few scant feet away, enmity and rage flowing off her in undulating waves.

With a flick of her wrist, I flew backward across the hard floor. I slammed into the nearby wall. The force of the blow knocked the wind out of me and sent a cloud of dust scattering throughout the space.

"Who..." I frantically sucked in air, fighting to catch my breath "Who are...you and...and why are you terrorizing people?" Goody's presence in this cabin, the reality that it had been her all along, causing the death and destruction surrounding Salem Village, made no sense. As far as I knew, she was a well-known, upstanding member in the village— a healer. Why?

She chuckled, a deep, throaty sound, abrasive and altogether grating. "Foolish child." She raised a hand in front of her, and with a sharp, quick flick of her wrist, I shot up off the floor, my body pinned to the wall, immobile. "I seek power, of course."

She glided across the small space as though her feet didn't touch the floor and stopped in front of a window, peering out into the milky fog. "I grow stronger with each act of violence, with each death."

She tapped a pudgy finger against the glass; a spider web of cracks grew from where her finger touched and spread across the entire pane. An icy chill slithered its way up my spine as she glanced at me over her shoulder, the corner of her mouth curled up into a wicked sneer. She faced the window once more, and with a quick breath, the ruined glass exploded, a million tiny pieces scattering through the air in slow motion.

I struggled to breathe, the unseen force she'd pinned me with squeezing the air from my lungs. I shook my head, the movement frantic and stunted. "But, you're a healer. I...I don't understand." And I didn't. People trusted Goody with their health, with their lives. That type of unfailing faith and confidence didn't come overnight. It had to be earned.

She flew forward with a high-pitched scream that shattered

the remaining windows and rattled the walls. "I was pathetic! A pitiful creature, a peon, unappreciated and unable to help anyone! For years I have toiled, battled illness and disease only to lose at every turn. I have struggled with the burdens of others while doing naught for myself. Do ye think I enjoy tending gangrenous toes?"

I winced, remembering Wyberg's pus-filled digits but remained silent, afraid anything I said would further fuel her anger.

"This life leaves few choices for women. To be sure, it leaves none. I held no power, no sway over anyone. I had thought my healing efforts would change this, but they did not. Every day was the same. Cook. Clean. Cower under the demands of the mighty reverend and his magistrate. I was as much of a slave as Tituba." The muscles in her neck and jaw strained as she ground her teeth together. "But no longer."

She narrowed her eyes and jutted her chin, looking down her nose onto me. "Salem Village is riddled with secrets—some easier to keep than others. When I caught wind Tituba was stealing away at night with a group of girls, conjuring and working spells, I seized the moment. 'Twas no surprise how easily she succumbed to my desires. The slave offered up her dark knowledge in exchange for my silence on the matter." She spoke casually, as if acquiring dark, killing magic was no big deal, and shrugged. "'Twas easy."

I gaped at her, disgusted and stunned by her utter selfishness. "So you blackmailed Tituba, got yourself some power. Wasn't that enough? Why did you—"

"Silence!"

An unseen force struck me hard across the face. I cried out, struggling to move my arms, to clutch my face, but it was no use. They were frozen in place, magically pinned to my sides.

"The inner workings of your pitiful mind cannot possibly comprehend my motivation." She turned her back to me and glided toward the fire. "Tituba's knowledge was limited—fortune telling, minor love spells and the like. When pushed, she revealed greater power and enlightenment could be achieved with the spilling of blood…a step she, herself, refused to take.

"Tituba was weak." Goody turned, her thick brows drawn together, pinching the skin between her eyes. "I, however, am not."

It was a stupid move, I knew it, but I couldn't keep the words in. "No. You're not weak. You're just a bitch."

Seething with anger, she extended her arms out from her sides, and with a deep, guttural cry, unleashed a large energy pulse. White light streamed from her hands throughout the small space, the force of the pulse crushing against me like an atom bomb and blowing the roof off the cabin. Fire exploded from the hearth, flames creeping along the walls, devouring everything in its path.

In pain and out of breath, I squinted, scorching heat from the growing blaze, coupled with the splintered bits of wood and debris raining down making it near impossible to see anything. Goody floated forward out of the sea of flames looking every bit the hell spawn she was. "As you can see, I am powerless no more."

Every muscle in my body simultaneously stiffened as she grasped my chin between her fingers and glared at me, eyes wild, plump features marred with rage. Hot, rancid breath wafted across my face. This was it. Bitch was going to smite me down and I was powerless to do anything about it. I slammed my lids shut and waited for darkness to overshadow me.

A loud groan filled the air. My eyes shot open just as one of the remaining support beams overhead buckled beneath the sea of the flames. Narrowly missing me, it crashed to the floor, taking Goody down with it.

Smoke from the roaring inferno burned my nose, choked the air from my lungs. Tears spilled from the corners of my eyes, drying seconds later as the scorching heat that was unbearable just moments before, now threatened to melt the flesh from my bones. Snapping coils of orange and yellow consumed the wooden slats around me, hungry for fuel, eager to devour me. My time was up. I was going to burn.

Hysterical, I cried out, thrashing against the magical bonds that pinned me to the cabin wall. "Let me loose! My God, Goody! Please!"

Body completely engulfed by flames, Goody lay pinned beneath the burning rafter, unable to escape. Her pain-filled shrieks tore at my gut, the vision of her arms and legs jerking and writhing as she tried to free herself permanently seared into my memory. Fire, it seemed, trumped her almighty power.

As her life force waned, so did her strength, and the magical hold she had on me faded with her last breathy shriek. Wrenching myself from the wall, I scrambled around Goody Godbert's blazing remains and dove out one of the shattered windows.

Lungs burning, skin slick with sweat and clothing singed from the fire, I leapt to my feet and ran—straight for Erasmo.

Truly, I wanted to hop on his back about as much as I wanted a sloppy kiss from one of Goody's demons, but my situation left me few choices. I needed to get to Gabriel, and Erasmo knew the woods better than I did. If there were any hope of me finding him, I'd need Erasmo's help.

Agitated, the great horse galloped back and forth in its small pen, crying out, eyes continually darting toward the treeline. Big Boy knew something bad was going down and wasn't happy about it. *Shit.* Was I really going to do this?

I gulped down the massive lump in my throat. With my heart pounding, I entered his pen, fingers digging into the wooden gate as the enormous beast cantered to me quickly. Half of me expected the horse to trample me to death; the other half was surprised when he came to a stop and merely sniffed me.

Okay, so maybe he's not going to eat me. I reached a shaky hand up and ran it along the side of his head, giving him a nervous pat. Clueless as to whether or not he'd even understand the words coming out of my mouth, I figured I'd give it a go and try to communicate. Stranger things *had* happened over the past few days. "I need to find Gabriel. Will you help me?"

The horse let out a whimper, lowered its head and nudged me as if to say "Dammit! Quit fooling around and hop on already."

If I thought about what I was about to do, I knew I'd bail, so I just went for it. I climbed onto the gate. Using the wooden enclosure as leverage, I sent out a silent prayer and heaved myself onto his hulking back. With no saddle, no stirrups and no reigns, I knew if I wanted to stay atop him I'd have to hold on for dear life.

Fisting large handfuls of his mane, I leaned forward. "Let's go, boy. Help me find Gabriel." I'd barely uttered the last word before he took off like a rocket, 1500 pounds of pure, rock solid muscle launching us into the forest at top speed.

The demon's wailing that had grown faint before, grew louder as we traveled deeper into the trees. More afraid for Gabriel than I was for myself, I tightened my grip on Erasmo's tangled mass of hair and gritted my teeth, determined to aid him any way I could. With no magic and zero resources, I wasn't sure how I planned to help him. I only knew he'd saved my ass more than once over the past few days, and it was time I returned the favor.

Fate had thrown me back in time for a reason: to find and fall in love with Gabriel. It was crazy. It didn't make sense, and I really didn't care. I'd found the one person I was meant to be with and I wasn't going to lose him.

An ear-shattering wail raised the tiny hairs on my skin, the sound so close I knew we were almost upon them. *Gabriel.* I swallowed hard, mentally preparing myself to face a bevy of fears head on as we barreled toward the pond where I'd been attacked the night before. What was it with this pond? Was it a gateway between the underworld and ours, or some kind of mystical demon magnet that drew baddies of all types to its watery depths? Either way, the area was filled with all kinds of bad mojo and it gave me the creeps.

A strange, electrical charge filled the air surrounding the pond. Magic. I'd witnessed enough of it over the past few days to recognize its lingering stamp.

A thunderous roar drew my attention across the murky water.

Leathery black wings drowned out the sun, their enormous wingspan casting dark shadows across the stagnant water. Face painted with deadly determination, Gabriel stood on the opposite bank of the small lake, hands raised defensively as he expertly dodged and averted the demon's fiery assault.

With a battle cry straight from the pits of hell, the demon swooped down toward Gabriel, opened its enormous muzzle, and breathed out a thick torrent of fire. No doubt anticipating the beast's move, Gabriel deflected the firestorm with a powerful succession of energy pulses. The flames ricocheted off each of the pulses, the blazing orbs rocketing backward over the water toward the demon—and me.

So engrossed in the battle, I didn't notice the blazing fireball sailing toward me until it was almost too late. No doubt sensing danger, Erasmo threw his head back and stood on his hind legs, bucking me off. I fell, ass first onto the muddy bank, the enormous steed bounding out of the way as the ball of fire shot over my head, colliding with a nearby hemlock. The force of the fiery pulse felled the tree, the loud crack and subsequent rumble temporarily drowning out the demon's cries.

I hauled myself off the ground only to duck seconds later when a large tree trunk, complete with roots and all, sailed through the air almost hitting me. The massive chunk of wood slammed into the base of yet another tree sending a family of birds into a tizzy before flying away. My ass needed to get out of the line of fire, and quick.

Grabbing fistfuls of wool and cotton, I lifted my heavy skirting, put one foot in front of the other, and hauled ass toward the opposite side of the pond, my eyes never leaving Gabriel.

Truly, the man was magnificent—a warrior in every sense of the word. A slick sheen of sweat shone across his bared torso, the thick muscles bunching and rippling with every strike. His movements were fluid, almost graceful as he engaged the monster in a deadly dance. Lunging and retreating, he'd strike the hovering beast with a stream of firebolts, then sift out of the way moments before it lunged forward, swiping at him with sword-like claws.

My movements, on the other hand, were anything but fluid. Still several yards away from the fight, I tripped over a rock, rolled my ankle and went down like a prize-fighter who'd just been dealt a KO punch. I skidded across the muddy embankment on my stomach with a garbled yelp.

"*Adonia!* You must leave!" Gabriel shouted. Focusing all of his energy on the demon, he raised his hands and blasted the beast with an energy pulse that sent it tumbling wing over tail across the pond.

One moment he stood yards away, the next he was scooping me off the ground, crushing me to him with a labored groan. "I cannot battle the demon and worry about your well being at the same time. I must get you to safety. One scratch from its diseased claws will end your life. I must—" He stiffened, and before I knew what had happened, I found myself crammed into a small hollow beneath an old fallen tree, yards away from the battle and safely out of view.

I dug my fingers into the dirt and peered out from the makeshift hiding space he'd sifted me to. "Gabriel? What…NO!"

I screamed until my voice gave out. Until my empty, burning lungs pleaded for air, begged for a smidgeon of life giving oxygen. Why was my heart still beating? Why wasn't I blacking out? Why was my body, my mind forcing me to endure this painful reality?

Gabriel lay pinned beneath the demon, blood pouring from the jagged claw marks slashed across his abdomen. He rolled his head to the side, his pained gaze seeking mine as the demon reared its head back and roared. With much effort, he extended a bloodied hand and silently mouthed the words "I love you" seconds before the beast showered him with a sea of flames. Dark eyes, riddled with pain, were the last things I saw before he sifted me to the Indian Bridge just outside of Boxwood Forest.

"No!" I dropped to my knees and tore at my hair, the pain of his loss, the guilt gnawing at my gut eating me alive. Gabriel had sacrificed himself…to save me. If I'd stayed away, had I not distracted him, he would still be alive.

I shook my head, the movements frantic and full of hysteria. "No no no! He's not. He's not dead!" I heaved, stomach bile burning the back of my throat with each painful retch. Too much. The ache in my chest, the pain... It was too much. It felt like someone had fired a cannon ball at my chest at point blank range.

Rough hands yanked me from where I lay, large fingers pinching and digging into my skin as I was pulled to my feet. My eyes were open, yet I saw nothing, felt nothing but overwhelming pain and emptiness. Fate couldn't be this cruel. Could it?

I screamed again, the rough hands that had seized me from the ground holding me up bodily. "Gabriel! He's not dead. He's not dead."

"Over here!" a loud voice shouted. "The witch has been found!"

I sagged against my faceless captor, the image of Gabriel reaching for me as a blanket of fire consumed him burned into my conscious thoughts: the only thing I saw. *Make it stop. Make it stop. Please. Wake me up. Put me down. Just please, someone end this nightmare.* "He's not dead. He's not dead."

I felt, but didn't see, another set of hands latching onto my arms. The cold, jagged bite of iron shackles digging into my skin followed soon after, and I was vaguely aware of being carried somewhere. "Not dead. He's not...dead. Not dead..."

The same voice that had bellowed a few minutes prior, hollered again. "Have the men sweep the woods to be sure. If the witch's mad ramblings are true, the warlock Gabriel Castillo is dead."

Chapter 21
· The Traveler ·

Whoever came up with the saying "time heals all wounds" was both an asshole and an idiot. Same went for the prick who first said "time flies when you're having fun." Time was my enemy. Always had been and probably always would be. When I needed it, there was never enough. And when I begged for it to end, it dragged on for an eternity.

Time eluded me, tricked me, messed with my head. I'd spent 300 years with nothing but idle time on my hands, cursing my existence and pissing away each day. I had no purpose, no reason for being. And in my utter uselessness, I had all the time in the world. Then, by some strange twist in the Fates' master plan, the light I'd lost so very long ago, swept back into my life like a raging torrent. Feelings, long dormant, reappeared, acting like kindling, igniting the fire within me, melting away the numbness that clung to me like second skin. Taylor, my other half, had returned only to be ripped from my arms once more and hurtled backwards through time.

The laws of physics, the rules that applied to the time/space continuum… That shit didn't apply to me. I had power. A lot of it. Yet, with all my power, even with my ability to travel *through* time, I couldn't slow it down, speed it up, or manipulate it when I needed to the most.

Time was a bitch, just like the Fates. But it was a bitch my weary ass wouldn't have to put up with much longer. I had one final move, one grand fucking finale to exact before my time was up. Then… Then maybe I could get some peace.

Chapter 22

· Taylor ·

Barren.

Hollow.

Empty.

A line of ants paraded across the dirt floor of the dilapidated outbuilding I'd been jailed in, tiny foot soldiers swarming over my shackled wrists and arms as though they were dying and I was their last meal.

I lay on my side, unmoving, and uncaring…numb.

The ants had it wrong. Technically, I was entitled to a last meal, not them. A feast of my choosing before death wrapped its arms around me. Or at least, that was the way of things in modern times. I wasn't kicking it in my own century. I knew that. And I wasn't hungry, anyway. I was already dead. At least, I felt dead.

I couldn't muster the will to live, to breathe, let alone brush away the army of bugs tracking up my arms and legs. Maybe they'd eat me alive, put me out of my misery.

Poor ants. They'd choke on my bitter flesh, wither away just as I was.

I was alone. In a dank, hay-filled shed, awaiting a mob of angry parishioners hell bent on taking my life. I wasn't the witch they thought me to be, but it didn't really matter. Any fight I had left in me died with Gabriel beneath the demon's deathly grip. If the fire hadn't killed him, the bloody gashes raked across his gut would.

He'd said himself, one scratch from its claws would result in death.

I shuddered. Sharp, stinging pain piercing the empty space where my heart used to reside, drumming up images I refused to recall again. *Keep your mind blank. Don't remember. Don't think. And don't sleep.*

Every inch of me ached, the drag of sleep a heavy burden my body begged to succumb to. But, sleeping meant dreaming. And I couldn't allow myself to dream. I couldn't allow myself to see Gabriel, to remember what I'd lost. Remembering meant feeling, and I couldn't face the pain.

Prudence died for daring to help me.

Gabriel died the same way.

And I... I was the coward who couldn't muster the courage to think about either of them because it was too damn painful. People didn't come more pathetic than me.

I focused on the ants crawling across my wrists, eyes straining until their miniature bodies became nothing but a blurry black ribbon cascading across my ivory flesh. The hollow vacuum I'd fallen into crept up on me again and I welcomed its silence, embraced the black void with open arms.

Just when I was sure the darkness had swallowed me whole, a warm, electrical surge jolted through my weary frame, Gabriel's masculine, earthy scent flooding my nose and filling my head.

"No!" I whimpered. I buried my face in my shoulder and sobbed. Dammit! Why? Why wouldn't my mind shut down? Why was I smelling him? Sensing his presence as though he were standing next to me? I was hallucinating. That had to be it. My brain had short-circuited; I'd gotten my wires crossed, and as a result, I was sensing and hearing things that couldn't possibly be real.

Warm hands caressed my face, swept across my wrists and arms. "Shhh, *mi dulce*. Don't cry, baby. I'm here."

"If only," I said on a breath. I kept my lids closed, afraid to open my eyes, afraid my whacked out brain had actually manifested a 3-D version of my recently deceased love.

The clinking of metal rang out as my shackles fell away. Strong arms gathered me off the dirt floor, sending my heart into my throat. "There's little time. Open your eyes, *mi dulce*."

I hesitated, but did as the familiar voice asked, positive the last shreds of my sanity had finally left me. Hallucinations weren't corporeal and warm, couldn't cradle you against their chest.

Vision blurred, I blinked rapidly as the person holding me slowly became clear.

Gabriel?

I sucked in a rapid breath and whimpered. Yep, I was right. I'd lost my friggin' mind. "You're not real." I shook my head and winced. "You can't be real. You… You died."

The world swayed as he set me on my shaky feet and grasped me by the shoulders.

His warm hand grasped mine and held it against his chest, his rapid heartbeat thrumming against my palm. "I'm very real, and very much alive. For the time being, anyway. We have to move quickly before they come for me."

I stared at his chiseled features, basked in the warmth of his eyes in complete wonder. How was it possible he was standing in front of me? And what was he talking about? Who was coming for him, and why was his time limited? Something wasn't right. I was dreaming. That had to be it. Body exhausted, I'd fallen into a coma and my mind was drumming up fantasies of my fallen love.

I swallowed back the lump in my throat, the sticky film coating my tongue making it hard to speak. *Damn,* I thought. *For a dream, this feels pretty real.*

His eyes narrowed and the corners of his mouth pulled down. "Dammit, baby. We don't have time for this. You've got to believe me when I tell you, you aren't dreaming." He blew out a ragged breath and ran a hand through his hair. "There's so much I need to reveal to you, and not nearly enough time to tell you in."

I stepped back and shook my head. "But, I saw the demon's claw marks. There was so much blood. No one could have survived that." Shaking, I sucked in rapid breaths, fighting against my body's urge to weep all over again. "I…I watched you burn."

Eyes never leaving mine, he grasped the hem of his shirt, lifting it toward his chest.

I gasped and covered my mouth with my hands.

Three distinct scars, collateral damage left over from his fight with the demon, were slashes across his heavily scarred torso.

I gaped at him, unable to put two and two together. The last time I'd seen Gabriel, his torso had been ripped apart, the demon nearly gutting him. But now, in the span of what could only have been a few hours, the once open wounds were thickened, the scars silvery and opaque as though they'd taken an eternity to heal. The aging disfigurements arced across a familiar mass of burn scars and old wounds like hash marks from just below his left nipple down past the waistband of his jeans.

I didn't understand what I was looking at. At all. If he had the ability to heal himself, why would he keep his scars? And on top of that, if he'd healed himself just a short time ago, why did the wounds look like they'd been around for centuries? I shook my head. "I…I don't understand. How are you alive? How did you escape the demon?"

He cleared his throat and shrugged. "I called in some backup after I sent you away."

I drew my head back and frowned. *He called in some backup? What is this, Crime TV?* "My God. The way you're talking… You make it sound like the whole thing was no big deal. That monster, that demon—"

"Is having its ass handed to it as we speak." He dropped his hands, his T-shirt falling into place as he frowned. "Xan, the guy who helped me heal you? He showed up and worked his healing mojo on me so I could finish off the demon. My younger self is ripping the fucker's head clean off its unholy body right about now."

I winced, refusing to picture him battling the demon again after the grave injuries it had inflicted, and entirely confused as to what he meant by "younger self." I considered myself a smart girl, but this shit was entirely outside my realm of understanding. It had sci-fi sorcery hoopla written all over it.

Aghast, I reached for his shirt, needing for reasons unknown to me, to see his damaged torso once more. I lifted the thin cotton, revealing the horrible burn scars, the scored lines etched into his chest. The marks that had been red and pink the night before were now a dull brown, mottled with silver. I frowned. Those wounds had aged—apparently overnight.

With one hand still covering my mouth, I reached a shaky hand forward and pressed my fingertips against his chest. The same spark that ignited my skin whenever I touched Gabriel tingled up the length of my arm. "Oh!" I said with a shock. "You feel…"

The same, I wanted to say, but couldn't find the words. How was this possible?

With a sob, I pulled my fingers down the length of his chest, reveling in the muscled grooves and indentations that were so familiar to me. If I couldn't believe my eyes, I could at least rely on my other senses to show me the truth. Breathless, I shifted in place, wanting so badly for my deepest desire to have actually come true— for Gabriel to be standing in front of me, alive.

The electricity, the glorious pull between us was the same. I wanted nothing more than to jump into his arms and lose myself in the safety of his embrace. His scent, his voice, his delicious accent—they were all the same. And yet, though his appearance was identical to Gabriel's, his features seemed hardened somehow, as though he'd been through a great deal of pain and come out the other side a changed man. Was he telling me the truth? Had he really survived the attack? Or, had I retreated into some unknown hell where my fractured mind conjured up vivid manifestations of my former love? I didn't know what to believe and was past the point of caring. His skin felt so good beneath my hand, I didn't care if he was a figment of my imagination. I'd take the brief moment with him, real or no and cherish it.

Unable to pull away, I trailed my hand down the length of his abdomen, ghosting my fingertips along the waistband of his jeans.

His body shuddered beneath my touch and he closed his eyes with a groan. "*Mi dulce.* For three centuries I've longed for your touch, longed to look upon you, and hear the sound of your voice. I—"

"Wait… What?" I yanked my hand away with a gasp, ignoring the ache that came with the loss of contact. My gaze traveled down to my filthy pilgrim garb, then back to him. Had I heard him correctly? Did he say three centuries? And what was up with his clothes? Eyes wide, my gaze traveled north of the vicious claw marks to the gray T-shirt I clutched, then up to his face. Something was off. The last time I'd seen Gabriel he was shirtless and wore breeches. A far cry from the low-slung jeans and wrinkled tee he wore now. What type of bogus flimflam was my subconscious working now?

I shook my head, utterly confused. "I…I don't understand. My heart, my soul, both tell me you're Gabriel. But, my head…I… you're…different." I stumbled over my words, barely able to speak and convinced I was crazy. "How?"

He closed the space between us in one quick step and clasped onto the back of my neck with his warm, calloused hand. Fingers fisting large handfuls of my hair, he leaned forward and slanted his lips against mine in a heart-stopping kiss that scrambled my already scattered thoughts and stole my breath away. "Fate," he whispered as he pulled back.

He traced a finger along my cheekbone, his warm gaze turning dark, serious. "Fate, combined with a dying woman's vengeful curse sent you backward in time."

The hardness behind his eyes softened, and he cupped my cheek. "But, it was our love, our unbreakable bond that brought me back to you after three hundred long years. You are my *alma gemela*, my soulmate. Nothing can keep me from you."

There were those words again. *Three hundred years.* Could it be? Had he come backward in time just as I had? I opened my mouth, afraid to say the words. "So, you're—"

A loud thunder-clap echoed overhead. Howling winds that seemed to come out of nowhere pummeled the small shed, threatening to tear it down.

"From the future," he said and gave me a single nod. "Just like you."

"Y-you..." My knees gave out and he caught me before I hit the ground.

He pulled me to him, crushing me against his chest. "We must move quickly, *mi dulce.* I will not lose you again."

Holy... I stared at him, a mixture of shock and disbelief racing through my veins. It all made sense. His aged scars, the hard, almost haunted look behind his eyes. He'd survived the demon attack and had spent the following three hundred plus years...*Oh, God.* His words played on an automatic loop inside my head.

I will not lose you...again.

My trip backward through time was a first for me. But not for the Gabriel standing in front of me. My stomach twisted, nausea and horror eating away at its ravaged lining. Gabriel had lived through this nightmare once before. And, from what I could gather, I hadn't survived.

Gasping for air that didn't come easy, I pushed past my frightening conclusion and pleaded for the answers I so vehemently sought. "You know where I'm from? Who I am?" Tears I was sure had long since dried up rolled down my cheeks as I fisted large handfuls of his T-shirt. "I can't remember anything. My memory—"

"Has been tampered with," he said, a mixture of pain and disgust tainting his voice.

Lightning flashed and thunder rolled in continuous waves, the ominous rumble a near constant roar.

Gabriel's gaze traveled from me, to the door, the muscles in his jaw and neck bunching with strain. "Fuck! Time! I need more time!"

I narrowed my eyes and palmed his cheek, forcing him to meet my gaze. "My memory's been tampered with? How? And what do you mean you need more time? What's going on, Gabriel?" Was he worried about Parris and Hathorne coming for me? Now that Gabriel was back, they were a non-issue as far as I was concerned. He could poof us to safety and we'd never have to see them again.

He heaved a deep sigh and grasped me by the shoulders, his firm grip digging into my flesh. "Do you recall the memories I shared with you of Nadya and Ivanov?"

I nodded, inwardly terrified I'd never be able to forget the grisly nightmare.

"Then you'll remember that just before she died, Nadya cursed me." He looked away, shame and disgust marring his handsome features. "She cursed my fated love…" He paused for a moment, and when he spoke again it was through clenched teeth. "She cursed you, *mi dulce*, to suffer untold cruelty and persecution before being taken away from me for all eternity."

I stood, open-mouthed, speechless. Nadya was evil, I knew that, but this…this went above and beyond any kind of cruelty I could imagine. Not to mention, the bitch was already dead. I couldn't exactly call foul and come after her. I was glad Gabriel ended her life, but part of me really wished I'd had the chance to give her a good beat down.

He slid his hands up from my shoulders and cupped both cheeks, forcing me to hold his gaze. "You're name is not Faythe, it's Taylor, and you're from the 21st century. Because of the curse, your fate skewed from its natural course and you were sent back in time by an evil vampire warlock."

Thunder strikes that sounded more like atomic bombs exploding shook the tiny shed. Blinding white light seeped through the cracks and crevices of the wooden outbuilding, its blazing heat permeating the space.

Gabriel pressed his forehead to mine and groaned. "My time is nearly up." He pulled back and traced his thumbs across my cheekbones, his gaze intense, wild. "Are you tracking? Do you understand what I've told you?"

The high-speed rate in which he'd doled out information was too much for me to process all at once and my poor mind couldn't keep up. I scrunched up my face. "I…" Words failed me. Taylor. My name was Taylor. Though foreign, the name felt…right.

I opened my mouth only to slam it shut soon after. My fate had been skewed? By an evil vampire warlock? *Great googly moogly!* Had I not witnessed countless amounts of magic and underworld activity in my short time here, I would have said he was nuts. As it stood, with the creepy light flooding the shed and the roaring thunder shaking the ground, I believed every scary word he said, regardless of how shocking it all sounded.

He brushed my wild mane off my right shoulder and ran his finger along the skin behind my ear. "The asshole that sent you back? He marked you, worked a spell to block your memory, and make things that much harder for you while you were here. My younger self noticed it this morning after he claimed you."

"A mark? I've been marked?" Frantic, I clawed at my skin. "Oh, my God! Reverse it! Make it go away. Please!"

"Infidel!"

The light that had been pouring into the shed flooded the space, drowning everything in a sea of white.

I dropped to my knees and covered my ears as preternatural voices echoed off the wooden walls, the heat from the light near unbearable.

"To alter time is to create chaos! You were warned, Traveler, what would happen should you choose to defy us and reveal your presence in this time."

"No!"

My eyes shot open at the sound of Gabriel's tortured cry. The light had dissipated enough that I could once again see, and the scene before me was nothing short of horrifying.

Three figures shrouded in bright, luminescent light stood in the center of the shed. The brightness shining off them was so intense I had to look away. Gabriel stood to my right, terror and anguish marring his features as he struggled to free himself from some type of invisible bond that rendered him immobile.

I, in turn, floated three feet off the ground, encased in some sort of strange energy bubble.

The sonorous voices bellowed an eerie decree. "Your Taylor, the woman known as Faythe Ellwood in this time, must die."

I felt my eyes widen in terror. "Die? Gabriel? What's—Ahhhhhh!"

I threw my head back and screamed as searing heat blazed from beneath my skin. Unimaginable pain coated every inch of me as I glanced down at my immobilized body. Bright orange and yellow light seeped from beneath my skin. Flames burst forth from my fingertips, skimming the length of my arms like a greedy second skin. I was burning to death, from the inside out.

Gabriel's voice boomed over my screaming, but the pain made it impossible for me to comprehend his words.

Just when I thought I couldn't scream anymore, the pain ceased and I fell to the ground, body limp, exhausted. The flames that had coated every inch of my skin had disappeared, my flesh untarnished and whole as though the episode had never happened.

"We accept your proposition, Traveler. Your life for hers. Your time is limited. Make haste, for the villagers come quickly."

The glowing figures faded, their bright light dulling to a mere pin-prick before disappearing altogether.

Gabriel was at my side before I could blink, scooping me into his arms. He swept a hand across my face and kissed me hard, a mixture of relief and pain radiating from behind his eyes. "You live, *mi dulce*. My God. You fucking live!" He crushed me to him and rocked me in his arms, his enormous body trembling against me.

I was alive, all right, though, I wasn't sure how. Who, or should I say what, were those glowing creatures, and why had they wanted me dead? And why, when I was halfway to the grave, had they decided to let me live?

Wait... The supernatural voices rang loud in my head as though they were still there.

We accept your proposition, Traveler. Your life for hers.

I pushed against Gabriel's chest and wriggled out of his arms. Scrambling, I lurched to my feet and backed away. "What did those voices mean when they said they accepted your proposition? Your life for mine?"

Gabriel pulled himself off the ground and stared at me, grim-faced and silent. He stepped forward and raised his arm for me, but I stepped back before he could make contact.

Dread smothered me, the weight of it crushing the air from my lungs. I let out a breathy gasp and shook my head. "No! Gabriel... what...what have you done?"

A wagon approaching and the sound of deep, male voices from nearby drew his attention to the nearby door, then back to me. "Our time is up, *mi dulce*." He vanished, appearing in front of me in an instant. Strong hands cradled my face as he claimed my mouth with a savage kiss. "I did what I had to to keep you safe, to keep you from hanging."

I shook my head, a breathy sob bursting from my lips. He couldn't...no...he wasn't saying what I thought he was. He just... He was going to die in my place? *No!*

He pressed a kiss to my forehead and stared down at me, his eyes resolute and full of love. "Nadya's curse is broken, my love. You will live, and I...I will finally have peace."

"No!" I screamed and pounded his chest with my fists. "I won't let you do this! We have time. We can still escape. Poof us, sift us, get us out of here. We can live somewhere else, alone, just the two of us. I don't understand. Why do you have to die?"

"Because," he said, casting me a sad smile, "Faythe Ellwood, you, *mi dulce*, are fated to hang. The Fates demand a life. I refuse to let them take yours, so I've given mine instead."

Heavy footfalls sounded just outside the shed, gruff voices barking orders.

"It's time to send you home," Gabriel said and kissed the top of my head.

"No, no, no, no!" I sagged against him, burying my face in his chest as I held onto him with everything I had. "Please, Gabriel. Please don't send me away." I fisted his shirt and molded myself against him, resisting his attempts to pry me off of him. "I don't want to go back to my time, to my home. You're my home, Gabriel. You. You're the only thing I need. Please."

A powerful surge of electricity jolted through me and I stepped back with a gasp. Body humming with magic, Gabriel's form began to shift, his body flickering like static electricity. "You have a rich life in the future, with friends and family who love you. Live, *mi dulce*. Live, and love, and…if it's not too painful, maybe think of me sometimes?"

Time slowed immeasurably, the events that followed seeming to happen all at once.

The door leading into the shed rattled as the wooden slat that kept it locked was lifted from its resting place.

I lunged toward Gabriel, arms outstretched, my body growing light and airy as I saw him mouth the words, "I love you, Taylor."

A soundless cry blew past my lips as the door to the shed burst open, the same moment Gabriel magically glamoured himself to look like me.

Darkness swallowed me whole.

Chapter 23

·Taylor·

I stared at the mouth of the trail, my tongue dry, a deep ache in my chest. "I don't know if I can do this," I said into my cell phone. "Everything is still so fresh, so…raw."

Jessica's voice carried through the receiver, her tone worried. "Taylor, honey, just come home. Please. The only thing you're going to find in those woods is a whole lot of heartache."

My roommate and best friend's worried voice tore at my gut, but not enough to change my mind. She was right, of course. My little trek to Danvers, Massachusetts—modern day Salem Village—wouldn't change what happened, and probably wouldn't provide me with the closure I so desperately needed.

Thing was, I couldn't stay away. Three hundred years has passed since Gabriel had sent me forward in time, yet, for me, the entire experience had happened just a short week ago. It made no sense, though little in my life seemed to as of late, but I knew that walking through Boxford Forest, standing in the place Gabriel once lived, would make me feel closer to him somehow. The pull I felt to be here was unexplainable, irresistible. I couldn't have stayed away if I tried.

With a heavy heart and a deep sigh, I headed for the mouth of the trail. "I can't explain it, Jess. I just… I miss him so much. I need this. I need to be here right now."

"Look out on your right!"

I bounded out of the way with yelp as a steady line of mountain bikers sped down the dirt path, disappearing into a sea of green and brown.

"You okay?" Jessica called out from the other side of the line. "What was that?"

I swallowed hard and sucked in a deep breath, willing my body to calm down. I felt jittery and jumpy, like I'd mainlined caffeine for a straight 24 hours. "Just a bunch of cyclists. I'm okay. Listen, I'm about to make my way into the trees, so I'll probably lose reception. I'll call you tonight. 'Kay?"

Jessica grumbled on the other side of the line. "I'm worried about you, Tay, but okay. Call me if you need anything. Love you."

After hitting the End button, I slid my phone into the back pocket of my jeans and took another deep breath. Dry leaves and debris crunched beneath my shoes as I made my way into the familiar copse of trees, unsure of what I would find.

Thank God for Jess. Gabriel had been right. I did have friends back home who loved me—unconditionally. And thank goodness, because I was a right wretched mess when I returned. Battle weary and exhausted with a head full of repressed memories coming to the surface, I'd had a hell of a time acclimating to my surroundings and had lashed out more than once in frustration and anger.

My thoughts traveled back to the day I'd returned to Hanaford Park.

I hit the ground with a scream, head dizzy, body aching and wobbly as though someone had stretched it impossibly thin like Silly Putty, then crammed it into a tiny ball before shoving it back in its container. I moaned, the thick carpet doing little to cushion my sore body as I rolled from my side onto my back. "Criminy, that hurts."

Wait a minute.

I dug my fingers into the soft pile beneath me. Carpet… I was lying on a carpeted floor. Was it possible? Could I be—

A high-pitched scream blared throughout the space, rattling my already aching head. "Taylor! Oh, my God! You're back!"

I opened my lids, my blurry vision barely making out the streak of blond running toward me at top speed. Vivid blue eyes hovered over me, tears marring the relief that shone clear as day. "Oh, my... You're alive!" She turned her head and hollered over her shoulder. "Martha! Come quick! She's back! Tay's back!"

Frowning, because her screaming really hurt my head, I moved to sit up.

That's when they hit me. My memories.

I fell back onto the carpet with a muffled yelp, picture after picture, memory after memory, downloading into my conscious thoughts like I was some sort of super computer. I clutched the sides of my head and moaned, the rapid onslaught of information too much for me to handle too soon.

I felt the blonde pull away with a breathy sob. "What's wrong with her, Martha? She looks...she looks like she's suffering."

So out of it, I hadn't noticed anyone else enter the room and stiffened when a cool set of hands slid over my forehead. "She's traveled through time twice, Jess. That shit can't be easy on a person. Let me see if I can help."

A small electrical jolt shot through me as her hands slid to each temple, the pain, the utter fullness crowding my head easing back exponentially. I whimpered and dropped my hands to my sides, thankful for the relief.

"There," she said. "That should take away some of the sting from re-entry."

I peeled my lids open, my eyes focusing in on a pair of piercing hazel eyes and a long fall of mahogany hair. Martha, my other roommate.

"Too many memories," I bit out. "They came back all at once, and it...hurt."

Martha raised a brow and nodded as if she understood. "I bet." Clearly fighting back emotion, she mashed her lips together to keep them from quivering and swiped at a stray tear. She squeezed my shoulder, the corner of her mouth turning up. "It's good to have you back, girl. We were worried about you."

A dam burst somewhere inside me, and my body shook as tears flowed. Jess pulled me into a sitting position and hugged me for all she was worth, while Martha rubbed my back, both patient and understanding, allowing me to work through the moment.

I remembered everything about my life in Hanaford Park. I remembered the incredible closeness I shared with Jessica and Martha, my two dearest friends. I remembered the hell Martha had gone through with Lucian and with Xan.

Xan... Xan had come to my aid at Gabriel's place.

Gabriel...

"Gabriel!" I wriggled out of Jessica's arms and shot to my feet. "I need to see him!" Oh, God. Was he okay? The last I knew, he was out ripping the head off the disease demon Tituba had summoned. I knew he'd survived, knew he'd been successful; the Gabriel from the future, the Gabriel who'd died saving me had bore the scars to prove it.

What had happened to the man I'd fallen in love with? Did he stay in Salem? Did Parris and Hathorne drive him away? Had he found another to love, raised a family? My stomach churned at the thought and I squashed that idea quickly.

My head ached, the constant pounding from the onslaught of memories making it difficult to think. I slammed my lids shut and focused. "Where... Where would he be now?" Fragmented pictures shuffled through my mind as I fought to recall what I knew of him in the future.

My hands shot up involuntarily. "Wait!" My gaze darted back and forth between the girls as I tied my thoughts together. "A club... A nightclub! That's it! Fire and Ice. He works at Fire and Ice!" What time was it? Was he there now?

I glanced at my surroundings, realizing I was standing in the front room of my apartment, then glanced down at my torn, filthy pilgrim *garb and bit my lip. I looked hideous, as though time had chewed me up and spit me out, but I didn't care. I needed to see Gabriel, and I needed to see him now.*

I lunged for the front door, forgetting there was a coffee table sitting in the center of the room. I tripped over the wooden furniture and careened forward, legs tangling in my thick skirting.

The girls rushed to my side as I clamored to my feet.

Jessica grasped me by the wrist. "Are you okay?"

"No! I'm not okay. I need to see Gabriel!" I yanked my hand away, my only thoughts of the man who'd risked everything for me, the man who'd sacrificed himself to save me. "Is he at the club? Is he with Xan?"

Jessica appeared stricken, her mouth slightly ajar, her gaze bouncing between Martha and me.

I turned to Martha, who stood in silence with her jaw clenched, looking as though she knew something she didn't want to share.

"Well?" I shouted, frustrated by their silence, an awful feeling of dread welling in my gut. "Where is he?"

Silence.

"Tell me!"

Martha lifted a hand and took a reluctant step toward me. "He's gone, Taylor."

I clutched my chest, a hollow ache throbbing in the area my heart resided. I shook my head. "Don't say it, Martha," I pleaded, mouth quivering, knees weak. "Please. Don't…don't say it."

I heard Jessica gasp, saw her hands fly up to cover her mouth.

Martha's face fell, her eyes full of pity, full of sorrow. She shook her head. "He went back in time, looking for you. Taylor, I'm so sorry. He hasn't returned."

I swallowed back tears as I pulled the map I'd purchased at the airport from my backpack. The majority of my time in these woods had been spent running from monsters, not really paying attention to which trail went where. And while I had a vague recollection as to the location of Gabriel's cabin, the map would only serve to help me get there quicker.

It had certainly helped me earlier while driving through Danvers. With no idea where Prue's body had been buried, I'd stopped by the victims' memorial with a bouquet of sunflowers. Known to symbolize timelessness, I left the bright flowers near the base of the memorial to signify my lasting gratitude and love for my fallen friend.

Largely the same, the difference between the forest now as opposed to three hundred years prior lie with the well worn trails that cut through the dense mixture of hemlock, pine and maple trees.

Squirrels scampered through the ferns underfoot and scaled the sides of trees, escaping human intruders by heading to higher ground. The familiar *rat-tat-tat* of woodpeckers drilling into the ancient hardwood felt both comforting and upsetting. Comforting, because my surroundings appeared largely the same. Upsetting, because *nothing* in my life would ever be the same. Not without Gabriel.

It had taken quite a bit of time, a lot of explaining, and a serious amount of patience where Martha was concerned to help me understand the logistics of why Gabriel was truly gone.

In my mind, there had been two Gabriels kicking it in the past with me. The one from the future who'd swept in at the last moment and taken my place at the gallows, and the Gabriel from the past, the man I'd fallen in love with. I'd reasoned that since Gabriel from 1692 had survived the demon attack, he'd be waiting for me when I came back through time. Well, I'd hoped, anyway.

My poor brain… It just couldn't comprehend the intricacies of time travel, couldn't accept the truth. The truth that there had only ever been one Gabriel. Determined to change my fate after mourning my loss for three hundred years, he'd gone back in time and taken my place in the gallows. He'd given his life to save mine—

the ultimate sacrifice.

Swiping away tears and confident I knew where I was going, I folded the map, shoved it back into my bag, and headed further down the trail toward my destination: the area just north of Bald Hill.

I hiked slowly, frequently sipping from the water bottle I'd brought with me, and marveling at the way the sun shone down through the trees, illuminating the wildflowers and shrubs covering the forest floor.

My stomach churned as I passed Crooked Pond, the scene of my brutal attack, the place where I'd witnessed Gabriel fight the disease demon. *No, thank you. Won't be stopping there.*

An elderly couple with a pair of binoculars, and a young man sporting an expensive looking camera, traipsed through the swampy area observing the local birds and taking pictures.

I shook my head and grimaced. If they knew what had once lurked beneath the still waters of that pond, they'd probably run for the hills.

These woods were rich with untold history, full of atrocities and truths—truths that had died in the fire that claimed Gabriel's cabin that fateful day. The demon attacks had ceased after Goody Godbert's death, Parris and the villagers condemning a slew of innocent women for her murderous deeds. The textbook account of what happened during the Salem Witch massacre, though horrific, was much easier to swallow than the unvarnished truth I'd lived through. The majority of the population was incapable of accepting the truth about the supernatural, and honestly, I couldn't blame them.

The jittery feeling that had abated as I'd meandered through the forest slammed into me as I came upon the area where Gabriel's cabin once stood. The air felt thick, full of magnetic energy.

I swallowed hard, convincing myself that in my need to somehow feel close to Gabriel, I was sensing things that weren't really there. In short, I decided my head was doing a number on me and I needed to ignore it.

Sugar maples, tall and proud, littered the area, just as they had centuries before, their green leaves rustling in the gentle breeze.

I stumbled forward, knees weak, chest hollow.

Gone. Everything was gone. The cabin, the small outbuilding, the pen that once housed his mighty stallion, Erasmo. I sucked in a quick breath, wondering what had happened to the powerful animal that had carried me to Gabriel that fateful day.

Jessica had been right, though I knew she'd never press the issue. Coming here, standing on this patch of earth, it wasn't bringing me the closure I so desperately needed. The loss, the empty ache I carried with me daily felt every bit as strong as it had before. Maybe even more so.

Gabriel's presence clung to this place, even after three long centuries.

I closed my eyes, letting the memory of his scent cascade over me with the gentle breeze, allowing the ghost of his electric presence to wash over me, fill me.

Faint whispers carried across the breeze, the surge of power that floated with them sending a chill rocketing down the length my spine.

His life for yours…

Ultimate sacrifice…

My eyes shot open and I spun in a circle. "Who's there?" My gaze darted around the open space, finding nothing out of the ordinary. Yet, the whispering continued, becoming louder, more powerful.

Enduring love…

Thread of life still intact…

The calm breeze that had cascaded over me just a few moments before, grew into a raging tempest, the powerful currents kicking up dirt and debris as it funneled in front of me with a fierce howl.

Three voices, ancient and powerful, echoed inside my head as the wind continued to spin.

"Abiding, unconditional love is a rarity, a gift not easily extinguished. Your Gabriel's utter selflessness, his unwavering decision to lay down his life in your stead both surprised and pleased us…"

I stood, frozen in place, unable to breathe, unable to blink, terrified of what the voices would say next. Terrified to hope.

"Be of ease, young mortal. We are the Moirai, the keepers of fate, the protectors of time. Nothing escapes us, and we are seldom surprised. Your union, your merging of souls through the act of love has protected your Gabriel's thread of life. It cannot be cut… and neither can yours."

My hands shot to my mouth, as I dropped to my knees. The whirling vortex floating in front of me slowly dissipated, the dirt, leaves and debris clearing away enough for me to see Gabriel, naked, eyes filled with shock and surprise, standing in front of me.

My shoulders sagged as I sobbed, confusion, doubt, joy and relief pouring out of me along with my tears.

"The bond shared between soulmates is unique, and a rarity in this world," the voices boomed. "Cherish your gift of immortality and use it to celebrate the love you've been gifted."

A final gust of wind swept over us before whirling into the sky, the voices fading away with it.

Could it be? Had the Fates truly returned Gabriel to me?

He sifted to me, a warm, electric shock surging through me as he lifted me from the ground and crushed me against him. Strong hands caressed my arms, my back, then cradled my face as he sucked my lips between his own, in a passionate kiss. "Faythe… Taylor…*Adonia.*"

I clung to him, my fingers digging into his back, afraid to blink, afraid to close my eyes and find him gone again. "Oh, my God," I said on a breath. I slid my hands up the length of his back and cupped his cheeks.

Green eyes burned into mine, intense, hungry and full of longing.

"Is this real?" I ran my fingers through his thick hair, then pressed my forehead against his, breathing him in. "Am I really holding you? Touching you?"

He wove his fingers through my hair and pressed a kiss to the top of my head before pulling back. "*Sí, mi dulce.* This is very real." His lips curled up into a wicked smile. "What can I say? I'm a stubborn bastard that's hard to kill."

I chuckled then, the sensation foreign, yet totally welcome. I couldn't remember the last time I'd laughed, and it felt good. Really good. "Yeah, well, you heard what the Fates said. You can't be killed. You're not just everlasting anymore. You're immortal now."

He brushed a strand of hair out of my eyes and tapped me on the nose. "As are you, my sweet." He shifted, sitting me atop his lap, then grasped my waist with both hands and squeezed. "Looks like we've got nothing but time on our hands, baby. Any ideas on how we should spend that time now that we don't have a curse to overcome, or demons to battle?"

I glanced down at his very naked body and licked my lips hungrily. Time. It had been the bane of our existence, an ever-present thorn in our sides. Now that we had it in spades, I knew exactly how we should spend it. "Mmmm," I moaned and trailed a finger down the length of his torso while rocking my hips against his growing erection. "Why don't you and I make up for lost time?"

A wicked smile crossed his lips as he rendered us invisible. "Thought you'd never ask, *mi dulce.* Thought you'd never ask."

Acknowledgements

There are so many people to thank, I scarcely know where to begin! First, I'd like to give a huge shout of thanks to my critique partners, Kristin and Killian and Kaiti. Your continued support, honest criticism and willingness to read my work astound me, and I'm so very thankful for you all. I wish you much joy and success in all of your endeavors.

Taylor and Gabriel's story wouldn't be what it is today without the help I received from Lisa Langdale and Brenda Pandos, the two best beta readers a girl can ask for. You ladies are the bomb, and are always there when I need you. Mwah!

A very special thanks goes out to my two favorite book bloggers, Michelle and Marissa from Novels On The Run. Your help with Taylor's Aussie slang was invaluable, and I'm forever indebted to you. I love our chats on Twitter and Facebook, and I'm so thankful we became friends.

Last, but certainly not least, I'd like to thank my husband, Ryan, and my daughters, Kendall, Taryn, and Irelynn for being a continued source of support and love. You've allowed me to follow my dream, and for that, I'm forever grateful.

CPSIA information can be obtained at www.ICGtesting.com
Printed in the USA
LVOW131635260512

283455LV00003B/1/P